Revelations ...

An act of revealing or communicating

divine truth; something that is revealed;

an enlightening or astonishing disclosure

Books by Mary M. Cushnie-Mansour

<u>Adult Novels</u>
Night's Vampire Series
Night's Gift
Night's Children
Night's Return
Night's Temptress
Night's Betrayals
Night's Revelations

Detective Toby Series
Are You Listening to Me
Running Away From Loneliness

<u>Short Stories</u>
From the Heart
Mysteries From the Keys

<u>Poetry</u>
picking up the pieces
Life's Roller Coaster
Devastations of Mankind
Shattered
Memories

<u>Biographies</u>
A 20th Century Portia

<u>Children/Youth Titles</u>

<u>Novels</u>
A Story of Day & Night
The Silver Tree

<u>Bilingual Picture Books</u>
The Day Bo Found His Bark/Le jour où Bo trouva sa voix
Charlie Seal Meets a Fairy Seal/Charlie le phoque rencontre une fée
Charlie and the Elves/Charlie et les lutins
Jesse's Secret/Le Secret de Jesse
Teensy Weensy Spider/L'araignée Riquiqui
The Temper Tantrum/La crise de colère
Alexandra's Christmas Surprise/La surprise de Noël d'Alexandra
Curtis The Crock/Curtis le crocodile
Freddy Frog's Frolic/La gambade de Freddy la grenouille

<u>Picture Books</u>
The Official Tickler
The Seahorse and the Little Girl With Big Blue Eyes
Curtis the Crock
The Old Woman of the Mountain

Night's Revelations

A Night's Vampire Series Book

Mary M. Cushnie-Mansour

CAVERN OF DREAMS PUBLISHING

Published in Canada by
CAVERN OF DREAMS PUBLISHING
www.cavernofdreamspublishing.com

CAVERN
OF DREAMS
PUBLISHING

ISBN 978-1-927899-64-9
Ebook ISBN 978-1-927899-65-6

Cover Photo by
Cathleen Tarawhiti,
bookcovers2buy@gmail.com

Cover Design by
Hilde Abrahamsen
https://www.facebook.com/Hildes.Designs/?modal=admin_todo_tour
&
Terry Davis
https://ballmedia.com/

Even if the hopes

you started out with are dashed,

hope is to be maintained

Seamus Heaney
1939-2013

Acknowledgements

No matter how many times I go over my manuscript, or how many times I might run it through a grammar program, there is still nothing better than a great book editor to "bring my story home!" Thank you to Bethany Jamieson at Cavern of Dreams Publishing for making my dreams come true; and, thank you to Cavern of Dreams Publishing for once again believing in me.

I may be the author of the story; however, many other extraordinary people have helped me through the different stages:

The cover for "Night's Revelations" was a collaborative effort of three individuals: Cathleen Tarawhiti from New Zealand, Hilde Abrahamsen from Norway, and Terry Davis from Brantford's Ball Media, who put the finishing touches on the cover. I guess I should also thank all my fans who voted on the original photos—you chose well!

Randy Nickman at Brant Service Press, who does a fantastic job of getting the finished copies to print.

I would be remiss if I didn't thank all the individuals who read my books and keep encouraging me to continue on this crazy journey of mine. Your positive comments about my writing are the fuel that keeps me chugging along.

Once again, as with all the books in the "Night's Vampire Series," I must thank the Talos family for the continued use of their home, "Yates Castle" as the location for my novels. "Yates Castle" was built in Brantford in 1864 by the Yates, a railroad family, and was sold to the Talos family in the 1920s.

Last, and definitely not least, I thank my family—you all know who you are—from the wonderfully, patient man I am married to, who puts up with my endless hours of writing; to my children, who have been inspirations to me throughout their years, to my grandchildren who excitedly tell everyone that their grandma is a writer!

ARE YOU READY FOR ME?

Prologue

drianna Daciana, better known as the Dark Wolf or the Black Witch, sat behind an oversized cedar desk. There was a smile on her face. She had waited a long time for this moment, but the time had never been right. Now, she felt she would be able to accomplish what she had dreamed of for centuries—revenge for what Dracula had done to her mother. A cloud passed over her eyes as she thought of her beautiful mother, of the story she had listened to over and over again when she was a child…

"He was not a handsome man, but there was something irresistible about him. I found him on a trail one day; he'd been hunting on my mountain and had fallen and hurt his leg. He was unable to walk, so I brought him back to my cabin and mixed some herbs and put them in a drink for him. He was dreadfully weak; it was several days before he could put any pressure on his leg and another couple weeks before he could actually walk on it.

"Of course, he needed to be bathed, and I had no choice but to strip him of his clothing to do so. I was shocked when I saw the scars on his body. They were like a map of destruction. Some appeared to be battle scars, easily detected, but others…"

Adrianna's mother always paused at this point and wept before she continued…

"The other markings were different. I recognized them as torture scars, and I asked him from where they had come. He told me he had been a captive in the Turkish Court for a number of years during his youth. His father had sent him and his brother,

Radu, there as a guarantee that he would not attack the Turks. Dracula's brother was given a luxurious room, but it was one to which the Sultan's son had plenty of access. Radu was a pretty boy; Dracula was not.

"The Sultan decided Dracula had other attributes, and he started teaching him the methods of Turkish torture, many of which he performed on Dracula. I cried when he told me some of what was done to him, but he would gently brush away my tears with his fingers and tell me it made him more of a man. And he remained a man, he would say to me. He never allowed one of the big Turks to violate him as they did Radu.

"But I could tell, sweet Adrianna, he was tainted in other ways. Many were the nights he cried out and thrashed about in the bed, and I would crawl in beside him and hold him tight to me and tell him all would be well. I dared not use any of my spells on him for fear he learned I was a witch, especially after I discovered he was Dracula, the king of Transylvania. Witches were outlawed, and I had seen too many of my sisters burned at the stake to open my mouth and end up the same.

"Then, one day, I caught him looking at me differently. Lust was in his eyes. He asked me to bathe him again, saying he felt dirty and sweaty. I told him I'd just bathed him the day before, but he smiled and said he sorely needed another bath. I felt his eyes on me as I heated the water and carried it to the bed where he lay. As I took the cloth and began sponging his chest, he grabbed hold of my wrist and pulled me to him…"

Another faraway look would creep into her mother's eyes at this point; she would pause and smile, and touch her lips with her fingers…

"Oh, Adrianna, he was so gentle, but his tongue lit a fire in the pit of my stomach and I returned his fire with one of my own. The days of bathing this man had stimulated what I hadn't had for far too long. We made love—again and again and again.

We made love the next day, and the day after, and every day until he said he had to leave.

"I was in love with him. I'd never allowed myself to feel that way for any man before; I'd only taken my pleasure and left them, not wanting to be hurt as my mother had been by my father when he left her alone in her bed every night to be with his whores.

"At his leaving, I told him I loved him, and you know what he did? He laughed at me! I thought at first it was a joyous laugh, but it wasn't—so I realized later ... later when he never returned to me. Later, when I discovered he had married the daughter of a Boyar. Later, when I felt the child—you, my dear Adrianna—growing in my belly, I knew I had been betrayed and used the same as my mother. Only I was the whore the king took to pleasure himself, not the wife.

"Feeling desperate, I went to Dracula's castle, confident that once he knew my condition, he'd embrace me. I asked for a meeting with the king and I was laughed at. I demanded to see Dracula. When I refused to leave, the guard finally told me to wait. He returned a few hours later and said Dracula would not see me and I was not to return, ever, to the castle or I would be burned at the stake. The guard was leading a horse, already saddled, and he handed me the reins, informing me Dracula was giving me this present so he could rid himself of my presence as quickly as possible—and as payment for services rendered while he was injured.

"So, I raised you by myself. When you were young, you showed immense powers, even grander than mine. I knew you were going to be a powerful witch, and I began teaching you everything I knew. You were also growing into a beautiful young girl.

"One day, a Gypsy maiden showed up at my door, distraught with grief. She told me the land was rent with war, and its leader, Dracula, was out of control. He killed anyone who disagreed with him, torturing them in the cruellest manners: impaling them on poles or by other sadistic means—even drinking their blood from goblets at the victory feasts! His talk of what happened to him in the Turkish Court returned to me; I was grieved he would do the same to his own people.

"The Gypsy's name was Tanyasin, and she was not just beautiful, she was extraordinarily so. She said she had heard I could cast spells and I gave power to individuals in exchange for things I wanted, and she offered me her beauty if I would give her the power to cast a curse upon the one who had murdered her husband and son. It didn't occur to me the individual who had done the deed was the same Dracula I had saved. I was getting older, noticing a few wrinkles on my face, and thought it wouldn't be so bad to take someone else's beauty in exchange for a simple curse. It wasn't until after the deal was made and Tanyasin left that I realized I might have made a mistake. What if the one who murdered her family was the one I still loved—what if it were my Dracula? After all, he was the king! And what would her curse be upon him? I soon enough found out.

"Suddenly, your once robust health began to fail, and you started refusing to eat food. You were only five. I was beside myself; I couldn't lose you. You were my life.

One day, I cut my finger slicing meat off the carcass of a deer I'd killed and you were watching me. You were hunkered under a tree, crying. I called over, asking what was wrong, and you said the sun was too hot, and you couldn't come to me. I walked over to you, and you grabbed my finger and began to suck greedily. When I pushed you away for a moment, I looked into your eyes, and they were flaming!

"It seemed nothing but blood would satisfy your hunger after that, so I put a spell on any deer that came around, and I would bleed enough blood from them to nourish you. I sent a *message to a friend who lived near Dracula's castle, asking if there were any rumours of a strange illness cursing the people.*

"A few weeks later, my friend appeared at my door and told me that a curse had been cast on the Dracul family and all that bore their blood. It was then I knew…"

Adrianna brushed away a tear and straightened her shoulders. It was challenging growing up, having to live in darkness. Her mother changed her life pattern to accommodate her daughter's, and together their powers had grown, but mainly hers. A change came over her mother, a deep sadness that would not cease, and she began to waste away. No matter what Adrianna did, her mother kept slipping further into another world, one which finally took her mind completely.

Then came the day when Adrianna walked into her mother's room and found her lifeless body. Adrianna had cursed. She had screamed. And she had vowed revenge on the one she knew was her father. She swore to one day give him his just desserts, to give him a death like her mother had suffered. Her witch powers grew as she used them more and more. Her vampiric powers grew as well.

Adrianna worked at her magic until, even though she was a vampire, she was able to walk in the sunlight. She kept the secret of her parentage well-hidden; no one, not even those who thought they had her ear, knew she was Dracula's child. When she'd reached an age she desired to remain at, she stopped her growth and ageing on the spot—forever beautiful—forever evil. Ready to take what she felt was rightfully hers.

Yes, she, Adrianna Daciana, known as the Dark Wolf, the Black Witch, decided it was time she presented herself to her dear papa.

Adrianna stood and blew a kiss to her mother's portrait. "This will be for you, Mama!"

Chapter One

Police sirens broke through the morning silence as they raced to the Station Coffee House, which was located at the Brantford train station. The police dispatcher had received a 911 call from the owner, who had found a dead body behind their café. The dispatcher made sure to tell the hysterical woman not to touch or move the body.

Officer Nathaniel Jones let out a long, slow whistle when he bent over to examine the body. Standing, he looked at his partner: "You aren't going to believe this. It appears all the blood has been drained from our victim."

"I thought they did that at the funeral home when they embalmed the body," Frankie chuckled. He was a rookie and known around the station for his *different* sense of humour.

"Don't be a smartass, Frankie!" Nathaniel admonished. "This is a dead body we have here," he added.

"Smells like an old drunk … are you sure his blood is drained?" Frankie asked curiously.

"He is an old drunk, a homeless one," Nathaniel informed his partner. "But he has a name—Vincent. I assume Vincent had a family at one time, maybe even a job; however, for the past ten years, he's been a permanent fixture in our downtown. We've picked him up several times, and he's spent numerous nights in our jail cells. He was harmless, though."

The sound of an ambulance screaming into the parking lot interrupted Nathaniel's story.

"What do we have here?" the female paramedic asked as she approached the crime scene.

"Dead body," Nathaniel replied. "How are you doing, Karen?" he asked. "Long time no see." Nathaniel and Karen had been an item in the past—a long gone past.

"How do you think I'm doing when my first call of the day is to look at a dead body?" she returned sarcastically. It had been a bad breakup.

Frankie snickered. Nathaniel threw him a dirty look.

Karen looked down at the body, then up at Nathaniel. "Do you see what I think I'm seeing? Appears someone drained old Vincent's blood."

"Yep, that's what I'm seeing," Nathaniel answered as he started unrolling crime scene tape. "Hey, Frankie," he called to the rookie, "grab the other end there."

"We need to call the coroner," Karen said, standing. "Can't move the body until they make the pronouncement of death," she stated, walking back to the ambulance.

"Looks like old Vincent finally got what he wanted," Karen said to her partner, Dave.

"Ah, shit!" Dave swore. "How did it happen?"

"Someone killed the old fellow; looks like he's lost a lot of blood, but strangely, there aren't any puddles around the body. Appears, whoever did this, drained his blood directly. We need to call Mitch at the coroner's office and get him up here right away."

"I'll make the call," Dave offered.

"Thanks." Karen climbed into the back of the ambulance and located her clipboard. She flipped through the papers until she found what she wanted, then, to save time later, filled in some of the spaces.

Angelique heard the early morning sirens. Usually, she wouldn't bother with them but there was something different this morning: the sound was close. She walked to her window and moved the curtain across.

"Oh, God!" Angelique's hand went to her throat as she saw where the police cars and ambulance were parked. She hurried from the room, leaving a sleeping Attila behind.

Transforming into a bird, Angelique flew to the Station Coffee House, settling on the dumpster behind the building. She gazed down at the body that lay crumpled on the ground. *Oh, Samara, what have you done?*

Another car pulled into the parking lot and screeched to a stop. The driver exited and strode over to the crime scene.

"Hey, Mitch," Nathaniel greeted the coroner just outside the crime-scene tape. "We got a strange one here."

Mitch didn't say anything, just raised his eyebrows questioningly. Mitch never said much.

Nathaniel continued: "Old Vincent … looks like all the blood has been drained from him … no puddles anywhere, though."

Mitch lifted the tape enough to stoop under. He crouched beside the body and whistled softly. Standing, he pulled a pair of latex gloves from his back pocket and slipped them on. Returning to a bent position, Mitch touched Vincent's chin and moved the old man's head to the side, where he noticed two puncture wounds. He shook his head, puzzled.

Angelique felt sick to her stomach at the sight of the victim's neck. *Just what we need right now. This couldn't have been done by anyone other than Samara. Mia went ahead of her and I followed her back to the house. Samara, you stayed behind … why would you do this?*

Karen came up behind Mitch. "Well, what do you say? Drained of blood?"

Mitch, his eyes fixed on the two puncture wounds, "Appears so. Look at these two wounds." He pointed to the marks on Vincent's neck. "This is where the blood was drained from." He paused and stood. With a serious look, "Do you believe in vampires, Karen?"

Karen grinned. "Really, Mitch? Vampires are made up characters for the book and movie industries."

"Well, whoever did this is playing at being a vampire."

Karen handed Mitch her clipboard. The page he had to sign confirming the victim's death was on top for him. Mitch accepted the offered pen and scribbled his signature and recorded the time of death—the unofficial time. Mitch knew he wasn't far off, though; rigour mortis had barely begun to set in.

No use hanging around here any longer; I've seen enough. Angelique took flight, returning to the house. *With any luck, no one witnessed what happened here, but the way our luck has been going lately...* She set down outside the little school room behind the house.

Angelique transformed back to her normal state. She looked around the yard. Something was bothering her, had been since Katalin's body had been found. All the pieces coming together suggested there were two individuals involved in the murder. She thought back to the liaison between Ildiko and Teresa all those years ago in Brantford, when they had teamed together to get rid of Virginia.

With what Angelique now knew—that Ildiko could possibly have been in the city the night Katalin died—and after hearing the conversation between Samara and Mia, noting Mia's unusual behaviour during said conversation, Angelique wondered if Ildiko and Mia were working together. Then again, why would either one of them want Katalin dead? Katalin was no direct threat to Ildiko, and the thought of sweet, little Mia killing her own mother was outrageous!

Angelique was drawn to the schoolhouse. She tested the door and found it open. "Strange," she mumbled. "Basarab never leaves outside doors unlocked." She stepped inside. Taking a deep breath, Angelique sauntered around the desks, running her fingers across the old wood.

Suddenly, she stopped and closed her eyes. The first visions she saw were Santan and Mia, then Virginia and Mia, then Basarab and Mia. But it was the last image she saw that disturbed her most—Ildiko.

Angelique waved her arms in the air and, within seconds, she was standing in the middle of the room she shared with her husband. Despite it being daytime, she shook Attila on the shoulder, waking him from a deep sleep.

"We need to talk," Angelique said as she began pacing beside the bed.

Attila swung his legs over the edge of the bed and sat up. "What is so important that you would need to wake me in the daytime hours?" His voice sounded gravelly.

"There's been another murder," Angelique wasted no time with her news. "Only this time, humans are aware of it. I believe our beloved granddaughter is playing with fire—again."

Eyebrows raised, Attila asked: "And you would know this how?"

"During the night, I followed Samara and Mia as they took a walk…"

"Samara and Mia?"

"Yes … I, too, thought it strange. I overheard an interesting conversation between them. Samara seemed to be trying to get Mia to confess to something…"

"To what?" Attila interrupted again.

"To murdering her mother."

"Really?" Attila perked up. He stood and joined in his wife's pacing of the room, his hands clasped behind his back. "To murdering her own mother? Did the girl admit to such?"

"Technically, no. But it was how Mia answered that caught my attention—plus her body language. She told Samara she'd overheard a fight between her parents; she heard her mother say that she'd rather see Mia dead than have to live as a vampire. Samara kept pushing, continuing to bring up the death of Mia's mom, but Mia, although she admitted she was pissed with her mother, said she would never hurt her, let alone kill her.

"Samara kept on … hinting that Katalin hadn't jumped because she was ill as Randy had told his daughter … told Mia her father was lying to her. Then Samara told Mia something she wouldn't know—that her mother had been killed by something—someone—who had ripped open her throat and drained her blood.

"Mia didn't blink an eye. She just stood and said she wanted to go back to the house, then walked away. I followed her instead of staying back with Samara, as I should have done. If I had, there wouldn't be a victim at the back of that café!"

Attila reached out and pulled Angelique into his arms. "Don't blame yourself, you couldn't have known what Samara was going to do," he said, trying to soothe his wife.

"There is more, Attila … something else that is bothering me … about Mia. When she met with Samara, her conversation indicated to me that she was glad to get away from Santan, out of reach of his watchful eyes … and … she asked…" Angelique was having trouble with what she needed to say next because she could barely believe what she had heard.

"She asked what?" Attila prodded.

"She asked if they could go somewhere and get a drink, she was thirsty. She asked Samara if she ever took blood from humans. At least our granddaughter drew the line at that, telling Mia she wasn't ready for that step in the vampire world."

Attila released Angelique and began pacing again. "So sweet little Mia is no longer so sweet is what you are telling me."

"Exactly." Angelique drew in a long breath. "There's more."

Attila stopped and waited for the next blow.

"When I returned from the coffee house, I stopped outside the schoolhouse. I was drawn to enter the room, and when I did, I had visions of its most recent visitors. Of course, we know about Santan, Mia, Virginia, and Basarab, but it was the final image that disturbed me—Ildiko."

"Ildiko? So, she was here in the house?"

"Appears so."

"Which means she is probably the one who murdered Katalin; Basarab is not going to be pleased about this. He promised Randy that when he found out who killed his wife, he would put them to death. Vampire law: no life is taken without reason, and if it is, the penalty is death."

"I believe Ildiko is partly responsible but is she the only one? I still have a gut feeling Mia played a part in this, despite it being her mother. Yes, Katalin hated vampires, and she never made a pretence about her feelings, but Mia loved Santan so much she wanted to change. Do you think she might have done something to prevent exposure of any kind, especially after hearing what her mother said?"

"We need to fill Basarab in straightaway," Attila said. "Before Ildiko arrives, especially. She has no idea what we know yet; but, if Mia is involved, it is going to open another Pandora's box; it would mean her death, as well. Santan will never accept that verdict!"

"Which paves the way for Samara to take the throne," Angelique interjected. "Maybe the reason she is trying so hard to get Mia to admit to having something to do with Katalin's death."

"With Samara's request to marry Lajos, and his connections with both Dracula and Ildiko, I am beginning to wonder exactly which one of them wants the power, or if they are all playing each other." Attila headed for the door. "I am going downstairs. There isn't much we can do until the sun sets, but I am too awake now to go back to sleep. I'll be in the library if you care to join me."

Angelique declined the invitation, stating she had a couple matters to investigate further. She would join him later.

Attila browsed through the books on the shelves until he came to a dog-eared, leather-bound one entitled, *The Musat Family History*. He pulled it out and sat in a chair. Opening the book, he was aware of how brittle the pages were and wondered if he should transfer the information to a computer for safe-keeping. Maybe when this current mess the family seemed embroiled in was over, he would do so.

Flipping carefully through the pages, he came to the section where he'd met Mara, Basarab's mother. A tear slipped from his eye, landing on the page, blending with the other tears he had shed while reading this part over the centuries.

"Ah, Mara, my love, I am so sorry all this happened. I want you to know, though, our son grew into a fine man—a great leader. And he has a son now … you are a grandmother … to two children … there is a girl, as well. Santan is like me, quiet. Some would say wise, too, although there are times I doubt my own wisdom. But he has Basarab's strength—an excellent combination. Samara, on the other hand, is wild and, most times, uncontrollable. I believe she may be more like her great uncle, Dracula.

"You must know by now, wherever you are in this universe, I found love again, in a most unusual place. But, it was in front of me all along; I was just too blind, for centuries, to see it. Angelique. She has been my salvation these past few years, as she was when I first met her, when she showed me the vision of you on your deathbed, allowing me a moment to say goodbye to you."

Attila flipped to the first page of the account…

The fate of our family has been sealed with that of Vlad Dracula. Time, action, and blood have forged our souls together for an eternity in hell … The God that we once prayed to in the great cathedrals of Wallachia, Transylvania, and Moldavia has forsaken us entirely, and the witches of Satan have cursed us with a never-ending night…

Attila skipped forward a few pages…

Stephen and I were shaken awake by Dracula, who was suggesting that we seal our brotherhood in blood … Dracula passed us his knife and told us what to do … we reached forward to mix our blood … fingertip to fingertip … Dracula grabbed hold of our wrists and stopped us. Then he took Stephen's hand, raised it to his mouth, and sucked the blood from the open wound. He repeated the action with me … this event, as I learned later, was the first substantial step that sealed our souls together, forever in darkness…

There was no doubt in Attila's mind that the lives of the Dracul lineage were sealed in darkness. He thought about the day the family was cursed by the Gypsy, Tanyasin, and turned the pages to that section of the book…

Dracula and I escaped, during the night, through secret passages that had been tunnelled through the mountains. What we came upon there, when we exited the mountain, sealed our destiny. Entering a clearing, we were confronted with a circle of wagons and a group of Gypsy women ... Suddenly, one of the hags turned to us, "At last you have come ... I have waited many moons to curse your bloodthirsty ways! You and this pup that runs at your side are not worthy to walk in the healing rays of our Mother Sun!

Attila smiled briefly at the vision of Dracula standing up to the old Gypsy, but she had cursed him and his lineage despite his bravado. He had done a great injustice to her family, taking the life of her husband and son, and she was going to make him pay! Attila ran his finger down the paragraphs until he came to the actual curse…

Vlad Dracula, better known, to all those less fortunate than you, as the Impaler ... I curse you to an everlasting hell! Your days shall be spent under closed lids, your nights in horrid shadows. You shall run in the night with the swiftness of the wolf; your eyes shall burn red like a cave bat, and you will coerce your victims into submission. You shall be as cunning and charming as the red fox while you lure your victims to your den of darkness. But, at the same time that you are exerting such power, no rest shall ever refresh your soul, and no peace will ever ease your mind. No man shall open his door to you or give you refuge at his table. You, that pup at your side, and all your blood descendants shall be burdened with this curse from now and into eternity! Those who stand here with me are my witnesses to this blight I cast upon you and yours!

Thus the curse remained. Attila thought about the early years and how he had buried himself in raising Basarab. He smiled at how headstrong his son had been, and he learned so much patience trying to live up to the one last request Mara had asked of him. The Dracul family learned to live with the curse, thanks to Angelique lightening the sting. There were tough times—many of them—but the family had survived.

They survived the attempted takeover by Radu, Dracula's younger brother, which had been one of the most difficult. Attila often wondered what happened to all the rogues Radu had gathered. He often wondered what happened to Radu, as well.

Attila had tolerated Dracula's indiscretions, knowing how difficult it must have been for him to have gone from a king—the ruler of Transylvania—to being subservient to the son of his little cousin. Even though that little cousin had been the only one to stand by him during the final days of the war against the Turks, it was still a trying state of affairs for one such as Dracula to swallow.

But now, it looked as though Dracula might be tiring of playing second fiddle. Was he looking for a way to control the throne without actually sitting on it? Attila closed the diary, stood, and walked to the bookshelves. He slipped it back into its resting place.

"Father?" Basarab's voice broke the silence hanging in the room. "What are you doing in here?"

"Thinking. A new *situation* has come into play and you are not going to like it. Why you are up so early?" Attila smiled at his son.

"I could not sleep."

"Well, maybe our wakefulness is good; we can have some time before the rest of the household awakens." Attila pointed to two chairs by a coffee table. "Shall we sit?"

When Attila finished relaying to Basarab what he had learned from Angelique, he saw the brokenness in his son's eyes.

"I never thought it would go this far—that Samara would go this far," Basarab said. "With everything else going on, how she could dare to be so reckless!"

"Ildiko will be here at sunset; how do you think you are going to handle her?" Attila asked.

"I will respond to whatever excuse she is going to give," Basarab replied. "I will lay the net below her, and when she steps into it, I will pull the ropes! She will have nowhere to go." Basarab rose. "I hope, for all our sakes, she has not done this!"

Chapter Two

Ildiko was nervous about her meeting with Basarab and the rest of the family. She wished Gara would arrive before she had to go to the house, but he'd only said he would see her tonight—he'd not given a specific time. Ildiko knew Basarab did not tolerate tardiness; she also knew if she weren't there for the first meal, it would shade her as guilty in his eyes.

Just as she was about to leave her room, the phone rang. Snatching up the receiver, "Hello."

"This is Leo from reception; I have a gentleman here, Gara, who says he knows you and would like to come up to your room. We take our security very seriously…"

"Send him up," Ildiko curtly cut the attendant off. She hung up the phone and smiled in relief as she waited for her brother. She unlocked the door.

A few minutes later, Gara entered after giving a light knock. Ildiko approached him for a hug but he sidestepped her.

"I see you are ready to walk into the den of lions, sister. I cleared my schedule to ensure I would be by your side—more so to ensure you do not screw this up with your impetuous temper. You will allow me to take the lead."

"Won't that make me seem guiltier if I do not speak for myself?"

"Oh, you will speak enough, but this is how it will go…"

For the next half hour, Gara explained to Ildiko exactly how they would proceed and emphasized the importance to her of sticking to the script.

An hour before gathering for the first meal, Basarab held a meeting with Kardos, a trusted member of his inner council. He had decided not to confide details to Santan because of the vague implications pointing to the possibility Mia may be involved. It would be interesting to see her reactions when specific subjects were brought up.

Kardos wasn't surprised by Samara's actions; he'd always known her to be unpredictable and a threat to the secrecy of the vampire world. He decided to speak his mind. "If I might be frank with you, Basarab…" Kardos began.

"Please do, this is no time to be affable. I need someone by my side besides my father, who has the best interest of the family in mind, not his own."

"First, I don't believe Samara had anything to do with Katalin's death, but in reality, if what you are saying about Mia——and there *is* a possibility she is involved somehow in her mother's death—Samara is ultimately responsible. Your daughter turned Mia and created a monster.

"Also, your little Samara—I know she has always been the light in your eye, maybe because she is a lot like you were in your *wilder* years—needs to be severely punished for what she has done here. Taking a life, draining it of blood, and carelessly leaving the body to be found by humans is unforgivable under vampire law. I know, for a fact, she has done this before, and I had to clean up the mess so there would be no trace of her indiscretion. Others know of what she has been up to as well, including your son. He has protected his sister in the past, but I get the feeling he is not of the same mind now after what she has done to Mia." Kardos relayed what happened behind his pub when Samara took the life of a human patron.

Basarab's heart was heavy. He knew what he had to do in such cases, and if it were anyone else other than his beloved daughter, he wouldn't hesitate.

"As for Ildiko," Kardos resumed, "I have never trusted her, not since the incidents in Brantford when we were fighting against Radu, and, to be truthful, long before that. She has always been resentful that you never chose her to be your bride—she believes you have spurned her twice for a woman outside our bloodline—human women—adding insult to injury in her twisted mind. Ildiko is unbalanced. Granted, she is a fierce warrior, but we now live in an age that has no use for her type of fighting. Ildiko has never moved with the times.

"We don't know exactly what happened the night Katalin was murdered, but we do know it was vampire, and we have two prime suspects: Santan's betrothed—newly turned and out of control—and Ildiko, who has always been on a mission to either sit beside you on the throne, or as it seems to appear now, to take the throne from you by whatever means she is able!"

The count and his confidant spent a few more minutes discussing what Kardos' part to play in the dining room would be, then went their separate ways until it was time to face the building storm gathering on the family's horizon.

Viktor opened the door and ushered Ildiko and Gara into the foyer. He raised his eyebrows when he saw Gara but said nothing. Basarab had only mentioned Ildiko would be coming.

"Follow me," he said as he headed down the hallway toward the dining room. "Everyone is waiting for your arrival." He glanced at Gara. "I shall set another place for you, sir."

"Thank you," Gara responded.

Basarab tried not to appear shocked when Gara walked in the room, as did everyone else. Dracula was first to recover.

"Gara, good to see you. What brings you to this hick place?" Dracula asked with a smirk.

Gara returned the greeting with a sarcastic smile. "I have business in Southern Ontario; Ildiko was going to handle it for me but ran into some difficulties. I felt it necessary to make the trip to this 'hick' town. And, since I knew my cousin was here, I thought to pay my respects."

Dracula chuckled. "Well, you are a welcome sight, as is your lovely sister."

Viktor entered the room and placed another wine glass for Gara; he'd also brought an extra bottle of blood and set it on the table. He glanced at Basarab, eyes questioning if there was anything else needed at the moment. The count nodded, and Viktor bowed and backed out of the room.

"So, what's new?" Ildiko asked as she took her seat.

Basarab frowned. Ildiko never usually cared about anything that might be going on in anyone else's lives.

Samara spoke up excitedly: "We're going to have a wedding in the family!" she informed.

"How delightful! When is the big day, Samara?" Ildiko inquired, assuming it was her little cousin's wedding. "But wait, it can't be you … Ákos disappeared … we assume he's dead … or has he been resurrected somehow?" she laughed nervously.

Gara laid a hand on Ildiko's shoulder. "I am sure if you stop talking long enough, sister, someone will tell us who the lucky couple is." Gara looked at Dracula and Kardos: "Not one of you two old confirmed bachelors, is it?" he asked with a look suggesting he didn't really care.

Once again, Basarab frowned, noting the change in his cousin's attitude. Gara never behaved so cynically.

Mia was the one to finally answer Ildiko's question. "It's Santan and me; we're to be married as soon as we all return to Brasov and then Santan is going to become a king … sort of … and I'll be his queen!" her voice was filled with youthful excitement.

"How nice for you," Ildiko noted through pursed lips. *So Samara, your plan isn't working out as you expected, is it? I know something that might help you … of course, I will want something in return.*

Basarab decided to change the subject. He was annoyed with Mia for confirming her impending marriage to Santan. If what he thought might have happened under his roof—on his roof—she may never see the day when she would walk down the aisle to his son! But would Santan accept the old laws when it came to meting out punishment to the one he loved? If she was involved, that is.

"We should sup before discussing serious matters," Basarab suggested as he picked up a bottle. Going around the table, he filled everyone's glass.

Santan, who had also been shocked at Mia's outburst, carefully studied his bride-to-be. She was changed—her personality. She was no longer the sweet girl he'd fallen in love with. Santan hoped that once Mia learned how to control her urges, she would return to being the girl he had fallen in love with.

Mia wasn't paying much attention to anyone at the table, but suddenly realized her father wasn't in the room. "Where's my dad?" she directed to Basarab.

Instead of the count answering, Virginia replied: "Your father is having his supper in the kitchen; he'll join us later." Virginia knew how much Randy hated watching the vampires drink blood. He'd managed to hide his discomfort for her after she'd turned, but now that his daughter was a vampire, Randy couldn't bear to watch anymore.

"Lovely," Mia clapped her hands.

Samara rolled her eyes at Mia's behaviour. The girl was proving more difficult to control than she'd thought. In fact, Samara was beginning to find Mia annoying. She had hoped to get more information from her when they'd talked, however, Samara knew Mia was hiding something. It was only a matter of time before the wannabe princess tumbled off her high wall—maybe just as her mother had.

A restless silence filled the room as everyone partook of their nourishment. It seemed no one was in a talkative mood, each absorbed in personal thoughts.

Gara was studying the group around the table, trying to discern just how much everyone knew about what was going on—what had gone on. That most were not being overly welcoming gave Gara cause for concern. He hoped his plan worked.

Ildiko was nervous but trying not to show it. She knew from experience how intuitive Basarab could be. *I didn't strike the first blow; Katalin would have died anyway!*

Attila held his thoughts in check. He knew what was coming was not going to be easy—on any front.

Angelique was worried. Samara was out of control and what she had done—killing the old drunk—was going to put the entire family in danger. She kept telling herself she should have stayed back and kept an eye on Samara instead of following Mia. That would have prevented one problem. Angelique tried to think of a way she could control the situation to alleviate any further investigations into the murder of the old man. Maybe later she could pay a visit to the morgue and replenish the body with a bit of blood. That would baffle the coroner when he had to drain blood from a body he thought had already been drained. Angelique didn't know why she hadn't thought of that before.

Kardos was uneasy. He knew there was a lot of betrayal happening, but exactly what and where the betrayals were leading caused him some confusion. He was annoyed, as well, at Samara for having acted in such a rash manner that could bring the authorities down on all of them.

Dracula was enjoying himself immensely. Events were taking place—albeit out of his control—that could undoubtedly lead to his goal: control of the throne. No one would stand by Basarab if he could no longer control members of his own family.

Virginia was worried about Randy. He hadn't been the same since she and Basarab arrived in Brantford, and he was more withdrawn than ever now that Katalin had been murdered. Virginia was also concerned about their friendship; Randy was avoiding her.

Santan was thinking hard about decisions he and his father had made, and how those decisions had led them here. Because of their choices, Katalin was dead and Mia was a vampire. Where was it all going to end?

Mia was dreaming about her wedding … of the diamond-studded gown she would wear down the aisle to be wed to Santan … of the train embroidered with real silver threads, trailing ten feet behind her … of the coronation of her vampire prince … of her and Santan sitting on the throne, she perched precariously on his lap, her arms wrapped around his neck, her head resting on his shoulder. It was a beautiful dream and she was smiling—the only one around the table who was.

Basarab studied everyone. *I am so tired. Which problem do I deal with first? Which problem, once dealt with, is not going to cause another bigger problem? Is this the legacy I want to leave to my son?* Basarab glanced at Santan and his heart filled with love. *You are so like your mother and my father. Strong and fair. Compassionate and wise. I don't deserve you.*

The bottles of blood finally sat empty on the table, and everyone seemed to be looking to Basarab to address the uncomfortable issues that needed to be dealt with. Basarab knew they were all wondering which matter he would choose first. He decided to deal with Samara's indiscretion.

"Samara," Basarab began, "It has come to my attention that a body was discovered behind the Station Coffee House, just across the railway tracks from here."

"How awful," Samara exclaimed, her hand tapping nervously on her chest.

"You wouldn't happen to know anything about that would you?" Basarab tried to give his daughter the opportunity to come clean.

"Of course not, Papa." *What does he know ... who would have seen me ... Mia wouldn't have seen anything, but if she did, would she tell my father? ... Why? ... To secure favour with him?*

"Strange," Basarab continued, "the body was drained of blood, not something a *human* murderer would do." The count stared down his daughter.

Samara, realizing she was probably caught, although she still had no idea who might have seen her, finally confessed. "Okay, Papa. I admit I had an encounter. I didn't realize the old man died, though ... I'm so sorry. I was out for a walk," Samara glanced at Mia, "with my brother's bride-to-be. She headed back here and I was thirsty. I saw the old man stumbling across the parking lot and thought to just have a bit to hold me off…"

Basarab's fist came down on the table toppling many of the empty glasses. "You would put our entire family in jeopardy just for a nibble! How dare you!" The count's fury startled a number of the vampires sitting at the table, especially Samara, whose eyes widened in shock.

Samara knew it was time to turn on the tears, a tactic that always seemed to work with her father. "Papa, I'm so sorry; I didn't mean to kill the old man—honestly." She looked around the table at the other vampires, and with tears now flowing freely, "Honestly, I'm so sorry." *The old drunk must not have had a lot of blood in him; I didn't take that much from him!*

"It seems you have a lot to be sorry for lately, Samara," Basarab's anger was building inside as he thought of everything he knew about his daughter. "Shall we go over the list?"

"Basarab, is it vital to embarrass your daughter like this?" Dracula spoke up in defence of his great-niece. "She has apologized. I don't believe for a minute there are going to be any police knocking on our door. Is there anyone present at this table who would tell the police, if they were to come, vampires are living here? I think not!" Dracula drove home his point.

Thank you, uncle. Samara sniffled for effect.

Angelique, noticing the fury in Basarab's eyes at his uncle's rebuke of how he was handling Samara, quickly intervened. "I think there is a way we can escape this storm," she stated. "I will find out where the body is, and, using my magic, I will return some blood into the body and remove the puncture wounds. That should keep the humans baffled and questioning their first observations," Angelique grinned mischievously.

"Wow! You can do all that?" Mia exclaimed innocently.

Attila smiled at the young vampire. "My wife is not a vampire, Mia dear. She is a powerful witch, but one with no ounce of blackness in her heart. She has saved this family from harm many times." Turning to Basarab, Attila suggested, "I think, in this particular case, it would be wise to allow Angelique to work her magic, giving us one less thing to worry about."

Despite what Samara had done, Basarab was willing to concede this round. He would decide his daughter's punishment later, in private. He nodded, giving Angelique permission to work her magic.

"Now, on to the next subject," he said, looking straight at Ildiko.

Chapter Three

Ildiko repositioned herself in her chair, meeting Basarab's gaze with her own. *Stay calm ... Gara's plan will remove me from all suspicions ... I just have to figure out a way to tactfully present the real culprit as a viable option to be investigated.*

"Ildiko ... I asked you a question," Basarab's voice infiltrated his cousin's thoughts.

"I apologize, cousin," Ildiko said, slightly unsettled that she had not been paying attention. "My mind must have been elsewhere. Could you repeat the question, please?" She smiled beguilingly.

"I asked, when did you arrive in Brantford?" Basarab repeated, an edge to his tone.

"As I told Angelique the other night, I only just arrived. I guess I failed to mention I was here earlier but had to return to Brasov to speak directly with Gara about the business he'd sent me to deal with. There were difficulties and I needed to show him some paperwork—something we didn't want to take a chance on being read by anyone else if I were to have faxed or emailed it." Ildiko leaned back in her chair, feeling assured her explanation was enough to alleviate the count's suspicions about her.

Instead of speaking further to Ildiko, Basarab turned his attention to Gara. "I had no idea, cousin, you have such important business ventures here in Canada, in this area. When did you acquire such, and do tell what it is." Basarab's voice was smooth—and threatening.

Without missing a beat, Gara replied: "I have several real-estate holdings in the surrounding cities—Hamilton, Toronto, London, Niagara—and I had placed a property manager in charge. It came to my attention, through a friend I had planted as an insider to keep an eye on the manager, this individual was skimming money off the top. I asked Ildiko to come over and look into it for me, but she couldn't find anything concrete to substantiate my suspicions. I decided I needed to have the accounts looked at by someone we trust—someone in Brasov—so I asked my sister to fly back with the accounting records.

"Unfortunately, she couldn't get hold of her private pilot to use the plane she had left at the Brantford Airport; she was forced to take a red-eye flight out of Toronto," Gara hoped that would end the conversation of Ildiko's whereabouts on the night of Katalin's death.

But it didn't. "Whatever happened to the pilot, Ildiko?" Angelique asked. "Did he show up eventually?"

Ildiko was quick to answer: "Yes, he did … apparently, he was otherwise engaged with a young lady," she informed, a malicious smile on her lips. "However, it won't happen again; he has been dealt with and won't be inconveniencing me any longer," she added.

Angelique knew Ildiko was lying about the pilot being unavailable; on the other hand, Ildiko was telling one truth about the pilot: he wouldn't be inconveniencing anyone ever again!

Attila joined the conversation. "Exactly when did you arrive and when did you leave? We would appreciate it if you would give us the exact dates and times of your comings and goings."

Gara stood up angrily. "I am getting the impression my sister is under interrogation for something here! You are insulting her with this line of questioning." He turned to Ildiko. "I think it is time to leave. I will not tolerate such insult upon my family!"

Ildiko stood, happy her brother intervened on her behalf. She'd had no idea how she was going to explain on the spot her comings and goings.

Basarab was shocked and angered by Gara's insolence toward him. His voice tightened with rage. "You will not leave until we have answers from your sister as to her whereabouts, so we might clear her name. If she leaves now I will have every reason to believe my cousin has something to hide."

Gara's fists clenched. He dare not defy the vampire ruler, especially when it appeared the odds were against him—against his sister. Calming his voice, "And what is it you think my sister has done?"

"So far, we have cleared the whereabouts of everyone who was under this roof on the night Randy's wife, Katalin, was killed," Basarab articulated.

Ildiko saw her opportunity to open a can of worms and take the heat off her. "Everyone?"

Basarab tilted his head to the side questioningly. "Such a strange question for you to ask, Ildiko. Are you suggesting we might have missed someone, and how would you know?"

Shit ... I walked into that one.

Dracula came to her rescue—sort of. At the least, he delayed her having to answer. "The thing is, Ildiko, it appears Katalin was murdered and the deed done by one of our own. Her throat was ripped open and the blood drained from her body."

Ildiko saw her opening. "Like the man the police found behind the café?" By hinting at Samara's recent indiscretion, Ildiko was putting the heat on the young temptress, something she would have to fix later. Maybe.

Dracula grinned. "You make a valid point, niece, but in making it, you are pointing the finger at our esteemed leader's beloved daughter."

Ildiko swallowed nervously.

Gara cleared his throat. "Would such be so wrong to assume, especially after what Samara has done, putting us all in the possible limelight with the local authorities? If the princess killed that old man … well…" Gara left his statement open for all to fill in the blank.

Randy's voiced crashed into the room. "What's going on here? The princess—and I assume you are talking about Samara––has killed someone? And you think she might have killed my wife?" Randy strode with determination straight to Basarab. "Tell me, count, if this is true. You promised. You know what you have to do now!"

Basarab felt trapped. He couldn't believe the way the table was turning on him, on his daughter. He didn't want to believe for one second that Samara killed Katalin. She'd stepped over the line many times, and yes, she killed the old man, but that was a moment of … well, whatever it was, it wasn't the same as taking the life of the mother of the girl her brother loved. It just wasn't.

The count stopped Randy in his tracks with a look. Randy cringed before the vampire leader, noticing the rings of fire in his eyes.

Turning to Samara, Basarab ordered her to speak: "What have you to say for yourself, daughter? Do these *insinuated* accusations have any merit? Tell the truth, for if you do not, I will know, and it will be worse for you!"

Samara had never seen her father so angry—never! She went to him and fell to her knees, tears streaming down her cheeks. "I swear on all I love … all whom I love … I did not kill Katalin. You must believe me!" Samara half rose and gazed around the table at all sitting there. "I was not even here the night it happened!" she added.

Attila decided to end what was going on before it went any further. "I think we should discuss this later after I have had a chance to speak in private with my son. We will reconvene in the count's dining room—all of us—within four hours, and we will hold then a proper vampire court over which I will preside."

The statement made by the elder count shocked those sitting around the table. His inference that no one should leave the house until after the "court" was clearly understood by all. Dracula was the first to stand and stride from the room.

Chapter Four

On the way out of the dining room, Attila took Angelique by the arm and directed her to the entrance. He leaned over and whispered in her ear, "Be safe with what you are about to do." He hesitated. "I hope, for all our sakes, your plan works."

Angelique laid her hand softly on her husband's cheek. "All will be well, my love. This is not the first time I have cleaned up one of Samara's messes, and I have the feeling, until her father gets her under control—if that is even possible—it will not be the last." With those words, Angelique kissed Attila on the cheek and slipped out the door into the night.

Basarab came up behind his father. "She has left to pay a visit to the morgue?"

Attila nodded affirmation, then pointed to Basarab's study. "Shall we?"

Once settled into two armchairs, father and son were silent for a few minutes, both deep in thought.

"I made a mistake," Attila began, his voice heavy with sadness. "I should not have erased the files at the airport. In doing so, it gave Ildiko a head's up that we were on to her."

"I agree; however, I fear there is much more to this than meets the eye. Is Ildiko hiding something?—I think so. But is she responsible for Katalin's death?—not sure. There is no reason for her to want Katalin dead; there is nothing to gain. Katalin was a human—a human, who, despite how she felt about us, we could have controlled."

"In truth," Attila began thoughtfully, "do you think we would have been able to control Katalin? She hated us. Hated us even more when she was told about what happened to her daughter. And there is something else we need to consider: where would Randy's loyalty have laid? He loved his wife, but if she were to threaten Mia … If Katalin was not willing to accept what happened here and threatened to go to the police anyway, would it be possible for him to have done this?"

"You're forgetting one thing, Father; Randy is not a vampire."

"True, but did the evidence not indicate there was the possibility of two individuals involved in Katalin's death?" Attila stood and walked over to the window, staring out into the night. "What if Randy struck the first blow? He did go to speak with Katalin, right? If they argued and he hit her … if anyone heard the argument … maybe they went in and finished the job … probably without Randy's knowledge." Attila laid out a possible new scenario. "His grief seems too real for him to have killed his wife intentionally … but … a crime of passion to protect his daughter?"

Basarab joined his father at the window. "It is possible, but I can't believe Randy would strike his wife. It isn't in him to do such a thing."

"There is more to Randy than we might like to think. Remember what he sacrificed for Virginia when he feared she was in danger from Tanyasin. Do you think for one minute, had Tanyasin had the opportunity to physically harm Virginia that day at the cottage in Port Dover, Randy would not have physically protected her? He loved her … still does from what I have observed. And he loved your children. He basically raised Santan the first couple years of his life. He would do anything—

would have done anything—to protect the children, too. Do you not think, if Katalin threatened to expose us, or even maybe threaten to end her daughter's life so she wouldn't live like a vampire, maybe Randy would have protected Mia—and Virginia? Consider this, son: Virginia was his first love … then Santan and Samara … Katalin was his wife, yes, but Mia is his daughter—his blood. He will protect the vampires and his daughter before all else. I truly believe this."

Basarab placed his hands behind his back and began pacing. "You present a decent, thought-provoking argument, Father. If you are right, and Randy did strike the first blow, we still must discover which one of the vampires under our roof drained her of blood, finishing the job."

"Or, which one of the vampires *not* under our roof—then, or presently."

"Katalin may have lived had someone found her in time and not decided to finish a job someone else started," Basarab stated thoughtfully. "Maybe we shouldn't have been in such a hurry to allow the Russian Vampires to leave."

"Personally, I don't think one of them had it in them to…"

"Was it not Manya who attempted to kill Ákos?" Basarab countered.

Attila's eyebrows rose. "True. But that was done out of love—lack of knowledge of what was really going on. Why would Manya kill Katalin? There is not one doubt in my mind that would make me think it was her, or for that matter, any of the Russian vampires."

"What of Délia? She hates us; hates me for betrothing my daughter to her son." Basarab paused. "And, we must consider this: *she* was the first one to come upon the body."

"But she has gone with Volodya and his family back to Russia. Shall we ask her to return here? Or maybe we should wait to have the trial back in Brasov with all the council present?"

"No, the trial must be here. I promised Randy we would get to the bottom of who killed his wife before I left for home."

Attila didn't like that they would be holding the trial in Brantford but Basarab had given his word. With what Samara had just done, killing the old drunk, it added an element of extra caution to the circumstances. The longer they stayed in Brantford, the more chance of getting caught up in a police investigation. He hoped Angelique would not have any difficulties with what she was going to do at the morgue.

"Well, I think if you insist on holding our court here, we should send for some other unbiased members of the council," Attila finally suggested. "Do we have access to enough supplies to hold us over for a week or two—whatever time we might need?" he added.

"I still have my sources," Basarab replied. "And I am sure Carla will assist us with whatever we need. As for bringing over the rest of the council, I think that might be a good idea. At the same time, we can try and get word to the Russian vampires and ask them to return. I still have doubts they are all completely innocent."

"Good, I will message Lardos, our lawyer, and he can gather the rest and get a message up to Volodya," Attila said. "When we meet with everyone shortly, we will give them all the good news that they will be remaining here for a while longer."

Basarab grimaced. "I know some who will not be pleased about that."

"Pleased or not, they must obey. As long as you still sit on the throne, your word is law. You have given your word to Randy. You will find out who murdered his wife before we leave here, and this is the only way we can do it. I only hope, in finding out who did the deed, it does not open another, bigger, can of worms for us!"

Chapter Five

Nathaniel sat at his desk filling out the police report on Vincent. He was troubled by the loss of blood the old fellow had endured, and by the two puncture wounds on his neck. "I don't believe in real vampires," he mumbled.

"Did you say something about vampires?" Frankie plunked down at the desk opposite Nathaniel's. He grinned. "You want my opinion?" he asked, then continued without waiting for his superior's reply, "I think it was some crazy, hyped-up guy on drugs, hallucinating he was a vampire … maybe even had a set of those fake vampire teeth … probably custom-made with some sort of steel … sharpened…"

"Really, Frankie?" Nathaniel interrupted, staring at his junior partner with disgust.

"Well, how else can you explain the old bugger's blood was drained out through two puncture wounds so close together? Completely drained, too." Frankie smirked.

Nathaniel ran a hand through his hair and leaned back in his chair. "Don't know, but when I've finished this report, I'm going to head to the morgue and talk to Mitch—see if he can shed any light on the situation." Nathaniel resumed typing.

"What can I do?" Frankie asked.

Pausing, Nathaniel looked up. "Well, for starters, why don't you gather a couple officers together and start canvassing the area on both sides of the railway tracks. Surely someone was up early in the morning and might have seen our killer lurking around."

Angelique wandered through the main floor hallway at the Branford General, then took the stairway to the basement level, where she assumed the morgue was located. She was in luck. As she exited the stairwell a sign was directly in front of her, pointing her to the left: *Morgue.*

Venturing cautiously past several closed doors, Angelique finally came to the big double doors leading into the morgue. She put her ear to the metal door and listened. She peeked through the small window, noticing two bodies laid out on stainless steel tables.

One of the bodies was still clothed, but Angelique saw he was wearing rags. The man also had a long scraggly beard, and what flesh was exposed was crusted with dirt. "This must be the one," she murmured.

Angelique glanced over her shoulder. The hallway was still quiet. Muttering a chant, Angelique transformed into a mouse and squeezed through the crack at the bottom of the door. Once inside the room, she scurried to the first table and climbed up the leg and onto the flat surface where the body lay.

"Phew! This has to be the guy I am looking for." She made her way up to the old man's neck, confirming the two puncture marks. Angelique scurried under the man's beard and, taking a deep breath, began a silent chant, the spell that would return the body to normal—full of blood, and no puncture wounds.

Suddenly, the door swung open and a heavy set of footsteps entered. "Hey, Mitch," the voice greeted.

"Nathaniel … what brings you here? Can't wait for me to finish the autopsy on old Vincent? Horrible way to go. Whoever did him in must be a real sadist."

"Got anything yet?"

Mitch, who was standing by the other table in the room, set his scalpel down, wiped his hand on his apron, and walked over to the table where Vincent lay. Angelique hesitated a moment, then continued her chant, quicker now, with a sense of urgency to finish the spell. She felt the presence of two bodies standing close.

Nathaniel reached over and touched Vincent's beard, close to where Angelique was hiding. She made her way into Vincent's shirt pocket just in time to avoid Nathaniel's hand. "I wonder when the last time was that the old fellow had a good bath," he stated. "Hope they clean him up before the burying," he added.

"Won't be a burial," Mitch said. "These are sad cases, the homeless. Cheapest way to deal with them is cremation; government funds pretty well cover that."

"Shame. Man is born … lives his life … falls on hard times for whatever reasons … dies a horrible death … then gets incinerated." Nathaniel removed his hand from the beard and leaned over for a closer look at the puncture wounds he had seen on the neck at the crime scene. "What the hell!" he exclaimed, stepping back in shock.

Mitch looked at Nathaniel, a puzzled expression on his face. "What's up?"

"I could've sworn there were puncture marks on Vincent's neck!" Nathaniel shook his head in disbelief. Thinking he might have looked on the wrong side, he turned the victim's head. Nothing. "There were puncture marks, right, Mitch? You saw them … everyone saw them." Nathaniel stepped back from the body, turning to Mitch, a puzzled look on his face.

Angelique took the opportunity to escape Vincent's pocket, and scurried to a corner of the room. Her spell had worked. She decided to stick around long enough to enjoy the fruits of her labour.

Mitch approached the body to get a closer look. "I agree with you, Nate; there were puncture wounds on this man's neck, yet there doesn't seem to be any now … and … no … it can't be!"

When Mitch didn't say what couldn't be, Nathaniel pushed for further information. "What can't be?" he asked.

"When we brought this body here, it was drained of blood, right?"

"So we figured."

"Then how do we explain the fact that his body is now full of fluid?" Mitch shook his head disbelievingly.

"What!" Nathaniel couldn't believe what he was hearing. "The next thing you're going to tell me is that Vincent isn't dead and that any minute he's going to sit up and walk out of here to the nearest bar!"

Angelique let out a mousy snicker. *Why didn't I think of that? It certainly could completely solve the problem.* She began another silent chant, a spell she knew would only be temporary, but would buy enough time to thwart the police from investigating further into the death of a man who really hadn't died. Finishing the spell, she scurried over to the big double doors, ready to take her leave, hesitating only long enough to confirm all was in place.

"Ohhhhhh…" a low moan came from the body lying on the table. Vincent's body twitched, slowly at first, then building up to heavy shudders. "Ohhhhhh … w-w-where the f-fuck am I … I-I n-n-need a drink…" Vincent was trying to sit up.

Mitch moved quickly, settling Vincent back onto the table. Vincent struggled—pretty powerfully for a supposedly dead man—but Mitch's hand was firm on the old man's chest. Nathaniel just stood staring at the scene unfolding before them.

Angelique made her way down the hallway, back toward the elevator. Checking to ensure she was alone, she transformed back into human form. Once on the elevator, she pushed the button for the first floor, then leaned against the wall and smiled. All was going to be well. She was positive the investigation would stop, and there would be no one knocking on the count's door asking questions.

Had Angelique stayed a moment more, though, she would have heard Nathaniel's phone ring, and heard him tell Mitch about the camera and tape the owners of the Station Coffee House had turned in to the police station.

Chapter Six

Samara was furious. Furious at Ildiko for insinuating she might have had something to do with Katalin's death, just because she had killed the old man over at the Station Coffee House.

"Who do you think you are, Ildiko?" Samara's voice rose in anger. She paced furiously back and forth in front of her window. "You think I'm not aware you've been trying to use me to gain control over the throne? Do you think I'm not aware you've encouraged my relationship with Lajos, thinking you control him, and thus will be able to control me once you implement whatever plan you've concocted to see me on the throne and to have my brother cast aside?

"I saw through you the minute you set foot in my father's house in Brasov! I played your game, but I'm better at it—much better. I've enjoyed my time with Lajos, and I know he's enjoyed his time with me … more than he enjoys bedding you!" Samara couldn't help but snort at her last statement, remembering Ildiko leaving Lajos' flat and her, Samara, enjoying further moments in the arms of a man who knew how to please a woman in so many ways!

"I'll bring you to your knees before me for what you have tried to accuse me of! I'll turn the table on you—suggest it was you who murdered Katalin—and when the time comes … yes, you'll touch the throne, but only the stone beneath my feet, with downcast eyes. I'll spit on you … I'll spit on you as you did on my mother! I have no great love for her, but what you tried to do … you and Teresa … trying to kill my mother in an attempt to steal the throne … Do you think I'm blind as to not see what you are? That I do not know how quickly you would eliminate me when you feel you are secure enough to take what you have always longed for? No … you'll never sit on my father's throne … it's mine … mine alone!"

Samara thought about Santan. Despite everything, she loved her brother. She felt he was weak, though, and in great need of her strength. Samara thought about what she'd done to Mia, at Mia's request. Mia worried her; the girl was proving to be an annoyance.

The tension in Samara's body was building. The more she thought about what was happening, the more the power within her rose—the tempest brewing. She raised her hands above her head and a streak of lightning shattered through the room, destroying the desk by her window.

Samara twirled around and around, her rage releasing within the four walls. Finally, she fell to the floor, exhausted, lying amongst the rubble she had created.

Santan sat quietly at his desk, pondering the events transpiring in his life. What he had wished for—a life with Mia—was complicated now by what Samara had done. Mia's turning had changed her, and Santan did not like what he saw.

A soft knock came on his door, followed by Mia's voice requesting entry. Santan walked over and opened his door, but stood blocking her entrance into the room.

"Can't I come in, Santan?" Mia asked, batting her eyes at him.

Santan did not hesitate with his answer. "I don't think it would be appropriate under my father's roof."

"But…"

"There's no but, Mia. What happened back at Carla's place should not have happened, even though I participated as willingly as you. We're to be married now—now that you are a vampire. I won't come near you again like that until then." Santan was buying himself time to discover what was going on with Mia. "I think you need to stay focused on learning control in your new life, and I think it would be helpful if you spent more time with my mother. She's the one to best help you with your transition, having gone through it herself."

Mia stamped her foot in frustration. "Why are you being like this, Santan? Isn't this what you wanted, for us to be together forever? I thought you'd be pleased. And, I thought I pleased you well…"

Santan's face was stern as he said, "I did want us to be together forever, Mia, and yes, I'll admit, physically, you pleased me greatly … but … but I'm not thrilled about the way you're behaving. This turning has changed you, and until you get a handle on yourself, I think it's best my mother helps you through." Santan stepped back into his room with the intention of closing the door, ending his discussion with Mia.

Mia wasn't about to be thwarted. She pushed her way into the room, almost knocking a shocked Santan off his feet. "I … will … not … be … cast … aside, Santan!" she shouted, her eyes burning red.

Despite the usual gentleness of his demeanour, Santan was infuriated by Mia's action. Collecting himself, he spun on her, his eyes now burning. He grabbed her by the shoulders, forcing her to look him straight in the eyes. Seconds ticked by before he spoke.

"Don't you ever think you are more powerful than me, Mia!" There was an icy pitch in his voice and he felt Mia stiffen under the pressure of his hands. "You will learn soon enough what kind of a world you are in, and what will be expected of you—should you ever make it to sit on the throne next to me!" he viciously added.

Mia cast her eyes away, cowering. This was a Santan she'd never seen before … more like his father.

Santan closed his eyes, envisioning where his mother was at the moment. He saw her alone, so transported himself and Mia to her room.

Virginia turned in shock at the intrusion. "Santan … Mia! To what do I owe this pleasure?"

"I have a request of you, Mother." Without waiting for Virginia to say anything, he continued. "I need you to watch Mia and help her finish her transformation. Don't let her out of your sight. I need you to teach her how to behave in our world, for her sake and ours!"

Virginia tilted her head questioningly. "What's wrong?"

Santan didn't want to say in front of Mia what his misgivings were, so he used another power he had discovered since the ceremony back in Brasov: he planted his thoughts in Virginia's mind. She nodded; she had heard him. Mia stood looking from Santan to Virginia and back, bewildered.

Heading to the door, Santan half-turned: "I will see you both in the dining room later."

Gara was annoyed at the inference Basarab had made toward Ildiko, but even more upset that he was being delayed in Brantford until the issue of who killed Katalin was solved.

"How dare Basarab detain us here!" Gara exclaimed as he paced the room he and Ildiko had been assigned to until Victor could clear the second one for them.

"He doesn't believe me," Ildiko stated. "What shall we do?" Ildiko had never felt at such a loss of how to handle a situation, and, for the first time in her life, she was afraid of Basarab. Really afraid. "There will be no exile for me this time if Basarab thinks I am the one who killed Katalin." Ildiko's voice was hauntingly terrified.

Gara's voice was icy, though: "You were the one who killed Katalin, sister. Even if you didn't strike the first blow, and the woman probably would have died had you left her alone, you finished her off and then foolishly threw her from the top of the house—an exceedingly stupid move on your part. Unless you come clean with who was there first and twist the truth slightly to remove the limelight from you, you are doomed. Basarab knows you were here in Brantford at the time of Katalin's death. He knows we are both lying," Gara finished, unhappy with the predicament he was in because of his reckless sister.

Ildiko's face darkened as her mood changed from demure to uncompromising. "I don't know why Basarab is so obsessed with finding Katalin's killer—she was just a human!"

"One who was married to the count's friend, I might remind you. And also the mother of the girl his son loves." Gara swallowed hard before his next thought was put into words. "Do you ever think of consequences before you act, sister?"

Ildiko felt trapped. She knew the only true ally she had was her brother—the twin connection bound them closer than regular siblings—and she had angered him with her indiscretion—again. Her only recourse was to humble herself to him, and humble was something she was not good at.

"I am sorry, Gara. Really sorry. I know I'm impulsive." She paused. "If I get out of this, with your help, I promise to work on that." Ildiko hoped she sounded sincere enough to convince her brother that was her intention.

"I guess we will see, won't we—if you get out of this one alive. You've had centuries to change, and the years have not tempered your impetuous behaviour one bit!" Gara didn't like that he had outright lied to Basarab, something that could—would—jeopardize the count's trust in him.

Dracula and Lajos were strolling around the grounds, Dracula having said he needed fresh air and would like the company. He needed to speak with Lajos about what was going on.

"I thought we were to stay in the house," Lajos alleged as they approached the spot where Katalin's body had been found.

"I don't believe walking within the property boundaries means we are leaving the house," Dracula stated matter-of-factly. "Now, if we were to go downtown and have ourselves a little fun…" Dracula chuckled suggestively.

The Lajos that Dracula knew would jump at the chance to break the rules, but lately, Lajos seemed changed. *Maybe there is too much stress being put on you … me … Ildiko … Samara … and you don't know where your allegiance lies anymore. I fear my niece—the temptress—has a firm hold on you, and maybe you now have your own aspirations for the throne!*

Dracula knelt down where Katalin had been found. He lowered his nose to the grass and sniffed, picking up all the scents: Délia's, Basarab's, Kardos', and his own. Plus the other two—Ildiko's and…

"Ildiko definitely has something to do with what happened," Dracula stated as he rose to his feet and faced Lajos, "but, that will be our little secret for now. Besides, she's not the only one involved here. I just can't place the other scent…"

"As you suggested," Lajos interrupted, "maybe it was Mia. Hers would be a new scent, one you are not yet familiar with."

"Maybe so." Dracula put an arm around Lajos and guided him away from the spot. "Let's go have some fun; I have a thirst."

"Basarab's orders were for us to remain here," Lajos protested weakly for the second time.

Dracula laughed.

Chapter Seven

Nathaniel raced back to the precinct, burst into the room, and went straight to Frankie's desk. "Have you looked at the tape yet?" he demanded.

"Nope. Thought I'd wait for you," Frankie grinned. "Especially since you told me to."

"Where is it?"

"Right here." Frankie took the tape from his desk drawer and handed it to Nathaniel.

"Is the T.V. set up?"

"Yep."

"Let's go."

On the way to the T.V. room, "Something else you need to know, Frankie…" Nathaniel filled his partner in on what had transpired in the morgue.

"Holy fuck!" Frankie swore. "You've got to be kidding me! The old bugger's alive?" He paused. "So why the hell are we wasting time looking at this tape?" he added.

"Something's not right about this whole thing," Nathaniel replied, shoving the tape into the VCR. "There's still a crime been committed."

"But you said Vincent isn't dead?"

"Frankie, were we not at a crime scene this morning?"

"Yeah."

"Did we not see a body, drained of blood, lifeless?"

"Yeah."

"So, like I just said, there's something not right here. Push play."

The tape, according to the owners of the Station Coffee House, was taken from their rotating camera, which was the best and cheapest way to cover more area around the parking lot. Nathaniel and Frankie watched as old Vincent staggered in and out of the line of the camera.

"Back it up a sec," Frankie said. As the tape rewound, "There! Stop it!" He pointed to a shadow moving across the parking lot seconds before Vincent appeared. "What's that?"

Nathaniel leaned in closer to the screen, squinting. "Don't know … probably just a shadow cast by the parking lot lights. There's a bird there, too … see?" He pushed play and they watched Vincent again coming in and out of view, but still quite a distance from the café.

The officers watched as the camera scoped around the back of the building, then the railway tracks. "Stop!" Frankie shouted for the second time. "Is that another shadow there, hovering over the tracks?"

Nathaniel studied the picture. "Could be. The only other thing in the picture, besides the scenery and the shadow, is a bird flying just behind and above the moving shadow. Probably nothing to get excited about." He pushed play again.

The next part of the tape puzzled both officers. They saw Vincent smile at something or someone, then the shadow appeared again and Vincent's face took on a look of terror. He seemed to be struggling with something, but there was nothing there but the faint shadow. Then Vincent crumbled to the ground and was being dragged—seemingly by the shadow—to behind the dumpster.

Frankie got up and circled his chair, frustrated. He put his hands on his hips, then pointed at the T.V. screen where Nathaniel had paused it. "What the fuck! How do you explain that? The old tramp was killed by a shadow?"

Nathaniel leaned back in his chair, tapping the remote on his knee. "Don't forget, a short time ago I was in the morgue where Vincent's body was laying on a slab, drained of blood, puncture marks on his neck—dead. No doubt about it. Yet when I left that room, Vincent was alive, there were no marks on his neck, and he was asking for a drink! None of this makes any sense," Nathaniel said, shaking his head back and forth. "No one took pictures at the crime scene, so we have no proof of Vincent's condition there, other than what we all saw."

"Yeah, big mistake not taking pics. I guess, Vincent just being an old tramp, it wasn't worth the bother, eh?" Frankie leaned on the back of his chair. "Push play."

The tape moved forward. The scene where the coffee house owners discovered the body unfolded. The two officers continued watching, looking for clues as to what might have killed Vincent initially, even though he was alive now.

"Stop the tape again," Frankie barked, suddenly leaning forward. He pointed to the dumpster. "There's that bird again— the one you pointed out earlier."

"Really, Frankie? A bird? When I noted the bird, I didn't mean it had anything to do with the crime!" Nathaniel snorted. "Birds are everywhere. Nothing strange about a bird flying around."

"I know, but once you pointed it out, I began to think about it ... the bird—*that* bird—was in a couple of the previous clips, and here it is again." Frankie tilted his head, ignoring Nathaniel's sarcasm.

Nathaniel chuckled: "Really, Frankie?" he repeated.

Frankie looked dead-serious as he pointed to the bird. "Look how it's perched on the dumpster, watching everything going on. Moves its head every time that shadow touches the old bugger. If I were a betting man, I'd say that bird knows—"

"Knows what, partner? Shall we put out an APB on the bird? You're losin' it big time here, buddy. It's a goddamn bird, for Christ sake! I think you need to go home and sleep off whatever you're on. I'll finish the report, add what was on this tape, but far as I'm concerned, as strange as it all is, Vincent is alive—saw it with my own eyes. Captain is going to tell us to close the case and move on."

Nathaniel shut the VCR off and pulled out the paperwork he needed to fill in. Despite what he'd told Frankie, he was still bothered by what was going on, and didn't intend to let it go.

Frankie wasn't totally convinced either. Not only did he know his partner probably wasn't going to let matters alone, he had a gut feeling there was more to the situation than met the eye. He felt a little follow-up at the crime scene wouldn't hurt; this whole case was too weird. He headed out of the station and drove to the train station and parked behind the coffee house. Getting out of his car, he walked around to the back of the building, to the dumpster, and scanned the area where the body was found, searching for clues.

Seeing nothing significant, Frankie walked in the direction the shadow in the video seemed to have gone—and the bird—across the railway tracks. He studied the ground as he went along. There had to be a clue somewhere. But, despite several footprints around the tracks, there didn't appear to be anything unusual.

He continued, walking into some long grass and weeds growing along the outskirts of the tracks. A flash of red caught his eye. Frankie bent over to see what it was. A small piece of material snagged on a bramble weed. Frankie reached into his back pocket and pulled out a plastic evidence bag.

"Could be nothing," he mumbled. "But who knows, might be a clue."

As Frankie made his way back to his car and was about to pull out his cell phone to call Nathaniel, his phone rang. "Yo," he answered.

"Where are you, Frankie?" Nathaniel's voice came over the line.

"At the train station. What's up?"

Without asking Frankie why he was at the train station, Nathaniel relayed his message. "Guess whose body was just found down by the river? Vincent's! Deader than a doornail. Hit his head on a rock, blood everywhere. Bottle of booze broken on the rocks."

"Any puncture wounds show up on his neck? Blood still in his veins?" Frankie interrupted.

"No puncture wounds but yes, blood still in his veins."

"Guess the old bugger is really dead this time." Frankie paused. "I've got something to show you … be there in a few minutes … wait for me." He shut his phone before Nathaniel could ask him any questions. The case was getting stranger, and the piece of material in his evidence bag might be the clue that would lead the police to a cold-blooded killer.

Chapter Eight

Lardom opened the envelope, which had been sent by special courier. There were two envelopes inside, a small one that read, 'open first,' and a second one that read, 'details.' Opening the first envelope, Lardom recognized the letterhead immediately and scanned down the list of names of vampires who were required to attend an emergency court at Yates Castle in Brantford where Count Basarab was presently staying: Vacaresti, Uros, Tardos, Sebes, Farkas, Bajnok, Kerecsen, and Laborc. There were added notes below the list of names: one, his presence was also requested, and two, the Russian vampire, Volodya, and his immediate family, as well as Délia and Ákos, were also to return to Brantford.

The letter ended with a firm request for everyone to be in Brantford within two days. No excuse for not showing up would be tolerated. The situation needing attention was dire.

Lardom wondered what the gathering of the council members was all about; what was the reason to have Basarab's innermost trusted vampires travel to Brantford for a vampire trial? Opening the second envelope, the details were revealed. After reading Attila's letter, Lardom leaned back in his chair for a moment, then picked up his phone and dialed, hoping he would be able to reach everyone on the list.

Basarab called Viktor to his study to ask him to prepare more rooms for guests who would be arriving within a couple days. "I apologize for putting so much work on your shoulders, but the issue of who killed Kaitlin must be dealt with before I leave Brantford. I have sent word for my most trusted council members to come here for a trial." The count paused. "Do you need any assistance? I could bring in someone to help with preparations."

Viktor knew from the way the count worded his request he would be obliged to deal with the opening of the extra rooms himself. "I will attend to matters and all will be ready. There is an entire wing I can open, which should accommodate everyone. We can also utilize some areas in the basement if need be."

"It may be," Basarab replied, handing Viktor the list of names.

Viktor smiled, bowed, and backed out of the room. "I'll get right on this," he said.

After Viktor left, Basarab paced. He was frustrated. He was more than that—he was furious! There was an uneasiness brewing inside him, something that could only be quenched by…

Basarab headed toward the front door and walked out into the night. There were still a couple hours before the vampires were to convene in the study. He knew the streets would be filled with revellers this time of night and he was not as foolish as his daughter. Whoever came in contact with him would never remember their encounter; their life would go on the same as before.

Samara picked herself up from the floor. She surveyed the disaster in her room but smiled. With each passing day, she felt her power growing, and she knew she was going to be a force to be reckoned with. Samara dusted off her clothes and walked to the door. There was still a while before the meeting in her father's study, and this time she would be more careful of how and where she quenched her thirst—she would leave no trace of her actions!

After filling out the police report about the most recent discovery of old Vincent's body, Nathaniel booked out and left for home. He hadn't thought the piece of material Frankie showed him was of any significance, telling the rookie it could belong to anyone. Nathaniel threw the baggie in the garbage after Frankie left.

Despite old Vincent being dead—again—and the case supposedly closed, Nathaniel decided to drive around the area on the far side of the railway tracks, despite it not being on his direct route home.

Travelling down Market Street, Nathaniel turned left onto Buffalo Street. As he was about to round the corner onto Usher, he noticed two men walking through the trees surrounding Brantford's famous Yates Castle. He slowed to a stop. Instead of sticking to the sidewalk, the men crossed the field and the train tracks.

"I wonder if they came from the castle or down the stairs from Terrace Hill," Nathaniel muttered. As he was about to put his vehicle in drive, he noticed another figure—a tall, well-dressed man—step out of the tree line. They, too, took off across the field toward the tracks.

Nathaniel scratched his head and cursed under his breath for not having a camera with him. He was wondering if the two parties were connected when a third figure appeared on the sidewalk, this time a female. He watched as the woman looked around before she, too, crossed the field to the tracks. He glanced at his watch. 1:30.

Resting his hands on the steering wheel, Nathaniel murmured: "I wonder what they're all up to … the bars are mostly closed or closing up at this time of night. Maybe they live downtown and are heading home? But why not together? Why all separately, yet in the same direction?"

Deciding to drive over to the train station parking lot, Nathaniel shoved his car into gear and did a quick U-turn. By the time he reached his destination, though, there was no one in sight. He shook his head, wondering how the individuals had moved so quickly, especially the female. Surely she wouldn't have had time to cross the field and the parking lot before he reached there. Making a mental note for him and Frankie to pay a visit to the castle, Nathaniel headed home.

Dracula and Lajos stood in the shadows outside a downtown bar as the patrons staggered out onto the sidewalk. Lajos could feel his thirst building. He hadn't wanted to at first, but now he was glad he'd accompanied Dracula.

Most of the people exiting were in groups. The vampires were aware of the consequences of attacking large numbers, so they waited patiently for one or two stragglers. Dracula tapped his fingers impatiently on his leg. As he was about to give up on the location, two young men exited the building, one of them turning and locking the door. When they passed the side of the building where the vampires were lurking, the men never knew what struck them.

As Dracula leaned over his victim, he warned Lajos: "Only enough to quench your immediate thirst, my friend. We don't want to be leaving any dead bodies around, as my niece did. I'm sure there will be others we can completely satisfy our thirst with." He sank his fangs into the limp figure in his arms.

Basarab walked down to the river, hoping he would find what he was looking for on a secluded part of the trails. He had before. He turned a couple times, feeling he was being followed, but saw no one. Continuing, he reached the large armoury building. Slipping around to the back of it, Basarab gazed down at the river, eyes searching.

Finally, he noticed a solitary figure sitting on a rock at the edge of the walking trail. Basarab glanced over his shoulder again, still suspecting he was being followed. Nothing. He shook his head, then made his way down to the lone person and sat beside him.

The young man stared at the intruder into his solitude. "What the…" he started.

Basarab looked into his victim's eyes: "No worries, son; this won't hurt, and you won't remember a thing."

Samara followed her father, making sure to keep a reasonable distance between them. She swallowed hard when he turned the first time, hoping she wasn't so close that he would see her. Luck was with her. Taking more care, she dropped back a ways. She watched her father go around to the back of the armoury building; she watched him go down to the trail by the river and sit beside a young man. Samara watched as her father leaned over his victim. She watched as he picked up the limp figure and placed him beneath some bushes, then headed back toward the building.

Samara moved quickly away from her hiding place, all thoughts of finding a victim of her own gone. She had what she needed to handle her father, and the satisfaction of this coursed through her veins. The vampire council would not be pleased with their leader's nocturnal activities—if she even needed to tell them.

With the fresh human blood in his veins, Basarab hurriedly made his way back to the house. There wasn't much time left before he would have to meet the family members in the dining room. Attila had agreed to take the lead, easing some of the pressure from his shoulders.

Chapter Nine

Nathaniel was already at his desk when Frankie sauntered into the office. "You're late," the senior officer regaled the rookie.

Frankie grinned sheepishly. "Slept in, boss." He went around to his desk and sat down, putting his feet up and leaning back in his chair. Noticing a distant look on his partner's face, "What's up? You look worried about something."

Nathaniel pursed his lips. "I drove by Yates Castle on my way home last night…"

"Why?" Frankie interrupted, raising his eyebrows questioningly. "You working another case in that area that I don't know about?"

"No … a hunch I had about Vincent's case."

"Really?" Frankie smirked. "I hear the place is haunted; do you think a ghost came out of there and killed the old bum?"

"Don't be a smartass!" Nathaniel leaned forward in his chair, "I saw something strange and thought we might want to follow up on who may be living there. I was under the impression the place is empty; the owner lives in Europe. Might not be the case." Nathaniel filled Frankie in on what he'd observed, then leaned back and waited for a reply.

"I see what you mean about it being a bit out of the ordinary at that time of night, but what does that have to do with the Vincent case? Like you said, they could have just been coming down the steps behind the castle, taking a shortcut from Terrace Hill.”

Nathaniel shook his head. “I don’t know, Frankie. But my old detective bones tell me something isn’t right, and since we’re going to canvas the houses in the area anyway, it wouldn’t hurt to stop in there and see if the owner or anyone else might have returned.”

“Maybe it was just a bunch of homeless cutting through the castle yard ... maybe they’ve even taken up residence there...” Frankie tried to suggest.

“None of the people I saw were homeless,” Nathaniel replied, “not the way they were dressed!”

Frankie stood and shrugged as he headed to the coffee machine. “Whatever you say, boss. Want a coffee?”

“No thanks, already had my quota for the morning. Get one to go, will ya; I’ll meet you in the cruiser.”

Basarab couldn’t sleep, despite the meeting going well. His father had handled the details of what would transpire once the council members arrived. Virginia was with Mia, and it appeared the young vampire was beginning to settle down under the experienced tutelage of her future mother-in-law.

As Basarab was about to return to his bed, to attempt to get some rest, his keen sense of hearing picked up the sound of tires rolling along the gravel in the parking lot behind the house. Then the sound of car doors and footsteps approaching the house. Basarab left his room and stood at the top of the stairs, keeping to the shadows, and watched.

A loud knock came to the door, and within a couple minutes Viktor appeared in the foyer and glanced through the peephole. Basarab noticed the butler sigh as he opened the door to two uniformed police.

"What can I do for you, officers?" Viktor droned.

Nathaniel was the first to speak. "Mind if we step in a moment, sir? There was a murder over behind the Station Coffee House, and we're canvassing the neighbourhood asking if anyone saw anything out of the ordinary going on there over the past couple days and nights."

Viktor's face remained blank. "I am sorry to hear of such a tragedy, but I don't know how I can help you. I don't go out much and am far too busy to be nosing out the windows to see what goes on in the neighbourhood. Besides, even if I did want to be a nosey neighbour, the trees block most of the view beyond our yard," Viktor informed.

Basarab smiled, despite worrying about why the police were coming to his door. As far as he knew, no one was aware he had returned. He decided to help Viktor out and started down the stairway. Viktor turned, surprise on his face, as the count approached. Quickly, he ushered the officers in and closed the door, knowing what would happen if the sunlight made its way into the foyer.

"How might we help you, officers?" Basarab asked smoothly. "I was just headed off to bed when I heard the knock. I was up late, reading … you know how it is when you get into a good book … can't put it down."

Nathaniel and Frankie couldn't take their eyes off the man in front of them. He towered well over six feet, and there appeared to not be an ounce of fat on the man. But it was his eyes that drew them in. They both noticed the blackness of them, and, to their surprise, a ring of red. Nathaniel thought the man was the size of the single individual who had stepped through the trees during the night.

Basarab smiled, as though sensing their thoughts. "I am afraid my eyes go quite red when I have been reading too long."

"Touché," Frankie returned, despite the discomfort that had started to creep through his bones. "Well, we just wanted to know if you noticed anything strange around…"

"Actually," Nathaniel intervened. "When I was driving home last night, I happened to pass by here and noticed some people coming out of the trees in front of your house. Thought maybe it might have just been some late revellers taking shortcuts across your property, but now that I know you are here … and possibly some family members?" Nathaniel raised his eyebrows questioningly, leaving the question hanging in the air.

"Yes, a few members of my family and I have come for a short visit to check on my holdings here. I am in the process of possibly selling this property and want to make sure I am making the right decision. It does hold a special place in my heart." Basarab smiled, yet the officers saw no warmth on his face.

"I see," Nathaniel said, regaining some semblance of control. "Would any of your guests have been out late last night, including yourself?"

Basarab's face remained steady, but inside he was wondering just what these men had seen, especially since they mentioned *guests*—plural. He knew he'd left the premises, but who else might have? Nevertheless, he continued smiling. "Most of my guests retire early," he stated. "To my knowledge, no one left the house. I will definitely check with them later when we meet for lunch, and if anyone did, I will be sure to let you know." Basarab glowered down at the officers. "Anything else?" he asked dismissively.

Nathaniel didn't like the tone of dismissal, but nodded and handed Basarab a card. "Give me a call if one of your guests might have ventured out. If that isn't the case, I would maybe take some precautions against people crossing your property so late at night."

Basarab took the card. "I will take your advice into consideration. But, for now, I must get to bed and grab a few hours sleep before lunch." He turned and moved toward the stairway. "Make sure the gentlemen get out safely, Viktor," the count said before starting up the stairs.

Viktor nodded, and, waiting until the count was well out of the line of sunlight, finally opened the door and ushered the officers out. He watched them make their way to their car and drive away before closing the door.

Basarab had remained partway up the stairs, and when Viktor turned after shutting the door, the count returned to the main floor. He stopped Victor, who was heading to the dining room. "A word, please."

Viktor turned, surprised. "Yes, count?"

"Did you see anyone leave the house last night?" Basarab left out that he, himself, had ventured out.

Viktor hesitated a moment. He kept a lot of secrets, and he kept them for good reasons. He liked his job, and the last thing he wanted was to lose it because of some wayward vampires, including the count. But he also knew where his loyalty should lie, and that was with his boss.

Finally, "I spotted Dracula and his friend, Lajos, walking around the grounds; however, I got busy and didn't notice when they returned to the house. Other than that, I saw no one else coming or going." Viktor waited for the count to reply.

Instead of asking anything more, Basarab turned and walked back to the stairs. "Thank you, Viktor. You have been very helpful."

Entering his room, Basarab began pacing. *What are you and your friend up to, uncle? Why were you wandering around the grounds when I specifically asked everyone to remain in the house? Are you the ones I felt following me? And is Viktor being entirely truthful with me? I noticed his hesitation...* Basarab was beyond frustrated. He didn't know how he was going to sleep now, but knew he had to. The next few days were going to be trying on everyone, and he needed rest in order to have his wits about him.

Little did he know just how trying the upcoming days—and nights—were going to be.

Chapter Ten

athaniel drove around the block before pulling over to the side and stopping the car. The only sound was the soft purring of the motor, and Nathaniel's fingers tapping on the steering wheel. Frankie stared out the window in the direction of the train station, pondering the visit and the strange people who lived in the big house.

"I think they're hiding something," Frankie broke the silence.

"I agree," Nathaniel returned. "I don't think we'd be remiss if we put a watch on the place."

"Might be a good idea." Frankie paused, unsure if he should tell Nathaniel what was really going through his head. Deciding he had nothing to lose, he dove in with his thoughts. "Did the big guy remind you of anything?"

Nathaniel looked puzzled. "Like what?"

"A vampire." Frankie's face was dead serious, and a soft pink flushed across his cheeks.

"Really, Frankie! A vampire! Get real, man!" Nathaniel guffawed, despite his own thoughts on the subject. "You better not be spreading those kinds of thoughts at the station or you'll be the laughing stock of the Brantford police force!"

"Just a thought," Frankie grinned, undaunted. "You have to admit, he did have an eerie presence about him—like Christopher Lee, the actor who played Dracula."

Nathaniel chuckled again. "Ah, my friend, there is the magic word—actor. Lee is an actor, not a real vampire!"

"Sure looks like one," Frankie mumbled, more to himself than to Nathaniel, and then shut his mouth and looked back out the window.

Nathaniel put the cruiser in drive again, heading in the direction of the station, forgetting all about checking in with any of the other people living in the neighbouring houses of Yates Castle and the Station Coffee House where old Vincent's body had first been found.

Dracula didn't like what he'd just heard. He'd been going down the stairs to the basement where his room was when he'd heard the knock on the front door. Curious, he made his way back to the basement door and observed the goings-on through a crack. Now Basarab knew that he and Lajos had, at the very least, left the house, even though Viktor had only seen them walking in the yard.

"There's something about you, Viktor; I don't trust you. I've been around long enough to be able to read people, and you were not telling your master the entire truth."

Dracula decided it best he speak with Lajos, so when Basarab asked what they were doing in the yard, they would have their stories straight. "Might be a good idea to just tell the count the truth," Dracula reasoned. "After all, Basarab knows I step out on occasion for fresh dessert," he laughed to the empty hallway as he approached Lajos' door.

After knocking twice and receiving no answer, Dracula decided just to enter. He knew Lajos was a light sleeper. To his amazement, the room was empty. Lajos had said he was going straight to bed when they'd returned from their adventures just before the sun rose. They'd entered the house through the secret passage, which ran from the schoolhouse to the living room on the main floor. He'd seen Lajos head to the basement.

"Perhaps, my friend, you have taken yourself to another bed, not being as fatigued as you presented to me?" Dracula left Lajos' room, intent on paying a visit to one of the upper floors where Samara would be.

Samara wasn't able to sleep. She was too excited, knowing what she now knew about her father's extracurricular activities. As she sat on the edge of her bed, a soft knock sounded on her door.

"Samara," Lajos called out softly from the hallway. "Let me in."

Samara grinned. "Just what I need right now," she whispered, perturbed at the disruption of her thoughts, as she made her way to let Lajos in.

Upon entering the room, Lajos grabbed Samara roughly, lowering his lips to her neck and taking a deep enough nip that he drew blood.

Samara pushed on his chest, shoving him away. "Take it easy, tiger," she grinned, then walked seductively to her bed and lay down, spreading her body invitingly. *May as well take advantage of the situation.* She smiled seductively.

Lajos didn't wait for a second invitation. He crawled onto the bed and onto the temptress, covering her with his passion. Holding Samara's wrists over her head with one hand, he fumbled with his clothing with his other, not seeming to be able to be rid of the clothes fast enough. Samara broke free of his hold and reached out to assist him, seeing how ready he was, her own heart skipping with anticipation.

Samara arched up to meet her lover. She knew the first coupling would be over quickly, and then they would temper the storm in their blood and ride the waves for as long as it took to satiate their overdue cravings.

It was three hours before the two lovers spent their fury, and they lay curled in each other's arms, Samara with her head resting on Lajos' chest, Lajos with his arms wrapped around the young temptress.

"I looked for you last night," Samara suddenly opened the conversation. She felt Lajos tense.

"And why is that?" he asked, a hint of nervousness entering his voice.

"Why do you think? I was hoping we could escape this place together, but I guess you had other things on your mind?" She hesitated a moment, running her fingers up and down Lajos' chest. "What were you doing, lover?"

When Lajos didn't answer immediately, Samara rose up on her elbow and looked down into his eyes. He could tell a storm was brewing within her, and not the kind of tempest he wanted to face.

"Were you with *her*?" Samara hissed. "Were you screwing, Ildiko?"

It was Lajos' turn to laugh now. "Don't be ridiculous, Samara! I've made my choice, and it isn't her!" Deciding to tell Samara the truth about where he was, Lajos continued: "Dracula and I went out for a walk and ended up being longer than we intended. I came to you as soon as I was able. Now," he moved quickly, pinning Samara underneath him. "How about I show you—again—how I feel about you?"

Samara giggled and surrendered. Again.

Dracula stood outside Samara's bedroom door, poised to knock; however, as he raised his hand, he heard what was happening inside the room. He grinned, turned, and walked away. He would make sure he spoke with Lajos before they reencountered Basarab.

Virginia stood looking down at a sleeping Mia. She felt awful about what had happened to the girl, knowing how difficult a transformation was. The past few hours had been problematic. Mia was utterly out of control, fighting physically against Virginia and spewing forth verbal attacks not exemplary for any young lady.

Finally, Mia stopped attacking Virginia and settled down and listened to her. For a half-hour before falling asleep, the new vampire had cried in Virginia's arms.

"I'm so sorry, Virginia. I didn't mean all those awful things I said … I'm sorry for striking you … I've been behaving like such a brat. Can you ever forgive me?" Mia sobbed as she stared saucer-eyed at Virginia.

Virginia gathered the girl into her arms and stroked her hair comfortingly. She whispered to Mia that all would be okay and that what she needed now was rest. Had Virginia seen the smile on Mia's face, she wouldn't have been so confident that the worst was over.

Angelique lay in Attila's arms. She sighed and stroked her husband's cheek. "I must admit, it was comical to see the look on the humans' faces when the old beggar sat up and asked for a drink."

Attila hadn't thought it was such a good idea for Angelique to resurrect Samara's victim, but it probably would confuse the cops enough to delay their investigation. "I am glad you got some enjoyment out of what you did," he chuckled. "It has been some time since I laughed like I did when you first told me."

Angelique snickered, but only briefly. "It was good while it lasted, but we both know difficult times are ahead of us. I also sense there is something even worse brewing on the horizon—worse than this situation with the old man, and ghastlier than Katalin's death. I've had dreams of something coming, but have not been able to see what, or who."

"Time will tell, my love," Attila whispered. "We have weathered many storms in the past, what is another one to us?"

Angelique shivered for no reason other than the memory of her dreams. "I hope you are right, Attila. Nevertheless, these dreams were murky, making it difficult to see who or what was in them, but the emotional state I am left with upon waking is of malevolence like I have never felt before. The storm is coming, husband, and I hope it is not a tsunami big enough to wipe out your family."

Attila was quiet for a moment after Angelique's comments. He drew in a trembling breath before speaking: "Maybe that wouldn't be so bad." He closed his eyes against the centuries of tear-wrought memories he held within his heart.

Angelique crawled slowly from the bed and gazed down at her sleeping husband. She noted the pain still etched around his eyes, the agony that had deepened over the years with not only his own sorrows but with each trial the family had faced. He gave her so much joy, though, something she'd never dreamed she'd ever know—an intense love with no demands.

Silently, she slipped out of the room, her turbulent emotions not allowing her to sleep. She made her way to the foyer, moved the thick tapestry away from the window, and looked outside to see what the day had to offer. No sun. Dense clouds, threatening rain. She let the material fall back into place, then left the house.

Angelique made her way across the lawn, past the tree-line, and across the street, in the direction of the Station Coffee House. So intent on where she was going, she didn't notice the unmarked black police car. She didn't see the officer behind the wheel pull out a set of binoculars and focus them on her. She didn't see him pick up his car radio and call the station to report to Nathaniel. Angelique didn't know the black car followed her and pulled into the parking lot at the train station, still observing her; it blended in with the other parked cars.

She wasn't there for any particular reason. Angelique noticed the police tape had been taken down, probably because, after discovering the victim was still alive, it was deemed unnecessary. Making her way to the front of the coffee house, Angelique noticed a bench and decided to sit for a spell. Despite the number of cars in the lot, it was quiet; everyone seemed to have already left on the trains and the coffee shop was not yet reopened for business.

"Poor people," Angelique sighed. "Must be traumatized by what they found behind their store the other morning."

Angelique's thoughts were interrupted by a group of boisterous teenagers walking along the train tracks.

"Hear about the old guy that got offed here the other morning?"

"Yeah, it was Vincent; nice old guy … gave me a coat last winter."

"Wonder if there's going to be a funeral."

"Doubt it. He was a nobody—like us."

A third voice broke into the conversation. "I heard he wasn't really dead. Friend of mine was up at Emerg and saw Vincent walk out of the hospital—well, more like stagger out."

Laughter.

"Yeah? Well if it was Kevin, he was probably so high he wouldn't recognize his own mother!"

"Fuck you!"

Laughter fading away.

Angelique stood and headed back to the house. The vigilant officer radioed Nathaniel.

"She's heading back … should I follow?"

Nathaniel scratched his head before answering. "This is what I'd like you to do…"

Angelique decided to take a long way back, heading out to the sidewalk along Market Street and turning onto Buffalo. As she approached the parking lot behind the house, she noticed a black car sitting there, its motor running. Hesitantly, she walked toward it, wondering what it was doing and if some of the family members had possibly already arrived from overseas. However, that wasn't logical, being daytime.

As she approached, the car door opened and a young man stepped out. "A word, miss?"

Angelique studied the intruder before answering. "To what do I owe the *pleasure* of your *intrusion* onto this private property? Did you not see the sign?"

The officer detected a hint of exasperation in Angelique's tone. He wasn't sure how much his boss wanted him to say, so he tried to think of something to stall time. Nathaniel was on his way and should arrive at any moment. As if on cue, a car drove into the lot.

Angelique turned, surprised at yet another intrusion. When she saw who got out of the driver's side of the vehicle, she swallowed hard. It was the officer who had been in the morgue when she'd revived the old bum. She looked away, giving herself a moment to recover, and then turned to face Nathaniel as he approached. She smiled aloofly.

Wow! What a beauty! Lucky man who has this woman in his bed! Nathaniel blushed at his thoughts. Out loud, "Good day, ma'am. I'm Officer Nathaniel Jones, and this is my partner, Frankie." Nathaniel flashed a badge and motioned for Frankie to do the same.

"What can I do for you, officers?" Angelique questioned, raising her eyebrows and looking them straight in the eyes.

Nathaniel cleared his throat: "We stopped by earlier today and spoke with a gentleman in the house—the owner, I believe—about some people we noticed coming through the tree line around the house last night. There was a group of two men, then one man, and lastly, just before we were about to drive on, a woman. Would that have been you by any chance?"

Angelique kept a straight face as she answered, despite the butterflies in the pit of her stomach. "I assure you, officer, I was in bed quite early last night. I had a headache and took leave of the family before supper was finished. My husband could vouch for me, or anyone else in the house, for that matter." She smiled amiably.

Damn! She has a husband! "Any other woman who might have ventured out at a late hour?" Nathaniel probed.

"Why don't you tell me what this is all about, *officer*," Angelique returned, furrowing her eyebrows and looking Nathaniel straight in the eyes again. "Has anyone from this house done something wrong that you know of?" she added.

When Nathaniel didn't answer right away, Frankie stepped forward. There was a smirk on his face when he spoke.

"I'm sure you must have heard on the radio or television, or read in the paper, there was a murder not far from here?" It was more of a question than a statement.

Angelique's face remained serious. "I assure you, no one in this household has heard or read anything about your murder. We do not own a radio or a television, and we don't waste our time reading the local paper. There are much better things to do with our spare time." She hesitated and stepped closer to the two officers. "Besides, we are only visiting here for a short time, so if that is everything you have to say to me, maybe you should get along and continue your investigation into who committed your crime."

Not giving either of the officers a chance to return volley, Angelique turned and quickly walked away, brushing past the third officer, who was just standing there watching the scene unfold.

Once inside the house, Angelique leaned against the door and took in three or four deep breaths. "Basarab must be informed about this incident," she murmured; however, she headed to her own room first to discuss the issues with Attila.

Chapter Eleven

Volodya was irritated when he received the demand from Basarab to return to Canada. He'd put behind him the disaster that had befallen his family, especially his daughter, Manya, and he wanted no more dealings with the leader of the vampire world or any members of his family! Manya was happy now, being reunited with Ákos, the love of her life, despite a deep brooding that had engulfed the young male vampire. Volodya put this down to the fact Ákos may still be pining for Samara, knowing what a hold the temptress might still have on him.

Vasilisa came up behind her husband and encircled her arms around his waist. "You know we have no choice, husband," she murmured against his back. She felt the shuddering release of breath as Volodya exhaled.

"We should have a choice, though," he spoke through gritted teeth as he turned around in his wife's arms. "We lived without the *family* for a long time—centuries—and now they come back into our lives and disrupt our peace. We may not be many, but we removed ourselves from Dracula and all those who supported him, right from the beginning. Basarab coming to power made no difference to us, so we still remained away. We have been happy. We have not been scorched by anything beyond our cave walls.

"We even took in, at significant risk, Ilias, and it was good, for a time. He fell in love with our Délia and took her as his wife, and she bore him a son before she turned. We never questioned Ilias about what happened to him in the mountains, despite how broken he was when he came to us. He healed under our care; and, even after we discovered who he was—his relationship to Dracula—we sheltered him.

"Ilias decided to take his son to Basarab for the final ceremony, which we could have performed here. He is ultimately to blame for all that has happened! Maybe it was the desire to see his mother and father again. I can't blame him for that, but what a can of worms he opened."

Délia had quietly entered the room while Volodya was speaking. She'd stayed in the shadows, allowing her king to go on. Deciding she'd heard enough, Délia stepped forward. It was time to reveal that Ilias had returned.

"He is home—my husband," she said as she approached her king and queen. "He is with our son at the moment, but wishes to speak with you, Volodya, at your convenience, of course."

Volodya nodded. "Tell him to meet me in the Great Room when he is finished his time with Ákos. I will wait for him there."

Délia bowed her head and backed out of the room.

Volodya waited patiently in the Great Room for Ilias to arrive. Finally, after about an hour, he appeared, with Rasputin.

"Volodya," Ilias walked quickly to his king and bowed. "I have returned by the grace of our friend here," Ilias motioned to Rasputin. "He found me in the mountains, almost expired from deprivation of nutrition. I had fallen on some rocks and was lying unconscious for … well, I don't know for how long.

"However, although I find it quite strange, I have memories of dreams, as though they were sent to me as a message to bring back to you, and I believe we must make sure the message reaches Basarab. I have the sense he is in danger, as is every member of his family."

Volodya raised his eyebrows and motioned for his two guests to sit. "Maybe you best tell me about these dreams."

Ilias' voice shook as he began, and Volodya could not detect whether it was from nervousness or from fear of what he was about to say. "I dreamed of a beautiful woman, but within her beauty there was something malicious, and extremely potent. She was familiar to me, as though I'd seen her before, yet I could not quite place where. She gathered me into her arms and carried me to a great fortress—also familiar—in the mountains, and handed me over to a group of men in white coats, who laid me on a stainless steel table. I felt I'd been there before, in the exact same situation.

"I could see her hovering in the background, a wicked smile on her face as she looked at me. The men turned my face so the woman was in my line of vision, and it felt as though she was boring into the centre of my core. A burning spread through me, and my entire body began to writhe on the table.

"The men in white tied me down, strapping my arms and legs to the table, then took big needles and began drawing vials of blood from me. She was laughing now, a diabolical sound that echoed in the room. The men expunged the blood into a granite bowl, then one of them took the bowl to her. He bowed as she took it from his hands.

"The burning in my body ceased temporarily as the woman set the bowl on what appeared to be an altar. Hovering her wrist over the dish, and without the benefit of a cutting tool, blood dripped from her flesh, mixing with mine. All the while, she chanted; I have never suffered such wickedness.

"As suddenly as the blood from her wrist began to flow, it stopped. She stirred the liquid with her fingers. She licked the blood from her hands before she approached the men in white, passing the bowl to them, watching as each one drank before handing it to the man standing beside them.

"I remember struggling against my restraints when I saw what was transpiring. As they drank the mixed blood their eyes began to flame, and their flesh became pale, almost transparent. So much so that I could see the blood flushing through their veins.

"In my dream, I was screaming, and straining against the ties as though my life depended on it. There was laughter all around me, hideous, grating on my nerves. I was sweating, dripping buckets of liquid, which fell over and began to fill the room. The water swirled around the table … the men in white hovered above it … the woman above them. It finally reached the table top and began to guzzle me, seeming to have multiple tongues flicking in and out of the waves, trying to devour me. I writhed in frustration as they taunted me with their insane laughter.

"As the water closed over me, I heard the woman speak. She said her time had finally come and that all those who bore the blood of Dracula would be sorry, especially him. She was coming to take what was rightfully hers! I closed my eyes then, giving myself up to fate, the sound of the creatures around me throbbing in my ears.

"It was then I felt a shaking on my shoulder and breath upon my face, as though someone was leaning over me. I heard a voice calling to me, calling my name. Rasputin saved me, not only from my death dream, but from where I had fallen, and he brought me home."

Ilias leaned back in his chair. Sweat beads bubbled on his forehead, dripping down his cheeks and neck, and melting onto his clothing. The room was silent as a tomb for several minutes before anyone spoke.

Volodya turned to Rasputin: "How is it you came upon Ilias?" he asked, puzzled about such a timely finding.

Rasputin was prepared for such a question. "I had begun to worry about Ilias when he didn't return after a few days, so I set off in search of him. I knew he'd been lost in the mountains before, a long time ago, and thought to search them. I was shocked by his condition when I found him, and it took a number of days to make him well enough to travel."

Taking a moment, Rasputin laid his hand upon his chest and moaned—a guttural sound. "What I witnessed when I found the body was trying even for one such as me—as our kind—to see. Ilias seemed to be almost completely drained of blood, his skin was flaking away. It was in the early hours of the evening when I noticed him on a rock, so I have no idea how long he was there; he must have had some exposure to the sun, but not enough to destroy him.

"I gathered him into my arms and wrapped my cloak around him. I had noticed a cave a short distance back on my travels and made my way down the trail toward it. Once inside the cave, I opened my veins and fed Ilias my blood, a bit at a time. Finally, he began to come around, but it took some time for him to gain enough strength, which is another thing peculiar for our kind—not to heal rapidly.

"During Ilias' recovery, he was quiet, except when he slept. Then he would toss and turn and speak of this dream that he just told you of. His face would be lined with fright, and he screamed out as though in pain—as though he were reliving the dream over and over again."

Rasputin ended his rendition of events there and folded his hands on his lap. The smirk on his face bothered Volodya. It suggested to the king that Rasputin was holding something back, but what? And were there not more important matters to attend to now? The warning about someone coming to take what was rightfully hers. The warning that all of Dracula's bloodline was in peril. Volodya had a decision to make, and it was not one he wished to do. He stood.

"We will be leaving for Brantford tomorrow," he stated blandly. "I was going to ignore Basarab's request for our returned presence regarding the death of Randy's wife, Katalin, but with what Ilias just relayed, despite his thinking it was nothing more than a dream, I don't think we can take the chance that was all it was. The family must be warned of imminent danger. I thank you both for your details and ask that you prepare yourselves for leaving." Volodya moved to leave.

"I will be accompanying you, as well?" Rasputin inquired, hiding his joy as best he could.

"Yes, you as well," the king replied on his way through the door.

Back in his room, Rasputin could barely contain his joy. It had been easy for him to find Ilias. In fact, he hadn't had to find him at all—he'd been there during the operation that Ilias thought was just a dream. He'd witnessed what was done to him. Rasputin was ordered to make sure Ilias was returned home safely. *She* was finished with him.

There had been no fall. There had been no cave. It had all been staged to maintain the dream-like state. Ilias had no idea how many days he had dreamed the same dream, but Rasputin knew. Rasputin also knew that the blood mixed in the bowl was done for two reasons: Ilias' blood was to turn the men in the room; her blood was so she could be in total control of her subjects.

Adrianna would be pleased he was going to Brantford with the Russian vampires, as she'd wished. It had been so easy.

Petya approached his father cautiously. He was bothered that Rasputin was accompanying them to Canada. "I don't trust Rasputin," the vampire prince stated.

The smile on Volodya's lips surprised Petya. "Nor do I," was the unexpected answer. "I have had misgivings about where Rasputin's loyalties lie for a long time. We took him in a long time ago, too many years to even count, but lately he is gone more than he is here—and without explanation."

"So why did you ask him to accompany us? His name was not on the invitation, or should I say summons, from Count Basarab."

"There is one thing I have learned over the centuries, son—keep your friends close and your enemies closer. That way, they will be facing you when they betray you."

Petya still didn't like that Rasputin was coming with them. He had enough fear in his gut about the reasons for being recalled to Brantford, with the pretence of holding a vampire court—inquiry—into the death of Katalin, the human's wife. He feared for Manya, and for his friend, Ákos. He even feared for Délia, who had found the body.

"Do you think Basarab believes one of us killed Katalin?" Petya straightforwardly asked his father.

Volodya observed his son, a thoughtful expression in his eyes. He chose his words carefully: "If we don't go, son, it may make them think one of us is guilty, but there is another reason we must go, one I have not told you yet. Ilias was given a warning in a dream—if that is what it was—he was told someone is coming for all those with Dracula's bloodline, and for this reason foremost, I must make sure Ilias is there to tell Basarab what happened to him, as our friend told me. If there is any foundation to his tale, the line of Dracula—which includes us— must stand together at all cost!"

Chapter Twelve

The Brantford airport had not seen or accommodated so many large, luxury planes ever, at least for as long as the oldest employee had been working there had witnessed, which was closing in on forty years. The landing of two jets on the same evening was bizarre.

Basarab had arranged for a large coach bus to pick up his guests and transport them to Yates Castle. The flight crew watched as the planes unloaded their passengers and they filed onto the bus.

Viktor had completed the arrangements for the guests, including setting up extra tables in the dining room. As the vampires arrived, they were ushered directly to their designated rooms and informed what time the meal would be served.

Basarab was not pleased by what Angelique was telling him about being questioned by the police officers, especially so soon after the same officers had shown up at his door.

"Did you get their names?" Basarab asked.

Angelique nodded. "Of course." She offered up the names.

"I have an old friend at the police station; I think I should pay him a visit and let him know some of his officers are harassing us for no apparent reason." Basarab walked over to the window, his hands gripped behind his back.

Attila came up behind his son and put his hand on Basarab's shoulder. "I hope your friend can do something because, with so many vampires here now, we cannot take a chance on those cops returning."

"I know, Father," Basarab returned, still staring out the window. "The sun has set again, but it is still early enough that I might be able to catch my friend at the station. If not, I am sure someone will know where he will be. I need you to entertain our guests until my return."

"Of course," Attila affirmed, then headed toward the door. Angelique followed.

Basarab waited a few more minutes before taking his leave.

Lajos finally left Samara's room, leaving her asleep. He knew Dracula would probably be wondering where he was. Approaching Dracula's room, he knocked softly and waited for an answer. It came immediately, and Dracula stood from the chair he'd been occupying as Lajos stepped inside the room.

"It's about time you returned," Dracula sneered, a twisted smile on his lips. "Are you satisfied?"

Lajos grinned. "Very." He strolled over to a chair and plopped down in it, his face turned up to the ceiling. "What's up?" he asked.

Dracula drove straight to the point. "Basarab knows we left the house last night. Viktor saw us in the yard."

Lajos leaned forward. "Did Viktor tell Basarab we left the grounds?"

"No, but Basarab is no one's fool. He will assume we might have; therefore, I want to make sure we have our stories straight." Dracula sat down and leaned toward Lajos. "We will tell the truth. We went out for a walk and found ourselves in the downtown area of the city. We can leave out the part of what we actually did."

"Will he not assume that, as well, if we tell him we were out and about?" Lajos wanted to ensure they were completely covered.

"Even if Basarab does assume we have stepped over the line and taken blood directly from humans, we did not kill them as our niece has done, so he has no proof." Dracula sat back in his chair. "I believe the council and some family members have landed for the trial—the Russian vampires, as well." Dracula paused. "I was watching out the window when they arrived and was surprised to see an old acquaintance of mine was with the Russians—Rasputin."

Lajos raised his eyebrows in surprise. "Rasputin! Now that is a vampire not to be trusted. What's he doing here?"

"Came with the Russians, I assume." Dracula stood and made his way to the door, opening it for Lajos. "Go, freshen up, my friend. The fun is just about to begin."

Samara stretched lazily when she heard her door close as Lajos took his leave. After a few more minutes of languishing under the covers, Samara threw the blanket aside and got out of bed. Heading to her closet, she decided to dress to impress for the guests. After all, she was Basarab's daughter, and if her plans came to fruition, she would be the next leader of all the vampires—with their blessings, of course. And what better time to sway them than now, when so many of the most important and trusted ones were under the same roof.

Virginia awoke from the chair where she'd fallen asleep. She glanced at the bed; Mia was still asleep. "Poor thing," Virginia whispered. "I hope the worst is over for her."

Mia stirred in the bed and moaned. Virginia walked over and sat down on the edge of the bed. Gently, she shook Mia's shoulder. "Time to wake and freshen up. I believe our guests have arrived and Basarab will be expecting us all to greet them in the dining room for our meal."

Mia rolled over and buried her face in the pillow. "Do I have to?" she mumbled. "I don't think I'm ready to meet all these vampires, even though I'm one now. It was hard enough at Santan's and Samara's crossing…"

Virginia didn't allow Mia to finish. "You will be fine; just stay by my side." She pulled the blanket off Mia and headed to the closet. Santan had been thoughtful enough to bring down a couple outfits for Mia to choose from for the evening meal. Virginia turned a moment, examining Mia's colouring, then selected the pale-blue dress. Setting it on a chair, "I think this will do just fine for tonight," she stated.

Proceeding to the door, Virginia hesitated before leaving. "I'll be right back; get dressed. When I return, I'll fix your hair."

With Virginia gone, Mia leapt from the bed, her eyes glowing red. She was thirsty. She looked around for a bottle of blood; seeing none, she cursed under her breath.

Mia picked up the dress. Looking at it, she snorted in disgust and threw it back on the chair. "She actually thinks I'm going to wear this little girl dress?" Mia's laugh bordered on hysteria. She opened the closet door, flipping through Virginia's outfits, hoping to find something more to her taste. She knew from past observations that Virginia had some pretty seductive garments. Mia was just about to give up when her fingers touched a soft material. She grabbed hold of the hanger and pulled out a red velvet evening dress. "Perfect!" she exclaimed.

No sooner did Mia have the dress on, the door opened, and Virginia stepped inside the room. She looked at her charge and grimaced. *If this is how you want to appear to everyone, well, so be it.* "I see you chose not to wear the blue dress," Virginia enunciated sharply. "Your reason?" she added.

"I'm not a child anymore," Mia returned with a pout.

You are definitely acting like one! "I see." Virginia approached Mia and circled her. "Don't you think this dress is a little too big for you?" Virginia noticed the trouble Mia was having keeping the strapless dress from falling off. "This dress was made specifically for me, my dear," Virginia continued, "and I might point out to you that I am much more endowed than you presently are."

Mia, even though she realized Virginia was correct, still didn't want to concede and have to wear the blue dress. She returned her attention to the closet, flipping through the outfits with one hand, and holding the red dress up with her other.

Virginia, feeling slightly sorry for Mia, "Maybe Samara has one more suited to you," she suggested. "You two are closer in size."

There was a noticeable sigh of relief from Mia.

"Give me a moment to change, and we'll go up and see what Samara might be willing to let you borrow," Virginia said as she reached into the closet to select her own outfit for the evening. On second thought, Virginia decided she wanted to wear the red dress, remembering how Basarab's eyes always lit up when she did. She turned to Mia. "Take it off," she ordered.

Shocked at the demand in Virginia's voice, Mia slipped out of the dress, which didn't take much effort. Virginia scooped the dress from the floor where it had landed and pulled it on over her head.

"Do you mind?" Virginia pointed to the back of the dress where the zipper was.

Mia's hands shook with fury as she zipped the outfit. Virginia sensed Mia wasn't happy. *Good ... you will need to learn your place in the hierarchy of this household, my dear ... you may as well start now, with this simple lesson!*

Virginia ran her hands over the material, smoothing out any wrinkles, doing so slowly for effect, and to prove to Mia that this dress was made, not for her, but for the wife of the Count Basarab Musat, leader of the vampires. Mia glared at Virginia's back, well aware of the lesson her future mother-in-law was trying to teach her.

You'll be sorry when I'm sitting on the throne beside your son and you must bow to me!

Virginia was cognisant of Mia's discomfort and, deciding she'd made her point, Virginia motioned to the door. "Shall we?"

Mia grabbed a blanket and wrapped it around her chest, then pushed past Virginia and headed to Samara's room.

Santan had not slept well at all. The dreams he'd had were sinister. He had visions of something dark hovering over the family, and it seemed the darkness had little to do with the trial.

He awoke several times, and each time he fell back to sleep, the murkiness would invade his mind again. Finally, Santan rose from his bed and paced around his room. He thought of going to speak to his father but decided against it. After all, it was only a dream.

Deciding to attempt sleep again, Santan returned to his bed and lay down. He pulled the pillow over his head, burying his face in the softness of the mattress. Closing his eyes, he re-entered his dream world.

This time, the scene that unfolded was of a court—a vampire court. His father and his council members were seated on a stage, and the room was filled with vampires looking on. There was a large chair by the table where the council sat, and between the council and the audience was another small table where a lone individual was rustling papers.

It wasn't a bad dream—yet—so Santan tried hard to remain in it. His father called witnesses to the stand and the man behind the small table was questioning them. Santan could not understand what he was saying, but each witness answered his questions—also unintelligible—then returned to their seat in the audience.

The dream went on and on; Santan saw himself sitting in the chair … he was dismissed … Samara was in the chair … she was dismissed … he noticed Randy standing at the back of the room, a scowl on his face as he watched the proceedings … Dracula took the stand and was dismissed … everyone who had been in the house on that fateful night when Katalin was murdered so far were being discharged.

Santan gasped in his sleep as Mia took the stand. He noticed how nervous she was. The vampire at the desk started questioning her and she broke down crying. Randy, seeing what his daughter was going through, ran to her and took her in his arms. He glared at Basarab and the council members, then lifted his daughter in his arms and carried her out of the room.

The dream faded.

Santan woke, a cold sweat breaking out all over his body. He lay for a moment more in his bed, then got up and dressed for the evening meal. He assumed, by now, the guests had arrived.

Chapter Thirteen

asarab returned from seeing his friend at the police station and went straight to his father's room.

"It did not go well, I take it, from the look on your face," Attila remarked.

Basarab snorted. "Oh, it was going quite well until one of the officers who were here popped his head into Captain Markus' office and saw me. He called Markus out into the hallway and spoke to him, and when Markus returned, he said there was nothing he could do for me. The officers were just doing their job." Basarab paused. "Markus was distant with me, not his usual friendly self I used to know," he added.

"You have been gone a long time," Attila suggested a reason for the old friend's indifference.

"I've often wondered how much some of my old friends really knew about me," Basarab pondered more to himself than his father.

Attila directed the conversation back to the present situation. "Markus saying there was nothing he could do for you probably means the police will be back around asking more questions," Attila stated, his voice stressed. "This is not good, especially now that everyone has arrived from Europe. I'm beginning to think it was not a good idea to hold this court hearing here, Basarab, mainly because of what Samara did to that old man. We have a big problem, I believe."

Attila paced—his back to Basarab. Returning his attention to Basarab, "We must convene court immediately, and as each individual is cleared, let them go."

Basarab stood for a moment, contemplating what might be their best move. With so many vampires in one place, and in such a small city, it could prove dangerous. On the other hand, he could pass the congregation off as a big family reunion and hold an after-dark party—maybe even invite some of the dignitaries he knew from when he'd lived here before. Possibly his police captain friend and the officers investigating the death of the old man. Basarab voiced his thought to his father.

Attila raised his eyebrows in surprise: "Really, Basarab? That is the worst idea I have heard you come up with, ever! Most of us are civilized enough to stay away from human blood directly from the source, however, you know there are those amongst us who are not! Need I say more to this crazy idea of yours?"

If there was ever a time Basarab had been thoroughly embarrassed, which he could not remember, it was now. *What am I thinking? My father is right—we just need to have this trial over and all get out of here before the police somehow tie my daughter to the incident at the train station!* "You are right, Father. I wasn't thinking rationally. We will inform everyone at mealtime that the trial will start immediately ... but everyone stays until it is finished."

Attila nodded. "As you wish." A pause. "We will need to ensure Lardom is fully aware of what has happened so he can question the suspects. He's one of the best lawyers I've ever come across, and if anyone can glean a confession, it's him," Attila interrupted. "I put a few notes in the attaché I sent, but maybe not enough for him to be fully aware," he added.

"It won't take long to go over a few preliminaries. We can actually start tonight, say around twelve o'clock," Basarab suggested.

"Who do you plan on calling first?" Attila asked.

"I'll let Lardom decide his strategy," Basarab replied, not wanting to commit. "I think it is time to go to the dining room; I hear some voices coming from that direction."

Attila nodded, and together father and son headed out of the room and down the stairs.

Upon entering the dining room, Basarab was greeted by his Aunt Emelia. He was surprised to see her since he'd not requested any family members to accompany the council members. "Oh, Basarab, it is so good to see you again," she said, giving him a tight hug. "I only wish it was under better circumstances. However," Emelia looked around the room, "it is nice to see so many of us here under one roof again, especially my son and grandson."

Basarab patted his aunt absentmindedly on her back. "Good to see you, as well," he mumbled, looking around the room at his guests.

Emelia, realizing her nephew's mind wasn't on her, smiled and backed away, then walked to where her husband, Vacaresti, Attila's half-brother, was seated. "Basarab is troubled," she whispered in his ear.

Vacaresti nodded. "As he should be," he mouthed back. "This situation is most distressing and out of the ordinary. I have a feeling a lot more than a trial is going to take place before we leave here." Vacaresti leaned back and sighed.

Basarab made his way to the head of the main table. He noticed his closest advisors, the chief vampire council, were seated there. Basarab observed the Russian vampires had chosen a table in the far corner, furthest away from where he was sitting.

Viktor was finishing setting the bottles of blood on the tables, and with the last one in place, he nodded to Basarab.

The count grasped the bottle by his glass and lifted it into the air. The talking that had moments before filled the room as the vampires caught up on each other's news, ceased, and all eyes turned to their leader.

Basarab's eyes swept the room again, taking in every detail. He was pleased to see that everyone asked answered his call, but at the same time, he was nervous about the situation Samara had created. She had been thoughtless about the trouble her rash actions could have. Having the police show up at his door, and then in his parking lot, was, without doubt, most disconcerting. And the fact he'd gotten nowhere with his friend at the police station didn't bode well with maintaining the anonymity he needed to protect his people.

Basarab poured blood into his glass, an indication the meal could now begin. Setting the bottle on the table, Basarab waited until everyone filled their glasses before opening the conversation.

"Welcome, my friends. I trust you are all settled comfortably into your rooms. I apologize for having to call everyone here, and I must warn you that some events that have unfolded over the past week have—*could*—put our kind in grave danger. Because of this, I must impress upon each of you the necessity to stay within the walls of this house until the trial is over.

"It is my hope that Lardom," Basarab directed a look to the vampire lawyer, "has somewhat informed you why you have been called upon. For the sake of surety, I shall fill you in more. Many of you were involved in the situation we faced several years ago here in Brantford when Radu attempted to usurp my throne. You may also be aware of my wife's dear friend, Randy, who, at the time, was instrumental in keeping her safe.

"Randy earned his way into our family, not by becoming one of us, but by his loyalty to us, and his friendship has meant a great deal to Virginia and me over the years. We were pleased when he married Katalin and filled with joy for him and his wife when they brought into the world their beautiful daughter, Mia. Many of you are most likely unaware that Mia has chosen to join us; she is in love with my son, Santan, as he is in love with her. It was not him, however, who turned her, but Samara.

"Mia's mother, Katalin, made no secret of how she felt about our kind and how she felt about Mia being part of Santan's—our—world. When she found out Mia turned, Katalin was beyond furious, and I knew I was going to have to do some damage control. However, before I could, someone slit Katalin's throat, drained her blood, and threw her from the widow's walk at the top of the house. Her body was discovered by Délia, who immediately came and told me.

"As you can imagine, my friend, Randy, is devastated by the slaying of his wife, and I have promised to discover and punish the perpetrator of this sordid murder. This was a senseless deed, and whoever has done it will be put to death, as is the custom when one of us takes such a disgraceful, unjustified path."

Basarab studied the vampires before him as he spoke, especially those who had been present, or possibly present, when Katalin was murdered. "Since we were unable to establish who killed her at the time and no one came forward, this trial became a necessity," Basarab continued. He looked at the table where the Russian vampires were congregated. "I apologize to you, Volodya, and to your family, for dragging you back here. I hope you understand. It is my intention to have this matter dealt with swiftly so we might all go home."

Volodya nodded to the count. "I would ask permission to speak when you are finished telling us what you need to," he began. "I have something of dire importance to relay to you and everyone here."

"You may have the floor now, Volodya," Basarab replied. "Come, stand by me, and tell us what is on your mind." The count motioned to his side.

Vasilisa put her hand on her husband's arm and nodded for him to step up beside the count and tell everyone what they needed to hear. Volodya patted her hand, smiled, stood, and made his way to the front of the room. He bowed his head as he approached the count, then, turning to the congregation of vampires, he bowed to them, as well.

Clearing his throat, Volodya began speaking: "I have distressing news … as you know, Basarab, Emelia's son, Ilias, was distraught with the death of his son, Ákos, and he left your castle in Scotland before the truth was revealed. Upon his return to Russia, he took himself to the mountains to try and deal with his loss. When he returned, he revealed to us what he thought was a dream—a very vivid dream. He said it all felt very familiar.

"He said in the dream was a beautiful, yet powerfully evil woman, who took him to a fortress in the mountains and laid him on a table. He was surrounded by men in white, and they tied him down and took needles and drew his blood. Ilias said the blood was poured into a bowl then handed to this woman, who in turn mixed her blood with his as she chanted.

"Upon finishing, she stirred the blood with her finger and licked it from her flesh before passing the bowl to the men who were surrounding Ilias. As each of the men drank the mixed blood, their eyes began flaming and their flesh paled. Ilias said he struggled against his restraints as those around him laughed.

"Ilias said he began to sweat, and the water fell in buckets from his body, filling the room. The men hovered over him, and the woman hovered over them. Her voice rang out, sharply … she said her time had arrived and all the blood of the line of Dracula would be sorry—especially Dracula; she was coming to take what was rightfully hers!

"At that point, Ilias awoke to Rasputin shaking his shoulder, and though he thought he'd been asleep, the dream had been more than real to him. Rasputin informed us that when he found Ilias, his body was almost completely drained of blood. I, personally, felt an obligation to inform you of this situation, Basarab, for, as you well know, there have been rumours throughout the years of a great sorceress—one more evil than any before or after her!" Volodya finished with a deep sigh.

Silence shrouded the room.

Chapter Fourteen

Adrianna Daciana stood by the window, looking out at the sheer rock walls of the mountains surrounding her fortress. She smiled, thinking about what she'd accomplished during Ilias' visit. She now had a small group of powerful low-breeds loyal only to her. The drinking of her blood mixed with that of the blood drawn from Ilias had assured their vampiric functions.

Returning to her desk, Adrianna tapped the centre drawer and withdrew a vial of blood. She held it up to the light. "You will do, won't you? Just enough for the two individuals who I intend to resurrect to assist me in my plan to attain the vampire throne."

Adrianna placed the vial in her pocket and left her study, moving quickly to the door opening to the stairs that would take her down into the deepest depths of her castle—the place where she kept, well-hidden, her darkest secrets.

The stone walls dripped moisture onto the floor of the passageway. Adrianna made a mental note to have the leakage seen to; it was increasing its flow. At the end of the hall was a large iron door. No knob. No keyhole. Adrianna murmured a few words and the door swung slowly open, revealing two coffins.

Walking to the first coffin, Adrianna ran her fingers over the polished oak letters: ELIZABETH BATHORY. Opening the casket, Adrianna peered at the body inside. Perfectly preserved. It had taken Adrianna some time to restore Elizabeth when she'd found her immediately after the episode in Brantford. Adrianna had hidden in the wooded area across the trail from the shack and watched Basarab rescue Virginia. She had been intent to interfere but then had stepped back to see what was about to happen.

Adrianna had hoped Elizabeth and Peter would destroy Basarab, but then all the others had come to assist their leader. However, the one she wanted to be there was not—Dracula! So she had stayed back, only going to the shack when all the vampires left.

Upon entering the building, Adrianna instantly saw there was no hope for Peter, his head having been severed. But the other vampires, even though they had ravaged Elizabeth, failed to finish the job. She was still alive! Adrianna transported Elizabeth back to her fortress in the Transylvanian mountains, nursed her back to full capacity, and then cast a sleeping spell on her until Adrianna was ready for her to awaken.

Now was the time.

Adrianna made her way to the other coffin and opened the lid. Inside was Dracula's brother, Radu. Adrianna had followed Radu's quest for the throne closely. She'd watched him build an army of rogues and observed his failure to usurp Basarab. Nevertheless, Adrianna felt that when she decided to make her move, Radu might be of some use to her. She'd found him licking the wounds of his defeat in his castle and had cast her spell, which put him into a deep sleep. She destroyed all Radu's rogues, transported him to her fortress, and laid him in the coffin next to Elizabeth until Adrianna was ready for him to awaken.

Now was the time.

Adrianna began her spell, her song echoing off the stone walls of the crypt. It was a spell that would awaken the sleeping pair, but would also keep them wholly under her control. Adrianna smiled as Elizabeth and Radu sat up in their coffins and looked sleepily around the room. "Welcome back," she said, helping first Elizabeth, and then Radu from their coffins. "Follow me," she ordered, "We have a lot to discuss."

Elizabeth and Radu followed Adrianna as she led them to the upper limits of her fortress. She'd instructed her disciples, as she referred to them, to prepare her conference room for a meeting to go over the details of what she expected of everyone over the following days.

Nathaniel walked out of Captain Markus' office and straight to his partner's desk. "Got a minute, Frankie?" he asked.

Frankie looked up from the paperwork he'd been going through. "What's up?"

Nathaniel cleared his throat. "I know the way old Vincent died leaves a lot of questions…"

"A lot of questions!" Frankie snorted, butting in. "The old bugger was drained of blood according to the original assessment, then suddenly, when he was layin' on a slab in the morgue, his body fills back up with blood and he sits up—according to you—and asks for a drink! Then, he's found down by the river with an empty bottle of whiskey beside him and a deep gash on his head—deader than a doorknob. This time he still had blood in his veins … oh … and no bite marks on his neck." Frankie raised his eyebrows. "Have I missed anything?"

Nathaniel chuckled. "And here I thought you didn't pay much attention to details. Well, as I was about to tell you before you interrupted me, after talking to the captain, he agrees with me that it might be a good idea to revisit that place—Yates Castle. I told him how strange the individuals we talked to were behaving. The captain surprised me by saying he actually knew the guy. Said it had been a while since he'd seen him, but when he was around, he'd been a good friend. Said if we do go back to the house, not to use undo pressure; we're to ask general questions and then move on. Captain said his friend had always been a bit strange, only attending evening events, but he also felt he had nothing to do with our situation.

"I don't think they're vampires like you suggested…" Nathaniel's brow wrinkled in mirth, "but, I definitely think there's more going on inside those walls than a family reunion! Probably more than our captain realizes too!"

Frankie glanced at his watch. "Well, I don't know about you, but I have a few hours before I want to hit the sack. Why don't we pick up some takeout and park near the place for tonight to keep an eye on any comings and goings? If someone leaves the house, we'll be close enough to stop and question them, and hopefully, it won't be that tall guy or the woman from the parking lot. We need to speak with someone a little more willing to talk to us."

In the late afternoon, close to the supper hour, the unmarked police car pulled into the back parking lot of a building across the street from the castle. Frankie's suggestion that he and Nathaniel pick up some coffee and a couple sandwiches had been a good idea. Nathaniel thought they could be in for a long night.

"Why don't we take turns keeping watch?" Nathaniel suggested. "Two-hour intervals ... that way we won't miss anything."

"Good idea," Frankie returned as he leaned his seat back. "You take the first watch," he grinned.

Nathaniel scowled and opened one of the coffee cups, rolled down his car window, and stared over at the old house.

He'd done some research on the building and discovered it was built by a wealthy railroad family in 1867, the Yates. Due to the magnificence of the house, it had been dubbed, "Yates Castle." As happens in numerous wealthy families, the younger Yates generation was not as ambitious as their predecessors and they squandered the family fortune. Lavish parties were held at the castle on a weekly basis and it was rumoured that the senior Mr. Yates had a massive stroke and was confined to a wheelchair in his later years.

The oldest son was quite a scoundrel, so the story told, and he locked his parents in the uppermost room of the castle. The father finally succumbed to his ill health, and the mother, being broken-hearted at the way she was treated and mourning the loss of her husband, was one day been found on the castle grounds, having jumped from the widow's walk.

It became evident to many in the community that their beloved landmark castle was falling into disrepair. One day, in the early 1920's, during another one of the oldest son's lavish parties, there was an explosion in the kitchen and the house caught on fire. All the guests managed to escape, including the younger siblings of the Yates clan, however, the oldest son was not so lucky. He'd been in the kitchen when the explosion happened, and rumours flew over the next several months that he might possibly have caused the explosion himself, having run out of money and thinking he could collect a significant amount of insurance money for the damage to the house. He succumbed to his injuries a week after the explosion.

The castle fell into total disrepair and the Yates son who was next in line put the property for sale. The records stated that someone from Europe purchased the castle and must have been well enough off because significant construction was undertaken, inside and out. Despite the revitalization of the house, it sat empty afterward, except for a couple of servants who were seen maintaining the property intermittently.

It wasn't until the late seventies that someone moved in, rumoured to be a European business man and his wife. No one knew what he actually did, and he was seen rubbing elbows with the elite members of Brantford society, but only during evening parties. Then, suddenly, in the nineties, he up and moved back to Europe and the house was once again left to the care of a servant. According to the records, the property was for sale but it never sold, and now, by the looks of things, the owner was back and was holding a huge family reunion there before making his decision of whether to keep the place or to finally let it go.

"Something just doesn't make sense here," Nathaniel muttered under his breath. He glanced over at the sleeping Frankie. "Maybe you're right, maybe they are vampires ... get real, Nathaniel; next thing you know, you'll be thinking Dracula has risen from some dark grave and is ready to take over the world!"

Nathaniel glanced at his watch. He was only a half an hour into his watch. He'd been so absorbed in his thoughts, he'd neglected his coffee and now it was cold. He took a sip anyway. "Not much happening over there yet," he mumbled.

Angelique had a dull feeling inside her stomach that something was amiss outside. She made her way to the top of the house and stepped out onto the widow's walk. Not much had been accomplished during the night, and many of the vampires suggested they begin the trial tonight, instead of on their first night of arrival. Basarab had not been overly happy about that, but Attila had taken the side of the majority, feeling it would be best.

Attila had also suggested a short conference with just the council members in order to organize a strategy, which in the long run would probably move the trial along quicker. Tonight was going to be most interesting.

Angelique surveyed the surrounding area. Nothing out of the ordinary for a late afternoon mid-week. Most people in the neighbourhood would already be sitting down to their suppers. As Angelique walked to the front of the widow's walk, facing Usher Street, she noticed a car parked at the back of the building across the street. She'd never seen anyone parked there before, the back of the building being kept clear for deliveries to the furniture company that owned the place.

After watching for ten minutes and not seeing the car move, Angelique decided to take a closer look. Changing into a bird, she flew down and perched on a tree branch overhanging the parked car.

There were two men inside the vehicle, one sleeping, and one looking at the house. Angelique's heart skipped a beat as she recognized who they were. *What the heck are you doing here? Why are you watching the count's house?*

Angelique decided to put a scare into the cops. She shook her feathers, enlarging her bird size to something bigger. *A nice, big, black crow should upset the mood a bit.* Angelique flew down and landed on the hood of the car, cawing directly at its inhabitants.

Frankie woke with a start and stared at the large crow eyeing him. He pushed the button on the car seat to put him back into an upright position. Nathaniel looked at the crow in shock, never having seen one quite so large. Angelique decided to have a little more fun, and hopped up to the windshield and began pecking on the glass.

"Turn your wipers on," Frankie suggested, "and spray some water. That ought to get rid of it."

Nathaniel did as Frankie suggested. Angelique flew off the hood, but instead of flying away, she hovered just outside the driver's side open window, glaring into the car.

"Christ!" Nathaniel swore, pushing the button to close the window. But the car engine wasn't on, so the window remained down. Nathaniel fumbled with the ignition key, his hands shaking. The crow started screeching, flying up and then diving toward the open window. Finally, the key turned, and Nathaniel managed to close the window just in time.

"Take a drive around the block," Frankie recommended. "We can circle back and park somewhere else to watch the house. That is one mean bird, and for whatever reason, it doesn't want us here ... maybe it has a nest nearby."

Nathaniel put the car in gear and drove out of the lot, spraying stones everywhere. He turned right onto Usher Street and away from the big house. "Good idea, Frankie. We'll circle around for a bit and then find a different parking spot. God! I've never been attacked by a bird like that in all my living days!"

As she watched the car drive away, Angelique flew to the sidewalk along the front of the house and transformed back to her human self. Had either of the officers in the car thought to look in the rear-view mirror, they might have seen her. But they didn't. Angelique returned to the house. The sun was beginning to dip into the west; the vampires would be rising soon, and the trial was about to start. She needed to tell Basarab the house was being watched.

Someone else observed the episode from a giant glass globe, several thousand miles away. She smiled; she knew the time for her revelation to the vampire world was even closer at hand.

Chapter Fifteen

Slowly, the inhabitants of the house came alive, so to speak. Viktor had bottles of blood and glasses set out on a side table, ready for the guests to grab a quick drink before moving on to the basement, where a room had been set up to hold the court proceedings.

Basarab had not slept well again. Virginia was still watching over Mia, which meant she was sleeping separately from him—not something he liked when he was under stress. Basarab made his way to the window and pulled the heavy curtain aside a crack. His room overlooked the front yard, and he noticed Angelique making her way across the lawn toward the house.

"Why are you out so early, Angelique?" Basarab pondered. "Where have you been?" The count stayed by the window until Angelique was all the way up the stone stairs leading to the front door, then quickly made his way out of his room and down to the foyer.

Basarab met his father's wife just as she stepped onto the bottom stair. "A word with you," he stated sternly and directed her to his study. "Close the door, please," he ordered as Angelique entered the room.

Angelique swallowed hard, wondering what the count wanted, or, what it was he'd seen.

"I am not going to waste any time," Basarab began, "what were you doing outside a few minutes ago?"

Angelique answered promptly. "I was actually coming up to tell you, Basarab. I was taking a walk earlier on the widow's walk and noticed a car parked behind the furniture building across the street. It sat there for some time, so I went to investigate. I disguised myself as a bird, something I often do when it is necessary to be incognito. You will never guess who was in the car." Angelique paused for a breath. "The two cops who have been snooping around here asking questions about the incident at the café by the train station."

Basarab's brow furrowed angrily. "How did you get rid of them or are they still there?"

"Let's just say they have a great fear of big black birds attacking their car. Having said that, though, there is no guarantee they won't be back, finding another spot from which to watch your house. We need to get this trial over with quickly and leave this place!"

"Does anyone else know about the cops watching us?" Basarab asked.

"I don't think so; it was still light out and no one else was up yet."

"Good." Basarab pointed to the door. "Shall we?" he directed. He took her arm as they were about to exit. "Tell no one except Attila," the count articulated with a stern look. "No one!" he repeated for emphasis.

Angelique nodded.

"I'll see you shortly in the dining room," Basarab said, heading down the hallway.

Attila was just getting up as Angelique entered their room. Seeing her, he smiled: "Where have you been, my love? I missed you."

Approaching her husband, "We need to talk before joining the others," she said.

Attila listened carefully as Angelique relayed what had gone on. He was silent for a few minutes before speaking. "You are right, my dear; we must make haste with this trial and get out of here."

Samara and Lajos exited her room. Before leaving, they had laughed about their liaisons and how no one had caught them yet. It was more exciting for them now that the house was overflowing with vampires; and, Samara was getting an extra rush, flaunting her relationship with Lajos in Ákos' face.

Lajos, as though reading Samara's mind, "So, your little lover boy has returned for this trial, eh?"

Samara tilted her head saucily. "Jealous, are you?"

Throwing his head back, Lajos guffawed: "Why would a man ever feel threatened by a boy?" He grabbed hold of Samara's shoulders and tightened his grip on her. "Shall we go back to your bed so I can jog your memory about the differences?"

"Down, boy," Samara snickered, putting emphasis on the word *boy*, as she pushed him away from the door.

Lajos went ahead of the temptress and waited in the dining room doorway for her, then offered her his arm and led her to a table. They sat quietly while the room filled with vampires. When Ákos entered, Manya clinging to his arm, Samara glanced at him and licked her lips seductively. He looked away. Manya, not missing what Samara had done, threw the temptress a contemptuous look.

The room filled quickly, everyone wanting to ensure they did not anger the count. Samara watched closely for Santan and Mia, wondering what they had been up to over the daytime hours. To her surprise, her brother walked in alone and went directly to the chair on the right side of his father's. A few moments later, Mia appeared with Virginia, but she directed the newly-turned vampire to a table that had been set up in the far corner of the room.

Samara noticed her brother only give a brief glance to his betrothed. *Trouble in paradise, brother?* Samara reached her hand under the table and fondled Lajos. He grinned and relaxed, leaning his elbows on the table.

Dracula watched intensely the goings-on in the room, especially the interactions between Samara and Lajos, and how Santan was ignoring Mia. *Misfortune in utopia, young prince? And you, Samara, playing with fire, as usual. If only you knew where Lajos' true loyalty lies!* Dracula glanced to Ildiko and Gara and saw the angry gleam in Ildiko's eyes as she, too, observed Samara's behaviour.

The chatter around the tables ceased as the count, along with his father and Angelique, entered the room. Basarab took his place at the head of the main table, Attila taking the spot across from Santan. Angelique made her way to the far corner to sit with Virginia and Mia.

Basarab remained standing, looking around the room, counting heads. "Good, we are all here." He paused. "There is a slight change in the location of our court. I instructed Viktor to prepare a room in the basement. We may have another unwanted visitor to our door, and I do not wish to have so many of us visible. My daughter, unfortunately," Basarab threw a disgusted look toward Samara, "has put us under the radar of the local police, and they don't seem to want to believe we know nothing of what happened at the little coffee house across the tracks from here."

A number of the vampires turned and gave Samara a look. Ákos snorted. Manya raised her eyes to the ceiling. Ildiko smirked. Samara stared at her father, flames in her eyes. *And I know a little something about you, Papa ... maybe the local police would be interested in your midnight escapades!* Santan watched the interactions between the different vampire factions, then looked to where Randy was standing by the door, leaning on the wall.

Randy caught Santan's eyes when the young vampire gazed his way. He swallowed hard and ran a hand through his hair, an old habit, and shifted uncomfortably—who wouldn't if they were the only human in a room full of vampires? His eyes wandered to the back of the room where Virginia and Mia were sitting, then filled with tears.

"Virginia," he mouthed. *Why did you choose this life when I offered you a normal one? None of this would be happening had you made the right choice. We could have had our own children ... and I could have taken you away, somewhere the count would never be able to find you. We could even have escaped with Santan and Samara, and they would never have had to go through that horrid ceremony that sealed them into the dark world they now exist in.* Randy blushed as he thought of the life he imagined he and Virginia could have had together.

Virginia noticed her friend looking at her and saw him blush. *Be careful, my dear friend ... such thoughts will not bode well in this room if one of these vampires reads your mind ... especially Basarab!* Smiling at Randy, Virginia turned her attention to her young charge, who was beginning to shake. She reached her hand over and laid it on top of Mia's.

Leaning into the newly turned vampire, Virginia whispered, "Hold tight, Mia; as soon as the count gives the word, you may have a drink."

Mia pouted but could protest no further as Basarab was speaking again. "Follow me, please. Viktor has also set out some refreshments for us in the room so we will be able to begin proceedings immediately." With that, Basarab led the way out of the room and down to the basement.

It took several minutes for everyone to get a glass of blood and settle into a chair to await further instructions. Basarab settled into the chair set up on a platform overlooking the entire room. A small table was in front of his chair, a bottle and glass on it. There was another chair beside the platform, placed there for the potential suspects to be questioned.

Lardom made his way directly to a second table that faced the platform and laid out several papers. The council members made their way to the front-row chairs in the room, and the rest of the vampires and Randy settled into the chairs further back. Randy sat in the back row, away from all the vampires, and folded his arms across his chest.

Virginia told Mia to stay put: "I'll get us some refreshment," she said, moving to the side table where Viktor had set the bottles and glasses.

Mia turned around and smiled at her father. Randy attempted to smile back, but his heart wasn't in it. Mia felt a jolt race through her chest, realizing for the first time since her turning how much her father must be hurting. She turned her face back to the front of the room, feeling inadequate to the only man she loved besides Santan.

"Are you okay, Mia?" Virginia asked as she handed Mia a glass of blood, noticing the young vampire seemed shaken about something.

Mia, not wanting to allow Virginia inside her head, "I'm fine," she replied taking the glass from Virginia and downing the contents in a single gulp. She looked at the count's wife, blood dripping down her chin, and smiled.

Virginia looked away in disgust. Even after all the years she'd spent being a vampire, she had a difficult time seeing such ill manners. She glanced back to the back row where Randy was sitting and saw the horrified look on his face as he beheld what his daughter had just done. He turned his face away from Virginia. She turned her attention to her husband, who was waiting patiently for everyone to be seated.

Basarab finally stood, raising his hands in the air, silencing any chatter. He began the ancient speech that opened all vampire courts: "Brethren, we are gathered here on this dark night with open minds to hear the testimonies of all potential involvements in the crime before us. We will judge, without prejudice, the words we hear, and we will take time to evaluate the meaning of all your words, and our decision of guilt or innocence will be based only on fact. If we establish on this night the perpetrator of the crime committed under this roof, we will move forward, without prejudice, with the rule of our law, which states clearly that no human life shall be taken by a member of the vampire family without provocation, or a dire need to feed when no other source of blood was available, and the penalty for doing so is death! Let it be known, again, we are here tonight to establish and then punish whoever murdered Katalin, the wife of our friend, Randy. Let us begin." Basarab nodded to Lardom.

Lardom shuffled a few papers on his table, then stood. "I would first like to call to the stand, Délia, from the Russian vampire clan."

Chapter Sixteen

Nathaniel and Frankie drove around for half an hour after the episode near Yates Castle. Both were shaken and confused by the bird's attack on their car.

"I've never seen the likes of a bird attacking like that for no reason. There was no tree close enough to our car that we could be threatening a nest," Nathaniel said as he turned a corner.

Frankie shook his head. "Yeah, really hard to figure. I'm in no hurry to return to that place … not that we shouldn't go back at some point … but I wouldn't mind a good hot meal in my belly before we find another hiding spot to watch from."

"Don't know if I could handle a meal right now," Nathaniel returned. "However, if you're hungry, we can grab something; I can always get takeout and eat it later when my stomach settles. After all, it was my side of the car the friggin' bird attacked." Nathaniel headed toward King George Road. "What do you feel like eating?" he asked.

"How about we go through Harvey's drive thru?" Frankie suggested.

"Sounds good."

They drove in silence for a few minutes, each absorbed in thought. As they pulled into Harvey's lot, Nathaniel reopened the conversation. "I don't think we'll do a stakeout tonight. I've got a gut feeling something is going on in that house, and I also got a gut feeling that someone in there knows something about what went on at the Station Coffee House. I think we'll simply pay them another visit."

"Under what pretence?" Frankie didn't like what his partner was suggesting. The tall guy in the house gave him the creeps.

Nathaniel pursed his lips. "Don't need a pretence," he smirked. "There was a crime committed, and even if Vincent miraculously came back to life in the morgue, there's no doubt in my mind he was dead when we found him behind the coffee house. How he came to life in the morgue is still a mystery— bordering on some sort of witchcraft maybe. I intend to go right up to the door, and demand to speak with everyone in the house!"

Frankie's eyebrows rose in frustration. "And if whoever answers the door says no?"

"Then I'll threaten them with a warrant, giving them no choice."

Shaking his head, Frankie voiced, "I don't like it, but you're the boss."

"Yep, I'm the boss … well, more like the veteran … and you're the rookie. Watch and learn, my friend … watch and learn!"

Nathaniel pulled up to place their order, then proceeded to the pick-up window. He handed the bagged supper to Frankie before continuing. Frankie opened the bag and pulled out a couple fries, popping them into his mouth.

"Can't wait, eh, buddy?" Nathaniel smirked.

"With what you're suggesting we're about to do, this might be my last meal," Frankie chewed out his words. And laughed nervously.

"Your last supper, huh?" Nathaniel played along, despite his own misgiving about who lived in the house on the corner of Buffalo and Usher streets.

As the officers proceeded toward their destination, Nathaniel's stomach grumbled. Not wanting to be too close to the house, he pulled into the entrance of the Greenwood Cemetery and parked. Reaching over for the bag of food, Nathaniel chuckled, "Maybe I better eat, too. Like you said, it might be our last meal!" Nathaniel took a bite of his burger. "But, oh, what a good last meal it is! Glad I didn't tell them to hold the onions; they could be our last line of defence!" Another chuckle.

"You might be laughing now, but that big guy doesn't look like a laughing matter to me!" Frankie took a swig of his pop. "And the creepy guy who answered the door … wouldn't be surprised if his name is Igor!" he added.

"Igor was Frankenstein's sidekick," Nathaniel snorted as he stuffed the final piece of burger into his mouth. Wiping his hands with a napkin, he rolled the window down and gazed out at the gravestones. "Lot of old stones in here, and over there, a mausoleum … wonder who's in there?"

Frankie looked at his boss, wonder on his face. "Next thing I know you're going to want to knock on that door!"

"Might not be a bad idea," Nathaniel started to open his car door. "Think I'll stretch my legs a little before heading over to Yates Castle … might be my last chance," he added, a mischievous gleam in his eyes.

"You might not be laughing later," Frankie returned sarcastically, remaining in the car. Leaning his seat back, he closed his eyes.

Nathaniel walked amongst the tombstones, thinking hard about his current strategy, whatever that may be. He began talking to himself: "What am I doing? There was, and yet wasn't, a crime committed … why is it I keep thinking there's something fishy going on in that house? Vincent was dead; how could so many of us have missed a pulse? How he came alive again is the biggest mystery … and fill up with blood … it's like witchcraft

… if I believed in witches and spells. Someone in that house knows something—I'm sure of it—but what is there to know? I know several people came through the yard, but were they coming from the house or from the stairs leading up to Terrace Hill? And that woman who walked over to the crime scene … that beautiful woman who dismissed me in the parking lot behind the house … why was she there, at the café? It's closed … been closed since the incident.

"And then the big guy came into the station to talk to the captain … what was that all about … I don't believe for a minute it was just to catch up with an old friend! Glad the captain saw it my way and didn't tie my wrists when I told him some of my suspicions… "

Nathaniel found himself in front of the mausoleum. He paused at the door, smiled, then knocked. "This is for you, Frankie … I assure you … nothing but the dead in this place." Nathaniel turned and walked back to the car.

"Wake up, buddy. Showtime," Nathaniel said, turning the key in the ignition.

Frankie straightened up in his seat. "Still doing this, eh?"

"Yep."

Nathaniel parked the car in the lot behind the house. Together, the two officers made their way through the yard toward the front door, guided only by the light of a full moon. They climbed up the broad stone steps and Nathaniel banged hard on the door. Frankie hung back in the shadows.

Viktor heard the knock as he was coming up from the basement. He sighed in exasperation, having wanted to go for a rest before he was needed again. Making his way to the door, the count's butler cursed under his breath. There was only one type of individual who might be coming to the count's door at such a late hour—the pesky cops!

Nathaniel was about to knock again when the door opened a crack. Seeing who it was, Viktor opened the door wider. "What may I do for you gentlemen at this late hour? I was just about to retire."

Inching his way across the door sweeper, Nathaniel answered Viktor: "Is your boss in?"

"He's unavailable," returned a curt reply. "Why would you think he might be available at this hour?" Viktor added.

Nathaniel was quick to reply. "Well, I thought maybe he might be up; he did say, on our last visit, he liked to read late."

"Not every night," came a sarcastic reply. "Now, as I said, I was about to retire." Viktor crowded closer to the doorway, hinting that he wasn't going to allow the officers any further into the house.

"When would be a better time?" Nathaniel insisted on prolonging the doorway intrusion.

Viktor's lips set in a firm line. As he was about to answer, there was the sound of a door opening and closing, and approaching footsteps. Two sets. Three sets of eyes watched the hallway to see who was drawing near.

Frankie uttered a guttural, "Wow!"

Virginia and Mia appeared from around the corner. Seeing Viktor at the door with two strangers, Virginia paused and shoved Mia behind her. "Go upstairs now!" she hissed to the newest vampire in the family. When she noticed the insolent look in Mia's eyes, Virginia toughened her words. "Now! No games here, Mia!"

Mia fled up the stairs, never having witnessed such resolve in Virginia's eyes or voice before.

Turning to the group at the door, Virginia sauntered up to them. "What is the problem, Viktor? Why are these men invading our privacy so late at night?"

Frankie couldn't take his eyes off the woman in front of him. *Are all the women in this place so perfect?!* The red dress Virginia chose to wear fit her like a tight leather glove, leaving nothing to Frankie's imagination. *Damn, I hope this one isn't married ... she doesn't look old enough to be that girl's mother.*

Nathaniel, noticing how much his partner was ogling the woman, gave him a shove on the shoulder. "Down, boy," he hissed in the rookie's ear. Frankie shook his head and refocused.

"These men are police officers," Viktor finally replied, having allowed Virginia's impression on the men at the door to play out. "They wish to see Basarab, but I have told them he is not available."

"So why are you still here, officers?" Virginia turned on the two men, curtly admonishing them for the intrusion. "Viktor told you my husband is unavailable, and the hour is more than late. If you have a card, I will give it to him, and he will call you at his convenience. He is a very busy man, so don't expect that to be any time soon."

While Nathaniel was thick in conversation with Virginia, Frankie noticed Viktor slip quickly away. He kept his ear open for a door opening and closing and was rewarded with a light clicking sound. Frankie returned his attention to what was going on at the door. He caught the tail end of what Nathaniel was asking Virginia—about the importance of meeting with her husband so he could set up meetings to speak with everyone who happened to be in the house the night of the murder.

Virginia replied with a resolute look on her face. "Are you insinuating someone in this house has something to do with whatever you are investigating? I assure you, you are barking up an empty tree."

"Well, ma'am, it's a tree I don't mind barking up, and if everyone here has nothing to hide, they won't mind speaking with my partner and me. We aren't treating you any different than anyone else in this neighbourhood." Nathaniel emphasized his last sentence.

Virginia was about to reply when she heard heavy footsteps approaching. All eyes turned as Basarab strode toward them with hostile intent written all over him.

"What is the meaning of this intrusion?" he demanded, turning his attention to Nathaniel. "Did I not tell you if anyone in this household knew anything of your *incident*, I would call you?"

Frankie put a hand on Nathaniel's arm. "Maybe we should…"

Nathaniel didn't give Frankie a chance to finish his statement. He brushed his hand away, then made a move to stand face to face with Basarab, which was difficult, him being a good six inches shorter. Nathaniel stared up at the count. "All I'm asking for is a few minutes with everyone in your house here. It won't take long. When would be a good time to come by to do that?"

Nathaniel's advance infuriated the count. Placing a hand on the officer's chest, Basarab removed Nathaniel from his immediate space. "I will speak with my guests, and if there is anything you or any other police officer need to know, I will call you. Now, kindly leave. My patience wears quite thin at this time of night and at unwanted intrusions!"

Nathaniel knew when he hit a brick wall, but he had one last card to play. "Okay, we'll leave. However, due to your lack of co-operation, we'll be back—with a warrant! Next time, you won't be able to push me out the door!" Before the count could comment, "Let's go, Frankie," he ordered, hustling his partner out the door.

Frankie almost stumbled as he and Nathaniel made their way down the stone steps. Taking a moment to look back, he was terrified by what he saw or thought he saw. *Holy shit! If there is such a thing as a vampire, that guy sure fits the bill!* Frankie couldn't shake off the sight of the red eyes, and what he perceived to be a smile ... with elongated incisors!

Chapter Seventeen

Basarab returned to the basement, frustrated with the police harassment. He had to do something about the situation before they returned with a warrant. But what? He hadn't had an opportunity to speak with Virginia because as soon as the cops left, she had hustled up the stairs to go and check on Mia.

When the count entered the courtroom, the murmurings in the room ceased. Délia was still on the witness stand, yet to be questioned. Basarab held up a finger to Lardom, indicating he wanted a moment to speak before the trial commenced. Taking his place on the podium, Basarab informed the vampire congregation of the circumstances.

"We have an issue," the count began. "The police have come around again, insisting on speaking with everyone who was in this house on the night their victim was murdered. What is bothering me, though, is why they are so insistent when Angelique brought the old man back to life. Technically, then, there is no crime.

"I cannot allow everyone who was here on that night to speak with the police, so after we are finished with this session of the trial, I will select who will participate, and we will go over what we say and don't say. The rest of you will remain hidden in this room while the police are dealt with."

Basarab looked around, trying to decide who his chosen few would be, who would be best to stick to the script. Shaking his head back to the present moment, he nodded to Lardom to begin his questioning of Délia. Lardom stood and approached Délia.

"Do you, Délia, swear to tell the whole truth in this vampire court, according to what you have witnessed in regards to the death of Katalin, the wife of Randy, guest of our esteemed leader, Count Basarab, revealing all that you know or witnessed of this dire deed?"

"I do."

"On the night of Katalin's death, you were the one to find the body, correct?" Lardom began the direct questioning.

Délia nodded.

"You must answer so everyone can hear you."

"Yes, I found the body."

"Under what circumstances?"

"I was taking a walk in the yard; I needed fresh air."

"Where did you find the body?" Lardom asked.

"On the lawn at the back of the house."

"Now, I don't want you to take offence to this next question, but I must ask it." Lardom leaned in close to Délia, looking her straight in the eyes. "Was Katalin still alive when you discovered her body?"

Délia stared at the man questioning her and her body trembled with anger. *How dare you! Is this turning into a witch hunt? What has been said about me that would make him ask such a question?*

"Is there a problem with the question, Délia?"

Délia shook her head. "No, no problem ... no, Katalin was not alive when I found her."

"Are you sure?"

"Very."

"How did you know?" Lardom's eyebrows rose questioningly. "That she was not alive?" he added.

"She wasn't breathing!" Délia retorted sharply.

"I am just trying to establish the exact condition of Katalin's body when you found her," Lardom smiled smoothly. "Did you lean down and touch the body in any way?"

"No, I saw her throat was ripped open; I didn't need to touch her to know she was dead. Her body was sprawled on the grass, and her eyes had a glazed over death-look to them. She was dead, and I didn't have to touch her to know that." Délia glowered at Lardom, then at the vampire jury. *You are not going to pin this on me, or any of the other Russian vampires. Volodya should never have returned here to be humiliated like this.*

Lardom continued with his questions. "What did you do once you established Katalin was dead?"

"I went straight to the house and sought out Count Basarab. He was with Dracula and Attila, but only Basarab and Dracula accompanied me outside to the body."

"And did they confirm she was indeed dead?"

"Yes, there was no doubt the woman was dead." Délia looked first to Lardom, then to the count. "Isn't that right, Basarab?" she added mockingly.

"What happened then?" Lardom continued. He already knew the account from Basarab's story; he just wanted to make sure the stories were the same.

"Basarab was distraught—more than he should have been over the death of a human—and he fell to his knees and raised his fist to the sky and shouted, 'Why!' Dracula took charge of the situation. He knelt down beside the body and sniffed around her ravaged neck, then claimed that more than one person was responsible for her death."

"Did he say who?"

"No. He said we needed to get her into the house. Dracula picked her up and said he was going to take her to the room in the basement, asking Basarab if there were still coffins down there."

"Did you follow them to the basement?"

"Yes, but I just stood in the doorway of the room where the coffins were. Basarab opened one and Dracula put the woman's body in it. They were talking in hushed whispers and I couldn't make out what they were saying, so I left and went upstairs."

"Just one more question, Délia … did you happen to see anyone else in the yard when you were out for your walk?" Lardom looked at her with an intensity she didn't care for.

Despite his piercing eyes, Délia answered without hesitation. "Not a soul."

"Thank you for your patience, Délia; you may return to your seat. I may need to call you again later." Lardom walked to his table and picked up a sheet of paper. "I would like to call Count Dracula to the stand."

Dracula sauntered nonchalantly to the witness stand. As he sat down, he grinned charmingly and leaned back in the chair.

Lardom took his time approaching the notorious count, seemingly reading something on the sheet of paper in his hand. After swearing Dracula in with the customary statement, Lardom asked his first question: "I have been led to understand the victim, Katalin, had no love for any of the vampires … is this a true statement, in your opinion of course?"

"I heard such."

"Hearsay or personally?"

Dracula leaned forward. "I'd say both, from hearsay and from observing the woman's actions around our kind." He leaned back again and smiled.

"Would I be correct to assume you didn't care for Katalin, then?" Lardom pressed on.

"I don't care much for any human, if you want the truth." Dracula's lips curled into a noticeable snarl. "I care even less for one who threatens our kind," he added.

Lardom turned to the jury, wanting to allow enough time for Dracula's last statement to sink in. "So, let me ask you where you were during the time frame Katalin was killed?"

"We finished our meal … I went to my room … then I returned upstairs to the main floor and met with Basarab and his father. As you already know, I was with them when Délia burst into the house to tell us the human woman was dead."

Lardom had a card up his sleeve that he didn't want to play just yet. With all the evidence he'd been given, he knew Dracula knew more than he was giving up.

"So, as Délia has told us, you went with Basarab to see the body, and you sniffed the area around the body and commented that more than one individual was involved. Is this correct?"

"It is so, but to save time here, I was unable to identify anyone … both scents were extremely faint."

"I see." Lardom shuffled his card to the bottom of the deck. "Okay, so, you picked up her body and together, you and Basarab, took the woman to the basement and placed her in a coffin. What happened then?"

Dracula smiled coldly and looked to the back of the room where Randy was sitting. "I advised Basarab that Randy and Mia should be informed of Katalin's death, and mentioned that Randy might become a problem."

"Did Basarab agree with you?"

Basarab looked at Randy and saw the anger building in his friend. *What are you up to, Dracula?*

Dracula turned to look directly at the count when he replied to Lardom's question. "Basarab said he needed to think on the matter. In my opinion, if I might be so bold as to give it, he did not desire to eliminate his friend. Randy has always been one of the count's weaknesses. Just like other humans, who seem to dig their claws into our *leader*," the word leader was said with a sneer.

Basarab glared at this uncle, fuming at his insinuations. He glanced at his jury and noticed them all looking at him with indifference. He thought back to the conversation he'd had with Santan when he told his son about Katalin's death and what Dracula had desired to do with Randy. He remembered his son's words: *Have you ever considered that maybe Dracula has in mind a means to control the throne ... not directly ... through someone else?*

Santan had gone on to point out Dracula's close relationship with Samara, how she adored her uncle, and how much the two of them were alike—both wild and reckless. It was no secret that Samara wanted the throne. Was she the one Dracula wanted on the throne? After all, there was no tangible reason for him to have come to Brantford, and with Lajos, with whom Samara was sleeping.

Basarab returned his attention to Lardom and Dracula, but not before noticing a worried look in his father's eyes. Directing his words harshly to Dracula, Basarab decided to show his uncle who was still sitting on the throne. "I believe you are attempting to discredit me, uncle; I suggest you stick to the case we are trying here, not to your feelings of my alleged inadequacy. Such jealousy does not become you!"

Lardom cleared his throat, caught off-guard by Dracula's statements. "I think we have heard enough from this witness for now. You are dismissed, Dracula, but be aware, I may call you again."

Adrianna chuckled as she watched the court proceedings from her mountain fortress. She was impressed with her father's arrogance and realized she might have inherited something of his genes. She would wait a bit longer, though, before making her final travel plans to introduce herself to daddy—after all, what were a few more days when she'd already waited centuries? Revenge would be sweet, no matter when it came.

Raising a glass of blood to her mother's portrait, Adrianna leaned back in her chair. "To you, mama … to you!"

Chapter Eighteen

Frankie hesitated before getting out of the car when Nathaniel pulled up in front of his apartment building. "I still don't get why you are pushing that guy," Frankie said.

Nathaniel was losing patience with the rookie. His voice was tart when he answered. "I have my reasons. Just follow my lead and learn from a master." He tapped his fingers on the steering wheel, waiting for Frankie to get out of the car. "Get some sleep, buddy; we'll be doing a lot of interviews tomorrow. Right now I'm going to see if I can get Judge Harris to sign a search warrant for me."

Frankie got out of the car, saying nothing further. He felt the frustration level he was at was best to be kept at bay. No sense pissing off his superior. "The judge is going to be pissed enough when Nathaniel knocks on his door at this hour!" Frankie mumbled as he entered his apartment building.

The tires squealed as Nathaniel hit the gas and sped out onto the street. He needed the warrant now so he could show up to the big house first thing in the morning. He didn't want to give the man time to remove any of his guests.

When Nathaniel pulled into Judge Harris' driveway, he expected the house to be in darkness and was thankful to see lights on in the living room. "Judge must be up late reading or watching the television," Nathaniel commented to himself as he made his way up the walkway.

Nathaniel knocked softly on the door, not wanting to ring the bell and awaken the judge's wife. It was several seconds before the door swung open and revealed Judge Harris in full nighttime attire.

"Nathaniel!" Judge Harris looked at his watch. "What brings you here at this hour?"

"May I come in, your honour?"

"Of course." Judge Harris stepped back, allowing Nathaniel to enter. "We can talk in the living room," he added, moving in that direction.

Once seated, the judge folded his arms across his chest. "Okay, let's have it; why are you here looking so worried, as if the world is coming to an end?"

Nathaniel drew in a nervous breath. "You recollect the incident that happened behind the Station Coffee House a few days ago?"

The judge nodded. "But I also heard there was some sort of mix-up, and Vincent wasn't really dead," he commented. "Weren't you in the morgue when the old guy sat up and asked for a drink? Must have scared the shit out of you! Would have me." Judge Harris chuckled softly.

Nathaniel grimaced. "You see, your honour, I don't know what is going on here. We all swore Vincent was dead, blood totally drained from his body! There was no way he could have been alive, that so many of us could have made such a mistake. Yet, I was there, as you said, in the morgue when his miraculous recovery occurred. Totally unexplainable."

Judge Harris was known around Brantford for being a get-to-the-point kind of judge. He had no patience for long, drawn-out stories. "What do you want me to do about this, Nathaniel?"

Clearing his throat, Nathaniel said, "I need a warrant so I can talk to the people in the big house—I believe most people in Brantford refer to it as Yates Castle—because the owner, who claims to be in town for a family reunion, is being evasive."

"I had no idea Count Basarab has returned," the judge interrupted.

A shockwave raced through Nathaniel. He hadn't thought of the possibility that the house owner might know the judge. "You know the man? A count?"

"I know him well," Judge Harris grinned. "Strange man, though. He was in the city several years ago and attended numerous after-hours functions. Bit of a nighthawk, if I remember correctly. Can't remember him ever attending any of our daytime events. I believe he mentioned something about a severe skin condition he was born with, so he'd just changed his lifestyle and only ventured outside after the sun went down. The rumour that went around when the count left so suddenly was there were some family difficulties in the old country—Transylvania, I believe—he had to deal with." The judge paused a moment. "Rumours—you know how they spread—said he took a wife and children back with him. The woman he married was not known to any of us. Lot of secrets the count had, I believe; but, he was a most likeable fellow in the social circles—and generous."

Nathaniel couldn't believe what he heard. First, his captain knew the guy, and now the judge! *Maybe Frankie is right! Could this guy be a vampire? The judge said he was from Transylvania! Hmmm ... still doesn't explain everything, though—or does it? Could he also work some sort of magic to cover a crime either he or someone in the house committed?*

The judge was watching Nathaniel's reaction to his account of an old acquaintance. "You okay, Nate?" he asked.

"Yeah … yeah … just had no idea you knew the guy, and he has such a history here in the city. Might explain his visit to my captain the other night."

"Hmmm … he might be making his rounds to see old friends. The count and Markus were pretty tight if I recall correctly. However, get to the point, please; I'm tired and would like to retire for the night. Big case tomorrow and I need my wits about me." Judge Harris wanted Nathaniel out of his house.

"I'd like a warrant so I can force this count to talk to me, and allow me to talk to anyone else who might have been in the house on the night of the crime," Nathaniel voiced his request, a nervous strain in his voice.

"Hmmm," the judge uttered for the second time. "Maybe I can do you one better. I'll contact the count and ask him to co-operate with you. How does that sound?"

"Well, it would sound good, but how are you going to do that? The man doesn't have a phone—or so he says."

Judge Harris chuckled. "He always was a bit strange in that way." The judge leaned forward and patted Nathaniel's knee. "Leave it up to me; you'll get your interviews. Now," the judge stood, "I need to hit my pillow. I'll contact you as soon as I speak with the count and set up a time for you two to meet."

The judge watched as Nathaniel backed out of his driveway. He felt troubled. He knew there was a lot more to Count Basarab than what he'd let on to the officer—a lot more. It was a judge's job to know things.

Nathaniel drove home, deep in thought. This case was getting weirder by the minute. *Maybe I should just listen to the rookie and let it go! But why can't I?*

Chapter Nineteen

Lardom decided it was time to reveal the fight Randy had with his wife before she was killed. He'd considered the possibility that Randy had murdered Katalin in a fit of rage and was a superior actor, exhibiting such a unique spectacle of sorrow and rage.

"I call Randy to the stand," Lardom called out.

A whispering murmur rose as all eyes turned to the only human in the room. Randy, himself, was in shock at being called to the stand. He stood nervously, hesitated, then made his way to the front of the room.

Lardom approached, a smile on his lips. "Randy … I know you are not a vampire, but since this is a vampire court, you will have to swear in with our code. Any problem with that?"

Randy shook his head, knowing well enough it would be useless to do otherwise.

"Good." Lardom repeated the swear-in ceremony. When Randy acknowledged, Lardom delved right into his first question. "Were you and your wife, Katalin, happily married?"

The question caught Randy off-guard, and he hesitated.

"Simple question, Randy … were you happily married?" Lardom repeated.

Randy shrugged his shoulders. He knew there would be no use trying to lie. "We were at one time," he answered.

"At one time?" Lardom tilted his head inquisitorially. "What happened to change your happy times?"

Sighing, Randy glanced at the count. "She hated the fact I was so bound to Basarab and his family."

"Why?" Lardom asked, even though he knew it was a rhetorical question.

Randy snorted. "You're all vampires! Isn't that reason enough for her to be upset?"

"But did she not know of your ties to the count's family before she married you?"

"No." Randy squinted at his feet and shuffled them fretfully. "I didn't tell her until after we married, when she began to question where all our money was coming from. I told her I had a benefactor—a wealthy businessman—who was the husband of my best friend. I confessed I had been in love with Virginia but she had chosen to be with the father of her children. I highly respect Virginia for her choice, despite it breaking my heart." Randy looked at Basarab, then around the room to see if Virginia had returned yet. She hadn't.

"That must have infuriated Katalin?" Lardom pushed. "To hear you were in love with another woman?"

"Not really. I'm not in love with Virginia; I only love her as a friend—my best friend. My wife was more hurt than anything, but she knew I was faithful to her and devoted to our daughter, Mia."

"I might guess Katalin knew you were faithful physically, but maybe not mentally? Despite what you say about Virginia just being a friend?" Lardom's eyes narrowed as he drove his next question home.

"Possibly." Randy ran his fingers through his curls. "We never talked much about my past after that. We did attend some of Basarab's special events but they were few and far between. I guess she tolerated them because I told her they were my family, the only people who'd ever given a damn about me!"

Lardom turned toward the jury while asking his next question. "So, Randy, exactly when was it you realized, decisively, your wife wanted nothing to do with your vampire family?"

Randy looked to Basarab again. "When we received the invitation to Samara's nineteenth birthday party, which also included an invitation to the final crossing-over ceremony for Santan and Samara. Katalin tried to convince me not to go, saying Mia shouldn't miss school. I told her we were going; I wasn't willing to offend the man who'd embraced me like family and was generous beyond our dreams. I wouldn't have been where I was if it were not for the count."

"So, you attended the party. I actually saw you there, having been invited myself." Lardom grinned. "Quite a spectacle, wasn't it?"

"It was." Randy shuffled uncomfortably in the chair.

"How did Katalin react?"

"Not well." Randy's voice was barely a whisper.

"Oh … what happened?"

"We were seated at the same table with Virginia, and she was almost as distraught as Katalin and I were, having not ever witnessed such a ceremony before. After all, Santan and Samara were her children, and despite Virginia having crossed over into the vampire world, she hadn't been fully prepared for what was happening. She told me it was different for a human crossing, from that of a child born with vampire blood already in their genes. She needed some air, so I went out to the balcony with her, leaving my wife and daughter alone at the table."

Randy's eyes found Santan in the crowded room. The vampire prince's face was expressionless as he listened to Randy's testimony. "Apparently, Santan approached Mia and asked her to dance, and Katalin told our daughter she would not dance with Santan that night, or ever! She left, dragging Mia with her."

"What happened when you returned to your room after comforting Virginia? How did your wife greet you?" Lardom's constant smile was beginning to annoy Randy.

"Not well," Randy admitted. "We fought. Katalin told me how jealous she was of Virginia because she'd noticed how I looked at her and how protective I was of her when it was my wife and daughter I should've been focused on. I tried to tell Katalin how distraught Virginia was, but she'd have none of it! It was then I got irate and told her more of Virginia's story, and just how deep our relationship went—what she and I had been through—what we'd had to survive … what Virginia had to endure. I reminded her of how Virginia—and Santan—had saved my life by giving me a purpose. I was a loner, going nowhere in life. We were just two lonely people who found a friend in each other.

"Learning even more of our history, Katalin relaxed a bit, and I thought the worst was over. But that wasn't the case. She told me about Santan and Mia, and asked what I was going to do about it." Randy looked at Santan again, who still sat stone-faced. "I told my wife I needed time to think about the situation because, in reality, Santan is an amazing person—kind, considerate, loving, and loyal—everything we could ask for our daughter. But Katalin had only one thing on her mind: Santan is a vampire, and she would never see her daughter in a relationship with such a creature!" Randy sagged in the chair, his energy drained, but he knew his ordeal on the witness stand was far from over.

The door at the back of the room opened, and Virginia entered with Mia. Randy had wondered where they'd gone but assumed it might have something to do with his daughter's transformation. He was glad of one thing, though—Virginia had not had to be privy to his witness-stand confessions. Lardom waited until the two women were settled before resuming his questioning.

"So, what we've established so far is that you were not honest with your wife before you married her, failing to inform her of your deep relationship with vampires, and also, you only told her enough to keep her at bay for a time. We have established that when she realized the full extent of what was happening within her happy little world, she became angry and wanted nothing more to do with your adopted family. Am I on the right track, Randy?"

Randy shrugged. "Pretty much."

"What took place next?"

"We left. Katalin insisted."

"Did you want to?"

"No … and yes. I was torn. To never see Santan again, whom I looked at as not only a friend but a son, was an awful thought."

"What about not being able to see Virginia again … how did that make you feel?" Lardom's smile was not as warm as it had been.

Randy hesitated, swallowed, and ran his hand through his hair again. Virginia, watching from the back of the room, knew her friend was nervous. Finally, "Yes, it would have bothered me to never see Virginia again … or Basarab," Randy quickly added the count's name.

"But you left anyway? You couldn't stand up to your wife…"

"It became more complicated than that," Randy butt in. "Basarab found out about Santan and Mia, and he approached me with a plan to move my family and me here, to Brantford, to remove the temptation from our children. The count said the union between Santan and Mia shouldn't happen, for my sake and hers, because if it did, Mia would most likely want to cross over to be with her husband for eternity. Especially if they had children, which could only happen while she was still human. The count felt that with time, Santan and Mia would move on.

"I told Basarab that Katalin wouldn't be happy about uprooting her life in Europe but she'd be pleased to get Mia away from Santan, so she'd almost certainly go along with his plan. I told the count my wife felt they were all monsters. He told me they were, despite how civilized most of the vampires appeared to be on the outside.

"Not surprisingly," Randy couldn't stop talking about what had happened in Brasov after the ceremony, "it wasn't Katalin who gave me a hard time about the move; it was Mia. She accused her mother of concocting something up to keep her away from the one she loved. She even threw blame on Basarab. I told her she was only sixteen and she'd listen to her parents and ordered her to pack her things. She screamed at me. Said she was going to hate me forever, and that Basarab and I couldn't keep her and Santan apart. She'd find a way to thwart our plan." Randy looked at his daughter sitting beside Virginia. His eyes filled with tears; hers did not.

Lardom returned to his table and sat down. He wanted to continue questioning Randy but he also wanted, while the timeframe he was currently in was fresh, to hear from the count, and possibly from Santan and Virginia, to ensure all the gaps were filled in. In a surprising move, Lardom asked Randy to excuse himself, but after examining a couple other witnesses, he would be expected to return to the stand and continue with the testimony of his failing relationship with Katalin.

"I call Count Basarab to the stand."

Basarab hadn't expected to be summoned to the stand so early in the trial. He actually hadn't expected to be called at all.

He reasoned Lardom was instructed to treat everyone as an equal suspect until the truth was revealed. Basarab stood and stepped over to the witness stand, and was sworn in.

"Thank you, count," Lardom launched into his questioning immediately. "Your friend, Randy, has revealed considerable information about what took place before, in his home, and at and after the ceremony where we celebrated the full cross-over of your son and daughter. Before continuing further, I would like to get a take on where you stand, if you don't mind?" Lardom was taking the time to stroke the count's ego by asking permission to question him.

"Ask away," Basarab said nonchalantly.

"Why did you invite Randy and his family to such an event?" Lardom's question shocked a number of the vampires in the room, in particular, Basarab.

The count paused for a moment, looking to the back of the room where Randy had seated himself. At length, he answered with a decisive tone: "It was a two-fold celebration … my daughter's nineteenth birthday and the ceremony. Randy is my friend and has been for a long time. It was only proper he be invited."

"How aware were—are—you of the special bond between Randy and Virginia?"

"Very aware," the count replied through tightened lips. "However, allow me to elaborate here: the bond between my wife and Randy is one of friendship. Nothing more." Basarab glared around the room. "Have I made myself clear about this matter?"

"Most clear," Lardom returned. "So, let's move on then. Were you aware of how Katalin felt about our kind?"

"Not until the night of the ceremony did she show her true feelings for vampires—to me, at least."

Lardom branched down another alley. "When did you find out about Santan and Mia?"

"Santan informed me that night. He came to me in the stables. We talked. Afterward, I told Virginia and communicated to her what we must do. I was sending Randy and his family to Brantford on the pretence of him being transferred by his company, and she and I were taking our family to the castle in Scotland."

"In your opinion, did Randy accept your plan well?"

"Well enough to realize we had no choice in the matter. As much as Randy loves Santan, I don't believe, in reality, he wanted his daughter to marry my son." Basarab found his son amongst the vampire throng and shivered at the look Santan gave him.

"I assume you wanted to get Randy and his family away as quickly as possible … when did they leave?"

"We arranged for them to leave just before sunrise when everyone else in the castle would still be sleeping."

"How did that go … what I mean to ask is, what was the atmosphere of their parting?"

Basarab thought back to the moment of Randy's departure. "Katalin tried to hide her disgust for me and Mia stared at me as though I were the devil incarnate. Randy seemed embarrassed by their actions."

"Did Santan not come down to wish Mia and Randy farewell?"

"My son was ill and had taken to his bed. The ceremony had not set well with his stomach. Santan had, and still does, I believe, a difficult time consuming too much blood in one sitting."

Lardom nodded, turned and walked back to his table. "That will be all for now, Count Basarab. I would like to call your wife to the stand now." He looked to the back of the room: "Virginia, will you come forward, please?"

There was another stir amongst the vampires, especially the ones sitting in the jury section. Attila and Angelique, as well, looked at Lardom surprised, as Virginia made her way to the front of the room. There were a few heavy sighs; it had already been a long enough night and it appeared Lardom was on a mission he wasn't quite ready to abort yet.

Chapter Twenty

efore going to bed, Judge Harris sent off two emails to acquaintances who had been in the same circles as he and the count had been part of more than twenty years ago. One email went out to the police captain, another to the man who had been an administrator at the Brantford General Hospital.

Dear Markus: I am aware you know that our long-lost friend, Count Basarab Musat, has returned to our fair city. It has come to my attention, via one of your officers—Nathaniel—that Count Basarab, or someone within his household, may be involved in the crime that allegedly took place behind the Station Coffee House. I use the word 'allegedly' because, apparently, the victim did not meet his final demise until a later date, despite the condition in which his body was first found—supposedly fully drained of blood and with puncture wounds on his neck.

There were only three of us—besides our informant, who is dead now—all those years ago, who actually knew who and what the count was. I am unsure if he is aware of our knowledge. Therefore, it might be safe to reason that the count, or, like I said, one of his people, may have been involved.

Your officer, Nathaniel, is convinced there is something 'weird' going on within the castle, as we refer to the home our friend owns, and he wishes to speak with all those who were present there the night of the crime. However, Basarab is not being co-operative. Subsequently, Nathaniel approached me for a warrant so he could force his way in to interview everyone.

I have stalled Nathaniel—he was shocked when he discovered I knew the count—telling him there is no need for a warrant, I would arrange the meetings for him. I am hoping, at your end, you can somehow convince your man to back off the count. The last thing we need is to have our friend overstay his welcome in our fair city.

I will be messaging Samuel, as well. It might be a good idea if we all meet before I speak with the count.
Respectfully yours,
Judge Harris

The judge pushed send, then began his second email to the former hospital administrator.

Dear Samuel: I hope this note finds you well. I know you stepped down from your administrative duties a few years ago, but I also know you keep in touch with a number of people at the hospital. Several years ago, we had a mutual friend that we learned a dark secret about. To my knowledge, he never realized just how much we knew about him.

The source that declared him to you before Markus and I knew—the man who used to obtain 'supplies' for our friend— passed away about five years ago; it is now only the three of us— you, me, and Markus—who are aware of who and what our friend is, to my knowledge, at least.

Count Basarab Musat is back in town and, apparently, there are some family members with him. I have no idea why he is here; he mentioned to a police officer that he was checking on his property and having a small family gathering at the same time. As you know, the count is on a specific diet, so this is where you come in.

I would like you to keep your ear to the ground for rumours of diminishing resources in the blood bank. One of the captain's officers is adamant our count has something to do with an alleged murder that took place behind the Station Coffee House. Apparently, the body was drained of blood—puncture wounds on the neck, too—however, somehow the man miraculously rose from the dead while lying on a slab in the morgue. You and Markus and I all know there is only one type of individual who might be able to commit such a crime, and I am suggesting we all meet before I speak with the count.
Respectfully yours,
Judge Harris

The judge pushed send, shut his computer off, and went up to bed. Count Basarab Musat was not someone he wished to deal with at this point in his life.

Nathaniel made a few notes on a scratchpad by his phone before hitting the sack. First thing in the morning, he was going to give Karen a call. She was the paramedic at the crime scene and had seen the body's lack of blood, same as he had. He had no idea why he was going to call her other than the fact that she could confirm what happened at the scene, but if he were to be honest with himself, he missed her.

Frankie cracked open a beer as soon as he entered his apartment, then moved to the living room. Turning on the television to catch a comedy show to lighten his mood, Frankie stretched out in his easychair. The comedy show never happened and the beer was never finished. Within minutes, a soft snoring filled the empty room.

Suddenly, Frankie found himself running through the graveyard off of West Street, the same one where he and Nathaniel had eaten their supper. He was sprinting between gravestones, stumbling to the ground occasionally, then picking himself up and continuing. Frankie could feel the adrenaline surging through his body as he was overcome with the fear that something evil was chasing him.

Finally, he staggered out of the graveyard and across the street, running toward the big mansion. Pushing through the guardian trees, Frankie raced across the lawn and up the stone steps of the house. He banged on the door, the fear almost choking him.

When the door opened, it was *him*! The vampire man!

"I've been waiting for you, Frankie. My children are hungry, and so am I."

Diabolical laughter enveloped Frankie. He tried to scream but the sound choked in his throat. He fell to the floor at the man's feet and then he saw them—several of them—converging on him. Smiles on their faces. Licking their lips between extended incisors.

Frankie awoke with a start, sweating cold. Sleep refused to come to him again—he wouldn't have allowed it anyway.

Chapter Twenty-one

Virginia settled on the witness chair, raised her head, and looked directly into Lardom's eyes. She wondered what he could possibly be going to ask her. She found out soon enough.

"Did you like Katalin?" Lardom inquired.

"I tried to," Virginia replied.

"Tried?"

"It was easy when Randy first married her, but as time went by, especially after he told her about us—his vampire family—she became withdrawn."

"How so?"

Virginia shuffled in her chair. "Well, Randy began declining our invitations quite a bit. I know it wasn't coming directly from him because he always enjoyed his time with our family. Especially with Santan, with whom he has a special bond."

"Did Randy ever confide to you directly how his wife felt about you and the vampires?" Lardom looked back at Randy, then to Virginia.

"No." Virginia swallowed hard, knowing she was telling an untruth. Her mind wandered back to the moment when Randy had visited the castle without Katalin and they had taken a walk in the gardens. It happened shortly after Mia's tenth birthday.

Randy had been morose, telling her his concerns about how adamant Katalin was about not spending so much time with the Musat family—the vampires. He'd said he didn't know what to do about it. Virginia had advised him to give Katalin some time to reconsider, however, it appeared she'd only gotten stronger in her conviction to try and keep Randy from his adopted family. Virginia was surprised when Randy and his family showed up for anything, especially Samara's party and the ceremony.

"Really, Virginia?" Lardom's eyebrows rose in confusion. "Are you telling this court that your good friend, Randy, never confided in you about his wife's feelings toward your family?"

Virginia's temper began to boil. Where was Lardom going with this sort of questioning? What did her close relationship with the man who was such a large part of her life have to do with the death of his wife? She and Randy made their choices in life—she'd chosen Basarab, the father of her children, and Randy eventually moved on and married Katalin. Their close friendship was accepted by Basarab because the count knew neither one would ever cross a line—there would be too high a price to pay if they did. It was none of anyone's business the moments she and Randy shared—the good times they shared publicly and the confidences they shared in private.

"Do you have a problem with the question, Virginia? Should I repeat it?" Lardom's voice held a hint of sarcasm. Virginia, being the wife of his leader did not negate the fact that many of the vampires in the hierarchy were not pleased when Basarab had cast aside his former wife, Teresa, for the human who had given him a son. Many believed he should have just kept the child and done away with Virginia. These were well-kept secrets within the minds of many of Basarab's loyal followers.

Virginia's lips set in a firm line. She glanced at Basarab, eyes begging him to stop this line of questioning. The count, reading his wife's expression and knowing how close she and Randy were, didn't want their relationship to be brought out in court. Besides, of what importance was it to the matter at hand?

Before either Lardom or Virginia could speak, Basarab intervened. "I don't believe the relationship between my wife and *our* good friend, Randy, has anything to do with the death of his wife. Randy has been an accepted part of our community for a long time, and I, as well as my wife, consider him family. Move on, Lardom."

Lardom looked first at the count, then to where the jurors sat. He hadn't expected to be curtailed in his questioning of witnesses; he was told he had free rein to do whatever it took to find the killer—or killers—as the case appeared to point to. The tension in the room was apparent, no sound other than the odd individual repositioning in their chair.

Looking at the count, Lardom finally spoke: "I believe we will take a recess. I would speak with you in private, Basarab."

Basarab nodded. "So be it. I believe we have all been through enough for one night and other matters need attention, as well. Everyone is free to go for now, but remember, you are all to remain within the castle walls. No one, and I repeat that with emphasis, must step outside—not even for a walk around the gardens." The count stood. "I will speak first with Lardom and then decide who will, along with me, speak to the pesky police officer, who insists someone in this house is involved in their crime across the rail tracks from here."

Basarab stepped down from the podium, gesturing for Lardom to follow him. As the two vampires walked to the door, Basarab signalled to Attila. "My father will join us," the count announced firmly, leaving no room for discussion.

Ildiko and Gara were both watching the proceedings with great interest. They'd agreed, before coming to the court proceedings, on what Ildiko would say when she was called to the stand. After Basarab left with Lardom and his father, the siblings slipped out of the room and headed to Gara's room.

"Lardom is on a witch hunt," Gara opened the conversation. "He's one of the best litigators I've ever met, and, because of what we are, he's had centuries of practice. Basarab has given him a task, and I do believe Lardom is surprising even our esteemed leader!" Gara paused and smiled sardonically.

Before he could continue, Ildiko spoke up: "It was all I could do to restrain myself from reacting when Virginia was on the stand."

Gara's face turned grim as he cut his twin off. "You will have to be even more controlled when Lardom calls you to the stand!" he snapped. "You are far from being out of the woods on this one, sister. Remember, you *did* have something to do with this human's death, even though it was just finishing her off. You are only to reveal what you know, if necessary, and I will give you the signal when to do so."

Ildiko gazed at the floor. It wasn't in her nature to prostrate herself to anyone—including her beloved brother—but under the circumstances, she knew there was no other option. She needed an ally, knowing she couldn't trust Lajos, despite their past. Nor did she have any faith in Dracula, whom she used to consider an ally, them being so close in character.

She nodded. "Go over everything with me again, just to ensure we are on the same page."

Gara nodded and began.

Santan followed his mother and Mia to Virginia's room. His primary intention was to get an update on how it was going with

Mia. So far as he was noticing, Mia was still not out of the woods, and could not be trusted to be left on her own.

Virginia walked straight to the small table by the window where Viktor had placed some bottles of blood and wine glasses. She poured a drink and downed it quickly. Santan noticed how shaken his mother was, guessing her nervousness was because of the questions Lardom asked her about her relationship with Randy. He glanced at Mia and saw her lick her lips, so he poured her a glass of blood and handed it to her.

Mia smiled as she raised the glass to her lips, her eyes telling him what was on her mind. Santan returned her smile but shook his head. She pouted.

"It will be daylight soon," Virginia commented knowingly. She turned back to the guests in her room. "Would you like some time alone with Mia?" she asked Santan.

Mia's heart quickened but was immediately crushed when Santan shook his head. "I only came to check on her, Mother. I think we should all get some rest; tomorrow night is going to be trying again for all of us. Lardom is not holding back anything with his questions, and I have my doubts that Father will be able to control his chosen lawyer."

"Can't you stay just a bit longer?" Mia pleaded, going up to Santan and trying to put her arms around him.

Santan plied her off him, holding her at arm's length. "No, Mia. I need rest, and so do you and my mother." He directed Mia in Virginia's direction. "She's all yours, Mother."

As Santan made his way down the hallway to his room, he heard Samara and Lajos coming up the stairs. He stepped back into the shadows of a pillar and watched as they made their way into Samara's room, glancing behind them to make sure they weren't being watched.

As soon as the door closed, Lajos picked Samara up and threw her on the bed. She giggled and started to pull her clothes off, anxious to have some fun before falling asleep. Lajos was stripping as well, his manhood anxious for release.

Flipping Samara over onto her stomach, Lajos took her from behind. She, anticipating what he was about to do, raised her buttocks invitingly just in time to receive the full force of his cock. She squealed in delight, matching his rhythm with a fury of her own. Within seconds it was over, and they both rolled, laughing, on the bed.

Laying there for a few minutes, side by side, the two lovers breathed in the air of their lovemaking. Lajos was the first to make a move, raising himself up on one elbow and trailing the fingers of his other hand over Samara's body. She closed her eyes, savouring every moment.

Teasingly, Lajos rubbed her mound, then tickled the entrance to her womb. She arched up to meet his penetration, but he pulled his fingers out and moved on, leaving a sticky trail along her inner thighs. Continuing his teasing, Lajos leaned over and found Samara's mouth, kissing her deeply, nibbling at her lips. Samara writhed in desire, reaching out to grasp hold of his pulsing instrument, squeezing it in her hand, feeling her partner shiver in anticipation.

Sliding down her body, Lajos licked at her love juices, swirling his tongue around her desire, surging her into a climax that didn't want to stop. Samara's body shuddered over and over, and she tangled her fingers in his long hair, pulling her lover closer to her, not wanting him to stop. Lajos' shoulders shook with laughter as he continued his conquest of the beautiful temptress.

Finally, Lajos pulled away from Samara, and shimmying up her body, trailing his lust across her bellybutton and between her aroused breasts, he pressed the crown of his cock to her lips.

Samara opened her mouth willingly, taking in as much of Lajos' manhood as was possible. He groaned in appreciation and moved rhythmically, slowly at first, increasing the intensity of his thrusts; Samara swirled her tongue and scraped her teeth along his flesh.

As Samara sensed that Lajos was ready to release his seed into her mouth, she pulled back, shoved him back onto the bed, and mounted Lajos with a hunger that devoured her lover. As he was about to release, she pulled off, laughed, then straddled him again. "Not so quick; I am not finished with you yet!"

For the next half an hour, Samara teased Lajos over and over until finally she allowed him his moment of consummation, timed to release with the last of her multiple climaxes. Laying upon his chest, Samara breathed heavily. Lajos wrapped his arms around the temptress and began kissing her again, close to her ear.

"Vixen," he whispered, taking a bite of her earlobe. "Fucking vixen."

Samara giggled and shifted off Lajos' body, turning her back to him. "Time for a nap, lover," she commented. "Best you return to your room. If you remember, Dracula wished to speak with you," she reminded him.

Lajos didn't like how he was being dismissed by Samara; however, she was right. He needed to meet with Dracula. Before taking his leave, Lajos drew a cover over Samara.

Dracula was waiting impatiently for Lajos to finish his business with the temptress. He wondered at times where Lajos' real loyalties lay. The man loved his women, one reason Dracula had chosen the virile vampire for the job. However, Lajos could also be unpredictable when it came to women, and Dracula had never known him to be loyal to any one of them—until now. Samara seemed to be living up to her name—the Temptress—digging her claws into Lajos to the point that, at times, he seemed to be nothing more than a whimpering puppy when he was around her!

I think it is time I laid things on the line to Lajos and remind him who his benefactor is! Remind him what I did for him when he had nowhere to go after his father died in battle. Remind him of the power he will have, through me, when he accomplishes his conquest of the princess, who wants the throne more than she wants anything else. Now, my friend, you are being played by Samara ... maybe I am, too. Possibly, I have underestimated my little niece, thinking the human part of her would decrease her power. It appears it has not!

There were no windows to the outside in Dracula's room, having been housed in the basement. Despite that, he knew the sun would be rising any time, and he was anxious to have his say with Lajos before grabbing a few hours of sleep. He was also keen to leave the house and revisit the downtown; bottled blood was not the same as taking directly from a human source.

A soft knock sounded on Dracula's door. Before he could answer, Lajos stepped into the room. He looked flushed. "What is it you wish to discuss, Dracula?" Lajos asked, walking across the room and planting himself on one of the chairs. He leaned back, stretching like a large, well-satisfied cat.

"What I have always wanted, Lajos." Dracula's voice was sharp. "Something you seem to be forgetting."

Lajos grinned. "Have I? You underestimate me, Dracula." Lajos stretched even further, hooking his hands behind his head. "I've been busy with Samara, as you instructed me to be. She is, I must admit, a handful, but she can't get enough of me!" Lajos knew he was only telling half the truth. He knew Samara was the one who controlled much of their lovemaking. He was a pawn in her hands always in the end. Proof of that was confirmed during their most recent session, where Samara took over and when she was satisfied enough, she dismissed him without a care.

Dracula was no fool, though. He sensed Lajos was not entirely truthful. His voice was saturated with sarcasm: "Do I underestimate you, Lajos? I think not. However, what I do think is you have misjudged Samara. Possibly I have, as well. But now is not the time to quibble, is it? We must be on guard. Lardom is asking a lot of questions, and he will get to the truth…"

"The truth as you know it, Dracula?" Lajos cut Dracula off in midsentence.

"Hopefully, because that truth will lead us directly to the throne, with you sitting on it and Samara perched adoringly on your lap!" Dracula drove his point home. "Now, just a few details before we sleep; you must be prepared for when you sit in the witness chair. Lardom is no fool, and neither are our fellow vampires sitting as jurors. You, my dear Lajos, are to appear as nothing more than a besotted lover of the beautiful princess…" Dracula continued with what was to be said and not mentioned, and soon the two conspirators parted company, each going to their beds.

Chapter Twenty-two

asarab motioned for Lardom and Attila to take a seat, while he sat down behind his desk. He thumped his fingers angrily on the arms of his chair. Lardom waited patiently for the count to open the conversation.

Finally, "What do you think you were going to accomplish by questioning my wife about her relationship with Randy?" the count scowled.

Lardom cleared his throat. He was not the least bit nervous; he'd been given a job to do, and Attila had told him he had free rein to get to the truth of who murdered the human woman. "Every aspect of every individual's life is important, especially that of those close to the heart of the crime." Lardom took a moment to allow his words to sink in. "Anyone, including you, your wife, even your father, who may have had reason to eliminate this woman, who openly detested our kind, is a suspect! You must allow me to do my job the way I see fit, and if you are not willing to do so, I will withdraw my services this instant, pack up, and go home. If that becomes the case, I can guarantee you, Basarab, a number of your most trusted council members will leave with me!"

Basarab didn't like the inferences Lardom was making. Nevertheless, he had a great deal of respect for Lardom, who had gotten many vampires out of trouble on several occasions. "I understand what you are saying, Lardom; however, I wish for you to understand this: my wife's relationship with Randy—past and present—is off the table. Virginia is not capable of hurting anyone, let alone murdering someone in cold blood. Ask what you want of me or anyone else, but keep your questions to my wife directly related to the subject at hand."

Attila noticed the dark look on Lardom's face and decided it was time he intervened before the situation blew up in his son's face. "Basarab, my son, you have always been wise enough to listen to good counsel, correct?"

Basarab nodded, not able to speak at the moment, he was so frustrated.

"Then we must not show favouritism. I know as well as you, Virginia is not capable of committing such an act, but we must allow Lardom to do his job to prove that. If she is innocent, as you and I believe her to be, then it will be proven by how she answers Lardom's questions—the same as anyone else. Have I made my point convincingly enough, son?"

Lardom watched the interaction between father and son closely. There had been times over the centuries when he had wondered who really controlled the throne, an unpredictable—at times—Basarab, or the wise and steady father, Attila. He thought it best to say nothing more until Basarab replied to his father's reasoning.

Basarab knew Attila was right, and he admonished himself for having made such a scene in the courtroom, realizing he might have prejudiced some of the jurors to think negatively of Virginia. He made the decision to concede. There was no sense in arguing further. Besides, now he had to make the decision on who would speak to the police.

"Very well. You have made a worthy point, Father." Turning directly to Lardom, "You may continue as you were; however, I can assure you that neither I, nor my wife, had anything to do with this murder, and all I ask is that you do take this into consideration."

Lardom smiled inwardly. Victory was his, but he would not allow the count to know just how pleased he was. Instead, he humbled himself. "I thank you, count, for the confidence you are showing me. As from the beginning, my only goal is to ensure whoever did this despicable deed is brought to justice." He stood. "I will take my leave now to get some rest. I know you have other matters to attend to."

Once Lardom was out of the room, Basarab tapped the desk with a pen. "Your advice, Father, on who I should select to speak with the officer?"

Attila thought for a moment before speaking. "The less, the better," he began. "I would suggest you, Virginia, Kardos, Santan, myself, and Angelique. These are the ones we know will be able to stick to a script."

"I agree," Basarab affirmed his father's decision. "We will meet before going down to continue the trial. For now, let us get some rest."

Father and son left the study together, each going their separate ways—Attila to the comfort of Angelique's arms; Basarab to an empty room. Virginia was still watching over Mia.

Adrianna called her people together and filled them in on what was happening across the ocean.

"Our friends are having a difficult time on several fronts, and, quite frankly, I am enjoying the spectacle. However, I think it is time to play my first card." Turning to Radu: "Be prepared to pay a visit to your brother."

Radu stared at Adrianna, a blank look in his eyes.

"This is what I have prepared you for, Radu. I want the whole lot of them to be off-guard. And to throw them off even more, you are to take Elizabeth with you. That should send a shockwave through some of them!" Adrianna almost choked on her own laughter.

Continuing, "Rasputin is already in place, having gone with the Russian vampires, and once you arrive at Yates Castle where many of Basarab's most trusted are staying, I am sure the count will not turn you away, being his long-lost uncle."

Radu smiled. Despite the control Adrianna had on his mind, he still had full recollection of what had happened all those years ago in Brantford when he'd tried to take the throne and had barely escaped with his life. "What is it you wish me and Elizabeth to do?"

"Just be yourselves; you've been in hiding these past twenty years, thinking about what you tried to do. You are sorry and wish to make amends with the family. You and Elizabeth have married…"

"How will my miraculous recovery be explained?" Elizabeth spoke up.

"They left you for dead but you weren't, were you? Radu was hiding in the woods nearby and rescued you, nursed you back to health, and then you left for Europe. That should be enough to satisfy any curiosities until I arrive."

"When do we leave?" Radu asked.

"I think tomorrow night should do just fine."

Later that same night, Rasputin received a message from Adrianna, informing him of Radu's and Elizabeth's pending arrival. She filled him in on what was to take place, and how he was to handle the situation. Rasputin assured Adrianna he would not fail her.

Chapter Twenty-three

*J*udge Harris received emails in the early morning from both Markus and Samuel. They cc'd each other, suggesting the three of them meet for breakfast at the Sunset Grill. The judge messaged both back immediately, saying that would be perfect; he would be there at eight o'clock, and he was buying.

Handshakes all around completed, the three men sat down and perused the menu. The waitress stopped at their table with a pot of coffee, offering to fill their cups. Markus and Samuel nodded yes, and Judge Harris ordered an orange juice. The waitress left, and returning with the judge's drink, took their orders.

While waiting for their breakfasts, the three men sat in silence for a few minutes. Finally, the judge opened the conversation: "We all are aware of who and what Count Basarab is, but I do not believe for one minute he had anything to do with the crime committed behind the café by the train station. The count never caused any problems for our community when he was here before, and we all knew him as an honourable and generous gentleman.

"Having said that, we cannot discount the possibility someone else in his household is involved. We know there is no sense dropping by during the day, so one of us needs to get there as the sun is setting to convince the count to allow Nathaniel to do his interviews either this evening or tomorrow evening. Unfortunately, I have commitments both nights. Is it possible one of you could approach the count?" Judge Harris leaned back in the booth as the breakfast plates were delivered to the table. He reached immediately for the salt and pepper.

"I have something going on tonight," Markus declared, "but I have a suggestion." Directing his next statement to Samuel, "How about you set something up tonight with the count for tomorrow night, and I'll accompany my overzealous officer for the interviews. Best way to keep things in check, in my opinion anyway. You okay with that Samuel?"

Samuel wiped some ketchup off his chin with a napkin and finished swallowing what he had in his mouth before replying. "I believe I can manage that. It will be good to see the count again; despite his propensities, he is a most interesting individual."

The judge finished the rest of his orange juice and set his glass on the table. "There were times I wished we hadn't found out about the count; made me feel uncomfortable around him."

"As far as we know, the count never discovered his contact at the blood bank caved and told us about him," Samuel said, "but I agree, after I found out, I did feel a tad uncomfortable around him, as well."

Markus pushed aside his empty plate. "I always had the impression he knew. At one of the after-hours events, I noticed the count pull a small bottle of red liquid from the inside pocket of his jacket and pour it into a wine glass. He caught me looking at him, raised his glass to me, and smiled. We never spoke of it."

"I remember his first wife … Teresa, I believe her name was … a real beauty." Samuel smiled at his memory of the gorgeous woman who accompanied the count to a small number of events. She'd barely spoken, but was always generous with her smiles. "I wonder whatever happened to her."

"The count left suddenly but returned a couple years later. There was another woman, apparently, who'd had two children—his, I presume—I believe the count took up with her," Markus informed.

Judge Harris frowned. "Well, my concern is not about the count's love life, so we need to make sure your officer doesn't piss the man off and cause him to do something catastrophic. We all know what his kind might be capable of if provoked."

"Strange, isn't it? How is it that a fantasy about a real-life character—Vlad Tepeş, also known as Dracula—created by an author, is a reality?" Samuel raised his eyebrows probingly. "There were times, after knowing about the count, I wondered how close to the truth Bram Stoker was."

"Well, we don't know for sure the count is a real, live vampire as depicted in books and movies. Maybe the guy just has a fetish for blood," Markus advised. "After all, we never found any evidence other than what we were told and what you saw at the one event, Samuel."

Judge Harris frowned and leaned forward, elbows on the table. "That is a valid point; nevertheless, just because we didn't discover any other evidence, doesn't mean the count isn't just extremely good at covering his tracks. Gentlemen, despite how much we might have liked the count, I want him out of our city as soon as possible." The judge lingered a moment, fiddling with his fork. "Are we all clear on what must be done to keep a lid on this situation?"

Both of the judge's companions nodded.

"Good … Samuel, send the captain and me a quick email once you have the meetings set."

"Will do."

The three men stood, shook hands, and left the restaurant, each going their separate ways.

Chapter Twenty-four

As the sun went down on another day, the vampires made their way into the dining room to partake of their first meal before heading down to the basement courtroom. Basarab entered and went straight to the head of the table when he was sure everyone was present.

"We will begin court proceedings shortly. I must speak with my chosen candidates in regards to how we are going to handle this irritating cop. Attila and I have discussed who will be present at the questioning: Virginia, Attila and Angelique, Kardos, Santan, and me. We decided the fewer individuals involved, the better. While this is going on, each one of you will be asked to remain in the basement. No one, and I cannot emphasize this enough, is to leave that room while the police officers are in this house!" Basarab looked around. "Have I made myself clear."

There were nods all around.

"Good. Now, the sooner you all finish up here, the sooner I can discuss strategy with the group selected to speak with the cop, and then we can let Lardom resume his questioning."

Numerous vampires picked up their glasses and filed out of the room, heading to the basement, an indication that most of those present were not keen on hanging around the city any longer than necessary. The rest followed suit. Samara took charge of Mia.

Finally, alone except for his chosen individuals, Basarab explained what they were to say when the officer showed up with his warrant.

"On the night the crime took place, we were all here playing a game of cards until the wee hours after midnight, then we all went off to bed and slept quite late, close to noon.

"We know Samara did indeed foolishly kill the old man, but we also know what Angelique did to form a smokescreen around the crime. However, Angelique, you did complicate the situation for us when you decided to bring the old man back to life. I am sure, at the time, you had no idea of the repercussions that might cause.

"It is my belief this cop is not aware of whether we know the old man mysteriously rose from the dead, which may or may not work to our benefit. We are not to allude to any knowledge of his miraculous recovery. We are to keep our answers short and to the point, and we must remain on script. I will insist we all be interrogated together. Any questions?"

Santan was first to speak. "Why have you chosen so few of us, Father? Will this police officer not suspect there are more of us here than just six?"

"As I already said, the fewer, the better. If asked if there were not more, I will answer that other family members who had been visiting have already left. It will be none of the cop's business who."

"What I don't understand," Kardos broached, "is why this cop is harassing us when the old man obviously was not dead. This cop himself saw that when he went to the morgue."

Angelique, too, was more than curious about Nathaniel's insistence. "I have observed the two officers in the neighbourhood and they did not go from house to house as they said they were doing. They've only concentrated on us. Very strange indeed."

"Hopefully, only a small hiccup we have to deal with," Attila added.

"Hopefully." Basarab pointed to the door. "If everyone is clear on what we are to do and say, let's get downstairs and continue with the other issue we are faced with."

As the group made their way to the stairway leading down to the basement, there was a knock on the front door. Basarab cursed under his breath. Viktor was making his way to the entrance, but the count raised his hand, indicating he would answer the door himself.

"Go on," Basarab directed to his companions. "I'll be down as soon as I deal with whoever is calling on us."

Before Basarab could open it, Samuel knocked again. He was nervous. It had been a long time since he'd seen the count.

The door creaked open slowly, and Samuel was shocked when he saw who it was. "Count Basarab!" he exclaimed. "You have aged well!"

The count swallowed his surprise; he'd been expecting the police officer. Extending his hand, "Samuel, I believe … what brings you to my home?" Basarab did not offer his guest entrance.

"Well, a police officer paid a visit to our mutual friend, Judge Harris, asking for a warrant to force you and whoever is staying here to speak to him about a crime committed not far from here. Once he knew you were back in town, the judge thought it was a bit outrageous and told the officer he would arrange the meeting himself; said you are an old friend."

Basarab chuckled inside. *You have no idea how old!* To Samuel, "How is Judge Harris? He hasn't retired yet? He was getting up in years the last I saw him." An outward chuckle.

Samuel shuffled his feet nervously, not understanding why the count wouldn't invite him in. Was he trying to hide something, or someone? "He's retiring next year," Samuel informed. "The years have been good to you; you don't seem to have aged a bit since I last saw you," he added, reiterating his initial shock at the count's lack of ageing.

"Ah … trust me, I have aged. Just that my family has never been prone to gray hair and I have a regular skincare regime that seems to keep the wrinkles at bay." The count laughed softly. "And you, Samuel? Are you still working at the blood bank?"

Samuel swallowed hard. "No … no … I retired about five years ago."

"I see." Basarab was anxious to get the man out of his house now that some preliminary niceties were out of the way. "Exactly why are you here, Samuel … certainly, you have not been sent to question my family and me yourself?"

"No. Judge Harris, Captain Markus, and I met earlier today and decided … if it were okay with you … the captain would come by tomorrow evening with the police officers, and he would sit in on any questioning. Does that work for you?"

Basarab was surprised at this turn of events. He'd been hoping to be able to toy with the police officer. Hadn't expected the captain, who was more knowledgeable about what he was, to be present. He was sure his three friends had no idea he knew of their knowledge of what he was. They also had no idea how the man who'd 'spilled the goods' on him had met his maker.

When the count didn't reply immediately, Samuel continued: "We three think the officer is going overboard; nevertheless, this particular officer, when he digs his teeth into something, doesn't let go until he gets to the bottom of things, so we have to pacify him. I hope you understand." Samuel realized too late what he said about digging in teeth.

"Well, I think tomorrow evening will be just fine," Basarab finally answered. "How say we make it at seven. I must warn you, though, I am packing up to return to Europe and will be leaving later tomorrow evening, so I will only be able to accommodate about a half an hour for this officer … I am sure that will be enough, don't you?" The count finished with a smile.

Samuel wasn't sure what to do next. The count gave him the creeps and he couldn't put a finger on why. "I'll let Markus know," he uttered nervously. "He'll set it up with the officer."

"Excellent. Now, if you will excuse me, I have other business to attend to." Basarab shut the door, leaving no more room for further conversation.

Samuel headed to his car, which was parked on the road at the front of the property. The first thing he did was pick up his cell phone and send an email to the judge and the captain, informing them that the meeting was on. He didn't feel like talking to anyone at the moment.

Chapter Twenty-five

ttila was waiting in the hallway outside the courtroom door when Basarab entered the basement. "Everything okay?" the elder count inquired.

"Everything is fine. The meeting is set for tomorrow night. Some old friends have gotten involved, and I have the feeling they don't think much of this officer who is harassing us." Basarab quickly explained to his father what was going to take place before they entered the courtroom.

Attila took his seat beside Angelique, while Basarab made his way to his chair on the podium. Everyone in the room settled down; the count nodded for Lardom to begin.

"I recall Virginia to the stand," Lardom called out.

Lardom didn't waste any time getting started once Virginia was in the witness chair. "Starting where we left off," he began, "you stated Randy never confided to you directly how his wife felt about vampires, and I asked you if you were sure about that. I ask again, are you sure Randy never confided such information to you?"

Basarab had spoken briefly with Virginia in private, relating to her what had transpired between him, Attila, and Lardom, and had instructed her to maintain that Randy had not specifically confided anything about Katalin's dislike for vampires.

"No," Virginia said firmly. "He never talked to me about his wife's opinion of vampires. Most of the time we talked about our children," she smiled.

"I see." Lardom didn't look pleased with Virginia's answer. He felt she was untruthful. Returning to his original questioning: "You said you tried to like Katalin, and after she found out about Randy's adopted family, it became difficult. Did you ever directly confront Katalin about this issue?

"No. We simply didn't say much of anything to each other … only polite, inconsequential conversation the few times they accepted our hospitality."

"I understand the issue heated up after the crossing-over ceremony, with Katalin making quite a scene in the hall when Santan asked Mia to dance. I believe her words to Santan were 'You will not be dancing with this young man, Mia—not tonight—not ever!' Is this true?"

Virginia nodded. "Santan told me such."

"Would you do anything to protect your son's feelings? I understand he and Mia are madly in love."

Virginia's anger surfaced. "Are you suggesting I would kill Katalin because she wouldn't let my son dance with her daughter? If that were the case, I could have done it in Brasov; why would I have waited until the possibility of meeting up with her later?"

"Why indeed?" Lardom asked smoothly, Virginia's fury not fazing him a bit. "Might I suggest that you had every reason to be rid of Katalin. She was threatening your son. She was threatening the existence of our kind. She hated us. In a way, through her threats, she was threatening your good friend, Randy. So, I might suggest yes, you had a lot of reasons!" Lardom glanced over at the jury and smiled.

Virginia had enough. Lardom was stepping over a line he had no right to. *What is your problem, Lardom? You have never treated me with such disrespect before. I don't care what my husband told me to do; I'm going to put you in your place!*

"How dare you even suggest I would do such a thing!" Virginia's voice rose to an angry crescendo. "Who do you think you are? I may have had several reasons to rid our lives of Katalin; however," Virginia leaned forward in the chair, looking straight into Lardom's eyes, "I am not the only one!" She leaned back, still staring Lardom down. "Or at least removed from our presence," Virginia closed with.

Basarab smiled at Virginia's spirit, one of the attributes that had drawn him to her in the first place. *Why was I even worried? She knows how to handle herself.*

Lardom grinned and looked around the room, resting his eyes briefly on those he'd already called to the stand and on those yet to meet his interrogation. Looking back at Virginia, "How correct you are, Virginia … several others might have had good reason to murder Katalin … but, who?" He turned again and faced the room full of vampires.

"Which one of you out there struck the first blow on this woman?" Lardom inquired. "Which one of you struck the second blow?" he added with a sneer. "You are excused, Virginia. Don't leave the room as I might need to call upon you again."

Lardom viewed the individuals in the room, going over in his mind the list he'd made of the order of call. He wasn't sure if it would be wise to summon Santan at this point, thinking maybe he should call upon some of the witnesses he'd already ruled out as even being close to being a suspect. Deciding the best route to take for now, Lardom skipped to the bottom of his list and began to call the Russian vampires, starting with Volodya.

Over the next hour, Volodya, Vasilisa, and Petya were questioned as to their whereabouts on the night in question. Their answers confirmed his thoughts: they had nothing to do with Katalin's death. Petya established that he, Manya, and Ákos had left the house in search of entertainment in the downtown during the timeframe of the murder. He pointed out Délia could confirm that because she was the one who'd encouraged them to go have some fun without her.

"So," Lardom stood in front of the witness chair, his hands folded behind his back, "the three of you were together the entire night?"

Petya nodded. "Yes."

"No one else from the house joined you? Other young people might have enjoyed a trip to partake of the downtown nightlife," Lardom baited.

Petya scowled, being wise enough to know who the lawyer might be referring to. "There was no one else in the house that would have been welcome to accompany us. Besides," he added, "I believe they had other things on their minds."

"Who might you be referring to?"

"You know quite well, who," Petya retorted. "We did not invite either of Basarab's children—especially not Samara! If Santan had been around, we might have considered him, but he wasn't."

"I see." Lardom looked to where Samara sat, hoping to get a clue from her body language. Nothing. Cold as ice. He continued. "You wouldn't happen to have seen Samara in your downtown travels?"

Petya pursed his lips. "As a matter of fact, Ákos mumbled something about having seen Samara and Lajos pass by the bar's door when it opened as someone was leaving."

Hmmm ... Petya is establishing Samara's alibi ... I anticipated she might have a lot to do with this murder ... just being seen downtown doesn't really rule her out ... she could have been the one to strike the first blow!

"Thank you, Petya. You may return to your seat." Lardom looked up at Basarab. "If you don't mind, I would like to take a small break to go over some of my notes."

Basarab nodded assent. Speaking to the congregation of vampires, "We will all meet back here in one hour."

With the room empty, Basarab looked around at the stone walls. He felt colder than he'd ever felt before. He wondered if this was the end of it all—the end of the vampires' existence. Samara, through her recklessness, had brought down the local authorities on them, much closer to home than ever before. However, what troubled Basarab more, and what he felt to be a far seriouser threat to the vampires' existence than his daughter's indiscretion, was the dream Ilias had relayed. Who was this woman? It seemed she was coming after the vampires—but why? How was he to prepare for such an unknown? And, if he remembered correctly, Tanyasin, Angelique's sister, before she died had also warned of a great sorceress stronger and more evil than anyone the vampire world would ever encounter!

Of course, over the centuries there had been times when the police questioned a vampire here or there, but such matters were dealt with quickly, and most of the officers involved in any of those investigations moved on to other suspects. Basarab smiled half-heartedly remembering some of the incidents.

Returning to his daughter, Basarab shed a tear—unusual for him. He'd always been known to have a steely demeanour, ruling with an iron hand; but Samara, as a little girl, the first time she'd looked up at him and called him papa, had wound her way through his heart and his head. There were more times than Basarab cared to number that she'd rendered him confused.

The sound of Samara's voice in the room startled the count. "Papa." Samara approached her father's chair, handing him a goblet filled with blood. "I saw you didn't leave the room and thought you might need something to drink."

Basarab wrapped his fingers around the goblet, enclosing his daughter's hand within his. There was a moment of silence between them, a moment when their eyes met and said it all. Despite everything Samara did, the count loved his daughter. She was so capable. She was so strong. She was a leader. The only thing she lacked was patience, and, sometimes, the prudence to make wise choices.

The count set the goblet on the table and gathered his daughter into his arms. His hand stroked her hair as he murmured, "My beautiful little Samara; what am I to do with you? What am I to do, period?"

Samara sighed and wrapped her arms around her father's waist. "All will be well, Papa. No one can hurt us. We are the family Musat, the most powerful of our kind!" *And when I sit on the throne, everyone will know that!*

Chapter Twenty-six

Lardom had his suspicions of who might have committed the crime, but there were so many variables to consider. Too many individuals had more than good reason to see Katalin dead, or at least out of the way.

What if the initial blow was struck as a warning? Would that mean the draining of blood was done recklessly, for the sheer joy of taking blood from the primary source?

And who is it we know who does things for the joy of it? Samara ... Dracula ... possibly Ildiko, although she has not really been involved with the family lately, so why would she do such a thing ... something I will have to dig into ... who else ... Basarab? The count has a lot to lose if Katalin went to the police ... he would have had to take drastic measures to protect the family ... would Attila have stepped in to protect his son from the pain by eliminating the problem?

Who do I call next to the stand? Am I forgetting anyone of any great importance ... should I call Randy again? Is it possible he's a great actor, feigning sorrow for the loss of his beloved wife ... he is in love with Virginia ... he's always been loyal to the vampire family that embraced him ... his beloved daughter turned to be with the one she loved ... and Randy loves Santan, as well ... could he have stuck the first blow as a warning to his wife to keep her mouth shut or he would come back and finish the job? Then, someone did the finishing for him!

As Lardom made his way back to the courtroom, he still hadn't made up his mind whom he was going to call to the stand next.

Nathaniel received a call from Judge Harris just as he was about to leave the precinct and go to his cruiser. Frankie was already waiting for him.

"Officer Jones," Nathaniel barked into the receiver.

"Nathaniel … Judge Harris, here. Got a minute?"

"Sure, but make it quick; I was on my way out." Then he remembered the judge was supposed to arrange the meetings with the mysterious count and his family. "Did you get the meetings set up or are you just going to give me a warrant?" Nathaniel asked.

The judge grimaced on the other end of the line. He respected Nathaniel, but the officer was being unreasonable in this case. There was no reason for him to want to interview the count and his family. It could lead to disaster. Clearing his throat, "The meeting is set for tomorrow night at seven. Captain Markus will be accompanying you. The count requested for everyone to be interviewed at the same time…"

"I'd rather interview them individually," Nathaniel cut Judge Harris off.

"Not going to happen. The count is a busy man and allocated you a half hour. Said he's packing to leave for home tomorrow night. So, you'll have to live with that,"—a pause—"or nothing." Judge Harris hoped Nathaniel would just back off and take the nothing.

No such luck. "Okay, I'll talk to the captain and arrange to meet him at the house tomorrow night. Thanks for setting this up for me." Nathaniel hung up the phone.

Judge Harris cursed under his breath, then turned to his computer and sent a quick email off to Markus and Samuel.

"What took you so long?" Frankie complained.

"Got a call from the judge; meeting is set for tomorrow night at seven."

"Meeting … not meetings?"

"My sentiment exactly. Apparently, this count is a busy man and is leaving tomorrow night for home. Evidently, he is also a good friend of the judge, so we're only going to be allowed one interview—and only with whoever this count wants us to talk to, I'm assuming."

"I still think we should just let it go. Vincent met his death down by the river," Frankie commented, not wanting anything more to do with the man in the big house.

"Yeah, that still baffles me. Should you, too. When we found the body, he was dead. No blood. Puncture wounds on the neck. Not moving." Nathaniel shook his head in frustration. "And when I first entered the morgue, Vincent was laid out on a slab and wasn't moving." He hesitated. "So how does a man like that, who's been examined by a number of professionals, including the coroner, all of a sudden sit up and ask for a drink?" Nathaniel went over the scenario he and Frankie had discussed on more than one occasion, and there was still no rationale to it.

"Frankie snorted. "And you think this count has the answer?"

Nathaniel nodded. "Him … or someone else in that house."

"Well, I guess the big mystery will be solved tomorrow night then." Frankie rolled his window down. His gut still told him they were making a big mistake, but Nathaniel was taking the lead on this case and he was Frankie's superior. Frankie had never been a religious man in any way, but his grandmother had given him a silver cross for his confirmation and he was definitely going to be wearing that when they went to interview the count and his family.

Lardom sat down and tapped his fingers on the table. He gazed around the room, still trying to make his decision on who to call next. His eyes rested on Ildiko, who was conversing with her brother. She seemed nervous—unusual for her. Lardom had always known Ildiko to be arrogant and self-assured.

His decision made, he summoned the next witness: "I call Ildiko to the stand."

Ildiko looked up in shock, not that she hadn't expected to be called—just not yet. She stood and made her way slowly to the witness chair. Sitting down, Ildiko focused her eyes on her brother, ignoring the rest of the room.

Lardom's first question wasn't asked until several seconds passed. "How well did you know Katalin?"

"Not well at all. I tend not to get involved with humans any more than I have to," Ildiko answered with a salacious grin.

"Did you know her well enough … let me rephrase that … were you aware of her distaste for vampires?" Lardom grilled on.

"I was aware; however, it didn't matter to me because I am not directly involved with the woman. She is—was—no threat to me, personally." Ildiko grinned and licked her lips, thinking how easy the questions were, and hoping they remained so.

Lardom returned her smile, then dropped one of his bombs. "You mentioned you do not get involved with humans any more than you have to; would I be correct in saying you have just recently returned from exile for having attempted to murder Virginia, the woman who bore Count Basarab two children and was set to become his wife?"

Ildiko swallowed hard at the unexpected question. She and Gara hadn't anticipated there would be any references to an incident that had happened twenty years ago. She glanced at her brother. Gara just stared at her, his expression not giving her any hint of how to answer.

"Did you not understand the question, Ildiko?" Lardom probed. "Should I repeat it?"

Ildiko's lips curled cynically. "No need." She glanced back to where Virginia was sitting. "Yes, I, along with Basarab's first wife, Teresa, was instrumental in the attempted murder of said human."

"Why?" Lardom's one-word question was simple.

Ildiko stood from the chair and pointing her finger at Virginia, "Because she had no right to the throne! She'd given my cousin what he wanted—a son. She was a human, not of our royal bloodline, and at the time, definitely not a vampire. There was no need for Basarab to set Teresa aside to take up with Virginia," Ildiko finished.

"That wasn't your decision to make, was it?" Before Ildiko could reply, Lardom asked his next question. "Was the count's first wife also not a human before he married her?"

"I think we all know she was … but what is your point here? What does something that happened so long ago have to do with Katalin's death?"

Lardom smiled, then turned and looked out at the sitting vampires. "I am just trying to establish your basic nature, but I guess we all know what it is, don't we? Volatile. Impetuous. Jealous. Just to name a few of your rudimentary qualities! We all know one of your goals in life is to sit on the throne beside

Basarab, don't we." He swung back to look at Ildiko, his question more of a statement than a question. "Therefore, I will change direction … were you in the city on the night Katalin was murdered?"

Once again, Ildiko glimpsed at Gara. He gave a slight shake of his head. Basarab watched the interaction between the twins closely and wondered what they were up to.

"No, I was not," she finally answered.

"Are you sure? Your plane was at the airport."

"I took a different flight home. As I told the count previously, I couldn't reach my pilot, and I needed to deliver some important papers to my brother."

"You returned when?"

"The next night."

"Alone?"

"No … well, yes. Gara followed me on a separate flight, and we met back at my hotel room, which I hadn't given up, knowing I'd be returning."

"Why were you here in the first place?" Lardom asked, despite knowing the answer.

"Gara sent me to attend to some of his affairs. He hadn't been able to make the trip himself initially."

"So why did he have to come now?"

There was the sound of a chair crashing to the floor and an ordinarily calm Gara shouted: "It is no one's business here what my affairs are! They have nothing to do with the death of this woman—a death you are trying to pin on my sister, who wasn't even here at the time the crime was committed!" Gara glared around the room, then directed his gaze to Basarab, hate toward his leader in his eyes. "Have you not punished my sister enough? Was the twenty years of her exile from the family not sufficient for her? You call yourself a leader?" Gara looked at the vampires sitting in judgement. "This man you have all bowed to for centuries, because a curse said he should be our leader, is spineless. He cannot control his own family, something that has been made evident on more than one occasion as he tries to clean up mess after mess—notably, the ones caused by his beloved daughter, Samara!

"Shall we go back to a time when there was relative peace … when Basarab was married to Teresa? We all loved her, even though she was originally human. Basarab honoured his deal with Max, his servant. And, let us not forget, Teresa, unlike Virginia, came to the count of her own free will! Virginia constantly sought escape, despite having the count's child growing within her womb. And, when she did escape, did she leave the count his son? No! She took Santan with her, and she shacked up with this man!" Gara turned and pointed at Randy.

"Of course, the two of them tell us their relationship was platonic, yet anyone observing their interactions can tell they are in love! If it wasn't for the fact Samara is so much like her Uncle Dracula in personality and her features resemble her father so clearly, I would have a difficult time believing she is Basarab's child!

"Virginia has always been out to protect herself—not us. She is the selfish one … the one who has manipulated events to her own gain!

"Speaking of Samara … she is nothing but a spoiled brat who does whatever she wants to get her own way—especially with 'daddy!' And as for the count's son, Santan—he is as spineless as his father, going after human women, not even looking to his own kind!" All the pent-up fury and frustration Gara had been feeling lately spewed from his mouth.

Basarab's voice rang out loud and clear, and furious: "Enough!" The sound of that one word echoed off the stone walls. "How dare you! How dare you attack my family and me! You have always held a place of honour in my household, despite what your sister attempted to do. Her crime was enough for me to have exiled your entire family, yet I did not!" Basarab fought back, justifying his decision regarding Ildiko. "Maybe I should have left her in exile, for she sits here, in this room, in front of her peers, and she lies through her teeth!" Basarab glowered at Gara. "Are you helping her to tell untruths here, cousin? Because, if you are, you will join her in whatever punishment she receives!"

Instead of answering the count, Gara turned and left the room, leaving Ildiko alone on the stand in a room where all eyes turned to her.

Attila stood and took control of the situation. "I believe we need to take a break. I suggest we meet back here in an hour's time."

Heads bobbed in confirmation, and the vampires hurriedly filed out of the room. Basarab noticed the look on many of their faces and, for the umpteenth time, he felt despair at what was taking place under his roof.

Chapter Twenty-seven

When the vampires returned to the courtroom, Lardom recalled Ildiko to the stand. There was a dull silence as everyone waited for her to take the chair at the front of the room again. Once seated, she looked over the heads of everyone, haughtily ignoring the stares.

Lardom slowly approached her. "Now, where did we leave off? Oh, yes … your reason for being here. If you want the truth, Ildiko, you are sitting on the witness stand because I believe you know a lot more about the death of Katalin than you are letting on—I believe you might have been part of her death. What say you to that?" Lardom looked her straight in the face, his own expression grim.

The lawyer's question startled a good number of vampires in the room, and they waited anxiously for Ildiko's answer. When it didn't come immediately, Lardom spoke again: "I suggest you be cautious with your answer when you are ready; I have a witness who will confirm you were still in the city the night Katalin was murdered—that indeed, you had not left!" Lardom looked from Ildiko to the jurors and back again. "What say you now?"

Ildiko was aware someone had been at the airport but she also discerned that was all they knew. They would not know if she had taken another flight from a different airport. At least, she hoped not. *I need to stick to the script Gara set out … where the hell is my brother anyway … why did he abandon me now?*

Finally taking the plunge to answer, "I fear your witness is not well enough informed to make such a statement against me. As I already told this court and the count on an earlier occasion, I was forced to take a red-eye flight…"

"Can you produce a copy of your plane ticket purchase?" Lardom cut Ildiko off in mid-sentence.

Ildiko answered without hesitation: "No, I didn't think it would be necessary."

Dracula was watching the proceedings with great interest, as was Angelique, both parties knowing Ildiko had been on the property, either on the night in question or very close to it.

"I see … well," Lardom smiled coldly. "You may step down, for now, Ildiko, but I will definitely be calling upon you again, and possibly, after you hear some of the other testimonies, you may change your mind and tell this court the truth!"

It was all Ildiko could do to restrain her anger as she made her way back to her chair and sat down. She glanced furiously at the empty seat beside her where Gara should be sitting, supporting his twin. *Damn you, brother … you have only made things worse for me by bringing up all the old shit that happened! And then, like the coward you are, you leave me to pick up the pieces. Well, it isn't the first time I've been left alone to deal with problems … twenty years of exile from the family provided me with quite an education!* Ildiko looked to where Samara and Lajos were sitting. *And you two have not heard the last of me yet! Lajos, I will have something special for you, and as for you, temptress, you will never see the throne as long as there is breath in my body!*

How do I tell this court what I heard that night, while Katalin was still alive? How the woman had told her husband that she would rather drive a stake through her daughter's heart than see her live as a vampire! That her daughter was already dead, and she told her husband she would find a way out of the house, and when she returned it would be with the police! To say all that, I'd be exposing that I was here the night of the murder!

Ildiko was so lost in her thoughts, she didn't realize Attila was sitting on the witness stand and was talking about his visit to the Brantford Airport.

"As I left, after confirming Ildiko's plane had not departed the airport since her arrival," Attila was saying, "I walked past one of our planes and noticed all the private pilots inside playing cards." He paused and looked directly at Ildiko. "Including Ildiko's pilot," Attila emphasized.

"Would it be safe to say, Attila, from your vast years of experience, that any pilot hired by our family is loyal and discrete to the point they would never leave their post?" Lardom questioned. "To always be ready to spring into action at a moment's notice?" he added.

"To my knowledge, and with my vast experience, no pilot hired by our family would abandon their post. They remain on the planes, on call twenty-four hours a day. Everything is supplied to them, so there is no need for them to stray away from their station."

"So, in your opinion, Ildiko's pilot should have been under the same rule of thumb?"

"No reason why he should not be."

Lardom looked explicitly at the jury as he asked his next question. "Is there anything else you might have *unearthed?*" Lardom paused for a moment of effect, "That you would like to tell this court?"

Attila cleared his throat. "After Ildiko told us her pilot was not available to her, I checked with the other pilots. They told me Ildiko had called her pilot away and he did not return."

"Away to her plane?"

"No, just away. Her plane did not leave the airport, and her pilot never returned either." Attila looked at Ildiko as he continued. "I decided to search for the pilot and found him on the riverbank, drained of blood. It appeared that someone had made a half-assed attempt to bury him, but the debris covering him could have washed up with the river water. He was just on the edge of the shore. Of course, I had to ensure the body would not be found by someone who would call in the police, especially because of the fiasco we still have to deal with, so I transported it to Ildiko's plane. There it still lies."

If a vampire's skin could become any paler, Ildiko's did! She'd thought that putting her pilot's body in the Grand River, he would be swept away by the current, far from the scene of the crime! All eyes in the room turned toward Ildiko, each one blazing indignantly. Kardos, who had been chosen as the jury spokesperson, stood.

"In light of this new evidence, I believe it is time we heard the truth from Ildiko. I also would like to have Gara present when she takes the stand, so if someone would be willing to go and seek him out and return him here, we will wait upon him. Gara needs to hear a truthful word from his sister's mouth, so he is able to make an educated decision on his next move—whether that be to stand by his sister, or to support us in the discovery of truth." Kardos looked to Attila to make the next move.

There was no need for further words; the elder count left the room to go in search of Gara.

Attila laid a hand on Gara's shoulder and sat beside him on the bench at the top of the stone stairs leading up to the front door of the house. Gara turned slightly, looking at the count, tears in his eyes.

"I know how problematic this must be for you, Gara," Attila stated matter-of-factly. "She is your sister—your twin— which makes it tougher on you. Nevertheless, you must face the truth. If you are unaware of all she has done, she is lying to you as she is lying to all of us!"

When Gara didn't comment, Attila continued: "I found the evidence myself that your sister is lying about, at the least, that she couldn't locate the pilot, and to save you the trouble here of trying to cover for her yet again, I will tell you what I found: her pilot, savagely murdered … drained of blood … washed up on the riverbank." Attila noticed the slump in Gara's shoulders.

"Ildiko is lying to you. She murdered her pilot, and there is only one apparent reason, to me, she would have done this—to cover up something else she is part of." Attila closed his eyes and leaned back on the bench. "You have been like a son to me over the years, living under my roof for much of that time. Your relationship with my son, Basarab, has been more of brothers than cousins, and you two have worked together to make our lives as vampires better. You know what your sister is capable of, yet you attacked those whom you have always loved and who have loved you back—the family that does not ask you to compromise your ethics, as Ildiko appears to be doing."

There was pain in his voice when Gara finally spoke: "She's my sister … you have no idea what she's been through … all those years of exile…"

Attila thought it wise to intervene before Gara said too much more. "Let me tell you what your sister was doing during her exile, Gara. Not what you think. Not mourning the loss of family ties, although I am sure she made you feel she was. Ildiko was enjoying her life, whoring her way around the world. You must remember, we have people everywhere—people who report directly to us.

"Your sister began a more serious relationship with Lajos, and then decided to use him … don't look so puzzled … yes, I know all about her plans to take the throne from my son since he never offered it to her directly by taking her as his bride. She thought she could set Lajos up with Samara and position both of them on the throne, with her manipulating everything from behind the scenes!"

Gara looked surprised.

"Don't think for a minute I do not have my son's best interests in mind. I know more than anyone could believe possible. You must remember, as well, who I am married to. Angelique has ways of discovering truths beyond even the power of vampires. We are lucky she is a white witch and not one with evil on her mind, as was the case with her sister, Tanyasin. And, as you well know, she has always had the best interests of the vampires in mind. If it were not for Angelique, the curse on our family would have been much worse!

"Now, I suggest you return to the court proceedings and hear for yourself what your sister has been up to…" Attila paused a moment, noticing the harried look on Gara's face. "You already know more than you want to, don't you?" Attila wondered just how much Gara did know, and how much Ildiko's brother was willing to tell.

Gara looked away, out to the trees encompassing the property. He was battling within himself between what he knew was the right thing to do and his love for his twin. It was a battle he'd been forced to fight all his life, and he was tired of it. Resigned, Gara turned to Attila, "I will return to the court, but I will say nothing against my sister. If she wishes to divulge to you that she has any part in this sordid affair, let the truth come from her mouth, not mine. I will stand by whatever the court might decide is fair in their judgement of her."

Chapter Twenty-eight

Frankie, despite being the rookie in the partnership, was still baffled as to what Nathaniel was trying to prove with the interviews at the big house. "Shouldn't we be concentrating on interviewing all the residents in that area?" He opened with as they parked under a large shade tree in Mohawk Park. They'd picked up a sandwich from the local donut shop and decided to find a private place to talk.

"I guess we could interview some of them," Nathaniel mumbled, his mouth full of food. He swallowed. "But what I'll be asking about is what they might have noticed going on at Yates Castle," he added.

"You really have a bee in your hat over this guy, don't you?" Frankie took a sip of his drink.

"He's hiding something … I feel it … and that woman we met in the parking lot … she's hiding something, too. I'm anxious to see how many of the people in the house we actually get to interview tomorrow night."

Frankie shuddered as he thought of the owner of the house. He wondered if it would be cowardly if he called in sick tomorrow night and just let Nathaniel do the interviews with the captain.

"What's wrong?" Nathaniel asked, noticing his partner's uncomfortable shift in the car seat.

"Nothing," Frankie lied as he rolled up his sandwich wrapper and got out of the car, heading to the nearest garbage can.

Judge Harris asked his secretary to call Markus and Samuel to set up a late-evening get-together. He wanted to know how Samuel's brief meeting went with Count Basarab.

"Where would you like to meet?" the secretary questioned.

"My place … no, wait … call the Olde School Restaurant … they have a nice piano bar there … we can talk and relax."

"Eight o'clock good?"

"Perfect." Before the judge left the office, he turned and added, "Tell Gus I would like one of the private alcoves on the upper level, please."

The secretary nodded and picked up the phone. The Olde School Restaurant was on her speed dial.

Gus, the owner of the restaurant, met the trio at the door. "Good evening, gentlemen," he greeted. "This way," he smiled, leading the way to the mezzanine and seating them at the table closest to the private back room.

Placing the menus on the table, Gus spread the napkins on their knees. "The usual drinks, gentlemen?" he inquired. The judge nodded, knowing he and his friends never varied their first drinks.

As Gus walked away, Samuel picked up his menu. "Let's decide what we want before the drinks come," he suggested.

"Good idea," Markus returned.

The restaurant was unusually quiet, the only sound being the odd, hushed conversation, and soft melodies floating up from the piano bar. After a few minutes, they each set their menus down and waited for their drinks.

Drinks served, orders taken, the three friends got down to business. Judge Harris opened the conversation. "You didn't say much, Samuel, in your email about how the count received you."

"To be truthful, he was short and to the point, couldn't wait to see me gone. Didn't even let me step inside," Samuel replied.

"Well, it isn't as if we ever did get to see the inside of Yates Castle when the count was here twenty years ago," Markus stated. "I remember the time we were looking for a place to hold a special reception to honour the new mayor, and I approached Count Basarab to see if he'd be willing to host us. The look he gave me sent shivers throughout my body; however, he masked it quickly and said his house was under repair and wouldn't be available to accommodate such an event."

"I remember that incident," Judge Harris remarked. "I found it strange because, driving by the house a few times afterward, I saw no indication of workmen coming and going." The judge leaned forward. "But, we aren't here to discuss the past—at least about the count not opening his house to us. I think we might have a problem with this officer of yours, Markus. I don't understand what his obsession is with Count Musat and his family and guests."

Samuel grimaced. "I don't think this is a man we want to piss off. There is something archaic about his mannerisms, and with what *we* know about him, we need to tread carefully."

"I concur," the judge leaned back as the appetizers were delivered to the table. With the waiter well out of earshot, he continued: "I think it is in everyone's best interest, Markus, for you to take the lead tomorrow night."

Samuel nodded his agreement as he popped a shrimp in his mouth.

"Nathaniel is one of those officers who, when they get a hunch about something, won't let go until they get the answers they want. He's got a good record for solving cases with our force, and with the Hamilton force that he worked for before coming to us. I don't know just how much I'll be able to control him." Markus laid his fork down, having finished his bacon-wrapped scallops.

Judge Harris scowled. "You are his superior, Markus—control him. I don't want trouble with Basarab, especially with what we know about him from Samuel's friend." The judge paused long enough for the waiter to clear the appetizer dishes. Then, "Does anyone know what happened to that guy?" he asked.

Markus shook his head no. "Disappeared without a trace."

"My point exactly," the judge specified.

"He could have just left town," Samuel suggested, even though he had a feeling that was far from reality.

"I doubt it." Judge Harris stood. "I must use the facilities; be right back. Think hard about what—who—we are dealing with while I'm gone."

By the time the judge returned, the meals had been served. His prime rib was done to perfection, medium rare, blood oozing into the vegetables. He picked up his knife and cut off his first piece and shoved it into his mouth. "Best prime rib in town," he said, chewing slowly, savouring the flavour.

Markus, who hadn't touched his lamb dinner yet, was thinking about the man who'd conveyed to them the information about Count Basarab. "I can do a search for the guy before meeting with the count tomorrow and see if anything turns up," he suggested.

"Good idea," the judge waved his steak knife in the air.

Samuel, who had been quiet up to this point, spoke up: "Even if you find out our source has passed away, it's not by any means a confirmation the count was involved."

"Unless it was foul play," Markus articulated.

"Whatever happened was twenty years ago, guys," Samuel continued with his line of thought. "I, for one, have no intention of trying to drag something up to incriminate the count in any way. I think we are pissing him off enough at the moment!" He looked over the brim of his glasses as if to say, "leave it alone and let's just deal with the matter at hand."

Judge Harris finished his last bite of prime rib and dabbed the corner of his mouth with the napkin. "You may have a point, Samuel. Maybe we should let sleeping dogs lie. Nevertheless, I still want you to investigate our man, Markus; I want to know what happened to him before you go to this meeting. Knowledge can give us an edge."

Markus polished off his vegetables and finally cut into one of the lamb chops. "What I would like to know, Harris, is what do we do with the knowledge if it points us to the fact that Count Basarab may have done away with whom he would consider a snitch? I agree with Samuel. We need to let that go!" He shoved a piece of lamb into his mouth. "Scrumptious," he commented.

Judge Harris moved his plate aside and picked up his drink. "I never said we would do anything about it; I just want to know." Finishing his beverage, the judge set the glass down. He noticed Gus approaching.

"Can I get you another one?" Gus questioned, noticing the empty glass.

"Sure, why not," the judge replied after a slight hesitation.

"How about you gentlemen … something else to drink?" Gus turned to Markus and Samuel.

"We're good," they said simultaneously.

The men sat quietly, each absorbed in their own thoughts, while Samuel and Markus finished their meals. Gus brought the judge his drink, and he nursed it while his companions ate.

Finally finished, they sat in silence for a few more minutes, enjoying the piano music.

"So, what do you suggest I do tomorrow night?" Markus directed his question to the judge, recollecting his honour's previous statement. "There's no way Nathaniel will be willing to give up the questioning to me; he'll want to take the lead."

"Then I suggest you keep a lid on Nathaniel. When a question is asked and answered, don't let your officer argue with the count. Don't let him make the count think, for one minute, he is not believed, or that any of his family or guests are not believed," Judge Harris replied slowly.

"I'll do my best," Markus said. "Won't be easy, though."

"Make it so." The judge stood, an indication the meeting was over. "Samuel and I will be waiting at my house, so when you are finished, come straight there and give us a full report." There was no asking; it was an order to be adhered to, given by a man who knew way too much about everyone in the city of Brantford!

Gus was standing by the door as the three men left; he shook their hands and wished them a good evening.

Markus couldn't sleep when he got back to his apartment, despite the lateness of the hour. He decided to fire up his computer and get a head start on what happened to their informant. Typing in the man's name in the Google search bar, Markus was surprised at the number of hits that showed up.

Scrolling through the links, Markus weeded out any he thought irrelevant. On the second page, he came across an interesting link—a newspaper article...

A hiker came across the decayed body of a man along the Grand River, east of Brantford, last night. The police have not confirmed yet if there is foul play. Further investigation will be forthcoming.

Markus ventured back to the first page, thinking he'd possibly missed a follow-up news article on the victim. "There … how did I miss that?" He clicked on the link:

The body, which was found along the Grand River, on July 10th, has been identified as Jack Guinness, a former employee of the Brantford Blood Bank…

Markus closed the article, not having to read anymore. Before shutting down his computer, he sent a quick email off to Judge Harris and Samuel, informing them of what he'd discovered.

As Markus crawled into bed, he prayed the judge would just let it go!

Chapter Twenty-nine

Attila ushered Gara into the courtroom, nodding to Lardom to proceed. "I recall Ildiko to the stand," Lardom announced.

Gara chose not to sit near his sister. Ildiko swallowed hard, wondering how much of what her brother knew he had revealed to Attila. However, knowing her brother as she did, she also knew he would not be the one to speak out against her.

"Did you murder your pilot, Ildiko, to cover up the fact that you never left town?" Lardom's first question was released with a vengeance.

This time, Ildiko knew she should not hesitate one second; her life depended on it. Hesitation made one look guilty. "No, I did not!" she scowled. Before Lardom asked another question, "Are there not enough other vampires in this room who were here in the city, who could have committed such a crime, in such a manner?" Ildiko gazed arrogantly around the room, letting her eyes rest briefly on Samara and Dracula.

Dracula grinned at her. *Don't be pointing fingers at me, darling ... I know you drained the body of blood and threw it from the widow's walk ... I just have yet to figure out who struck the first blow! You should admit the truth now before it is too late ... that is the only way I will be able to help you.*

Ildiko moved uncomfortably in her chair as she caught the look in Dracula's eyes. *He knows I was part of the crime, yet he says nothing. Why? Why, uncle?*

"You are aware, since we have the dead body of your pilot in our possession, we will eventually be able to detect who killed him?" Lardom asked.

Ildiko realized she could not continue the façade of total innocence. She looked to her brother but he avoided her eyes, indicating he was not going to assist her in any way. Shrugging her shoulders, she finally admitted some of what she'd done. "Okay, I killed my pilot, and I threw his useless body in the river." She glowered at Lardom.

"Why … what was your purpose for doing this?"

Ildiko was willing to give up something, but not everything. "I was hungry," she stated simply, "but unfortunately, I went too far and killed him."

"So you killed your pilot because you were hungry?"
Ildiko nodded.

"Well, well … isn't this an interesting turn of events now." Lardom's statement was filled with sarcasm. "Why don't you just tell us the entire truth and get this over with?" Lardom turned to the jurors. "Do you want to know what I think? Ildiko committed this crime and is trying desperately to get away with it. I also think her brother knows she did it, but doesn't want to go down with her. And I think there is at least one other person in this room who is aware of her involvement." Lardom looked up at Basarab. "I believe we have heard enough for tonight. I would like to reconvene tomorrow night, and I hope," here Lardom's eyes swept around the room, "everyone here is considering well the evidence that is piling up, and also thinks about the evidence that might still be brought forth based on everything they have heard." With those words, Lardom walked to his table, gathered his papers, and left the room.

Rasputin had sat in a back corner of the room during the proceedings. He'd observed everything with an eagle-eye and had a few ideas of his own. He'd noticed the most recent interactions between Dracula and Ildiko and was positive Dracula knew much more than he was telling. Rasputin had also seen how restless the newest vampire in the family was, how Mia shook every time Lardom was about to call someone to the stand.

He enjoyed watching the little games Samara and Lajos played with each other as they sat side by side, bodies touching as much as they assumed would be allowed in open. Seeing them together, he came to the conclusion that neither one had anything to do with Katalin's death; they were too much into each other. Besides, Lajos had nothing to gain by it … unless he was to have done it for someone else who held something over him—a possibility. But no, he had an alibi; he was with Samara at the time of the crime.

Rasputin focused his attention on Délia a few times, considering her a possibility. After all, she was the one who claimed to have found the body. Or had she returned to the human's room to make sure what she'd started was finished, and then thrown her off the rooftop before going down to fetch Basarab, and feigned total innocence? Possible.

Then, there was the prospect Randy and Virginia committed the crime together! Randy could have struck his wife in anger, then went to Virginia to help him cover up what he'd done, knowing there was no hope Katalin could live. She, seeing Katalin lying fatally wounded, possibly talked Randy into allowing her to finish his wife off, solving two problems for them. One, Katalin would not be able to betray the family to the local authorities, keeping everyone safe, including Randy's beloved daughter; and two, it would leave her and Randy free to pursue a love liaison—behind Basarab's back, of course. Another possible?

Rasputin noticed Santan standing beside Virginia and Mia. Despite that vampires thought the young prince to be weak, Rasputin sensed differently. Santan had everything to lose if Katalin went to the authorities, especially his beloved Mia. It was possible he committed the whole crime. *He's a smart young man.*

Basarab was also smart—too smart to get his hands dirty by doing the deed himself. However, there was a chance he ordered it done by one of his faithful followers. Kardos, maybe. Kardos was here in the house with the family at the time. It was known around the vampire world that Kardos would do anything the count asked of him.

Rasputin had multiple theories running through his mind, all of which he wanted to impart to his mistress, Adrianna. She had contacted him through his dreams, letting him know Radu and Elizabeth were on their way, and what he was to do when they arrived. Rasputin looked around the room as the vampires began to file out the door.

You all have no idea who is coming for you! No idea, at all!

Night made way for the day, and as Nathaniel and Frankie made their way around the neighbouring houses of Yates Castle, the residents behind its walls slept—most of them restless, but for many different reasons.

Chapter Thirty

The families in the first five houses Nathaniel and Frankie approached had seen or heard nothing strange going on around Yates Castle. In fact, one elderly lady said she didn't want to talk about the house. She was close to ninety and knew the castle when it was considered to be haunted.

"That man who bought the place might have fixed it up to its former glory," she'd mumbled, "but doesn't mean it ain't still haunted," she added. "Best to let the ghosts be."

"Weird old bird," Frankie laughed as they headed to the next house.

"That she might be," Nathaniel said. "However, we may have to go back and pay her another visit. I'll bet my bottom dollar she's seen a lot. If not recently, twenty years ago for sure, when the count was here before!"

At the next two places they approached, no one was home. House number three, though, was opened by a young mother with three children—all under the age of five—clinging to her legs. There was a fourth child, a baby, in her arms.

"What can I do for you gentlemen?" she asked, trying to shake a couple of the children off her leg.

The officers flashed their badges and identified themselves. "We'd like to ask you some questions about the big house," Frankie stated, pointing in the direction of Yates Castle. "First, could I have your name for the record?"

"Iona."

"Okay, Iona, how long have you lived in the neighbourhood?" he added, thinking there was no sense asking her too many questions if she'd not been around long enough.

"Moved here … Johnny, let go! … I swear, there are days I could just pull my hair out … don't know why I ever wanted kids in the first place … where was I? Right, you asked when I moved here … five years ago … Johnny!" Iona opened the door wider. "Why don't you come in … give me a minute to turn the television on for this bunch so's maybe we can talk without interruption … well, as few interruptions as possible," Iona said heading out of the room. As she did so, she called back: "There's some coffee in the pot if you want to help yourselves, officers. I know how much cops love their coffee," she laughed lightly. "Cups in the cupboard overhead. Won't be more than a couple minutes," she added.

"How old are the kids?" Nathaniel asked when the young mother returned with only the baby in tow.

"Five, four, two, and six months," she grimaced, but then gave a half-grin. "Don't get me wrong, officers; I love my kids. Just that some days it gets overwhelming." Noticing Nathaniel and Frankie hadn't helped themselves to a drink, "Didn't you want a coffee? I thought you guys lived on the stuff!"

Frankie chuckled. "Well, we get enough at the local coffee shops … I've already had my daily quota, thank you."

Iona blushed.

"As my partner already mentioned, we'd like to ask you some questions about the big house," Nathaniel said, hoping they could get further this time.

"What do you want to know … I don't get out much, and I don't know who even owns the place. It was empty when I first moved here, but I think someone is in it now."

"Do you recall when you first saw someone there?" Nathaniel continued.

"Well, a couple months ago it looked like a family of three arrived and set up house there. I think they have some sort of butler or servant, as well, because I saw a man all dressed in a black suit helping the family carry luggage up the front stairs and into the house. I was walking by the front, on Usher Street, heading home, and one of my kids ran into the big yard. I remember the fellow in the suit scowling at me. I didn't hang around and wait for him to come after me, though. Got my kid and moved on as quickly as I could with my little mob."

The baby started to fuss; Iona reached for a soother that was sitting on the table. "Here you go, love," she said as she bounced and rocked him all at the same time. The officers watched the magic as the baby closed his eyes and was soon sleeping peacefully in his mother's arms. "Best of the bunch so far," she whispered.

Nathaniel wanted more information. Obviously, the man in black the woman had seen was the count's butler, whom they'd met on their last visit. But, who was the family of three? "Can you describe the three people you saw?" he asked.

"Well, let me see … two of them, at least; the man and the teenager. The man was really tall and had curly red hair … the teenager had hair the same colour, but it was long … halfway down her back … I remember wishing I could grow my hair like that … the woman was already all the way up the stairs and kind of behind one of the posts … probably waiting for the butler, or whoever he was, to open the door. Didn't get a good look at her."

"Did you ever see anyone else arrive at the house besides these three?" Nathaniel asked.

"I don't want you to think I'm a nosy neighbour or anything, but sometimes I'm up late at night … even into the wee hours of the morning … kids, you know … none of them sleep through the night yet … I have seen several cars coming and going the odd night, and people getting out and going into the house … but, like I said, none of my business."

"Can you describe any of these people you saw?" Frankie inquired.

Iona thought for a moment, then, "First one I noticed was a really tall man all dressed in black. It looked like he was directing the others who were with him … a woman with red hair … I could see it was red even though it was dark out because there was a light on in the parking lot. And there was a younger woman, possibly their daughter, but I couldn't really tell what she looked like … she stayed out of the light. Then my baby needed feeding, so I had to focus on him."

"Good … good," Nathaniel said as he wrote some notes. "Any other time you notice comings and goings from the house?" he asked. "Take your time."

Iona blushed again, embarrassed that she watched the old house during the night when she was up with the children, but it had, over the past couple months, been something she looked forward to. "Well," she began, "I've seen several people coming and going, but only during the evening or in the early morning hours before sunrise."

"No one during the day?" Nathaniel probed.

She shook her head. "Just that first day when the guy with the red hair arrived with the woman and girl. I've never seen any of the others during the daylight hours."

"So how many different people would you say you've seen and were they male or female?" Nathaniel was writing furiously on his notepad.

"I believe there were more men than women … but I really didn't keep track."

A brawl broke out in the living room, distracting the woman. "I'm afraid I'm going to have to break that up," Iona said, getting up from her chair. "I hope I've been of some help to you. Please just make sure the doors are closed on your way out. Don't want one of the rug-rats getting out and terrorizing the neighbourhood!" With that, she rushed out of the kitchen, and the last thing the two officers heard was her yelling at her kids to settle down and then the wailing of a six-month-old who'd been awakened by all the noise.

Back in the cruiser, Nathaniel tapped his pencil on the notepad. "It'll be interesting to see just how many men and women are at our interview tomorrow."

Frankie stared at his partner and shook his head. "It doesn't mean anything … we already know the count is having some sort of family reunion. Told us himself, didn't he? Anyway, I'm not sure if I'm into the witch—or is it vampire—hunt you're on."

"You don't have to come along, Frankie; the captain will be with me," Nathaniel snarled, having had enough of the rookie's attitude.

Frankie didn't reply. As Nathaniel put the car in drive to return to the station, the rookie stared out the window, still trying to make up his mind if he was going to accompany his partner and captain to the big house with the mysterious man who gave him the creeps.

Chapter Thirty-one

ngelique couldn't sleep, so she quietly left the room, leaving Attila alone in their bed. Making her way to the top floor, to the room where Katalin was before she was murdered, Angelique shuddered at the eerie silence that filled the narrow stairway. Stepping into the room, she looked around. Despite not being used since the incident, Angelique got the sense someone else was in it recently.

Walking around the furniture, she scrutinized the floor, looking for what, she had no idea. Angelique wondered why no one had thought to look closely in the room for clues; she knelt down and lifted the quilt to see under the bed.

"What's this?" she said, reaching for a shiny object and grasping it with her fingers. "A diamond? Katalin didn't have any diamonds that I knew of." Angelique looked closer at the stone in her hand. Her hand rose to her throat, and she gasped. "This is Samara's!"

Angelique noticed a diamond missing from the necklace her granddaughter was wearing about a week ago but thought nothing of it at the time—but now! Standing, Angelique looked around the room again, noticing the blood stain on the carpet.

This is where the first blow was struck ... by the same one who threw her off the widow's walk or someone else? Angelique closed her hand over the diamond. *Samara, would you ... are you*

... capable of doing this? Angelique drew in a deep breath. *I believe you are ... but you did have an alibi ... Petya could be just saying that but for what reason? He hates you for what you did to Ákos, and his sister, Manya... he would never lie to provide you with a way out.*

Angelique made her way to the outer door and stepped out onto the widow's walk. The sun was shining, it was mid-morning, but clouds were trying desperately to gobble up her glory. Leaning against the railing, Angelique closed her eyes and concentrated, conjuring up images of whoever might have stepped foot on the uppermost area of the count's house.

Her first vision was of Virginia—a very pregnant Virginia—pacing the perimeters, stopping every once in a while to gaze out across the top of the trees. Angelique noticed the pain on Virginia's face and saw the tears streaming down her cheeks. The next vision was Samara, but Angelique couldn't put a timeframe on it. As she was about to open her eyes, another figure entered—Ildiko.

Angelique watched as Ildiko approached the door, and put her ear to it. She stayed there for a few minutes, ear to the door, as though listening to something going on, on the other side. Then, she pushed the door open and stepped out of view. Angelique kept her eyes shut, waiting, almost knowing that Ildiko would reappear. Several minutes passed, and finally, Ildiko stepped onto the widow's walk with Katalin's lifeless body in her arms.

Ildiko, her mouth smudged with fresh blood, looked around before progressing to the edge of the roof. She looked up and gave a small howl, then threw the body over the railing. For a brief moment, Ildiko looked down at the yard, then smirked and licked her lips. The vision dissipated.

A fourth vision crossed before her eyes, but it was too foggy for Angelique to be able to see who it was. There were two figures intertwined, appearing to be flailing their arms at a third apparition.

Angelique opened her eyes, a foreboding washing over her. *What are you going to do, Basarab, my friend, for there are those I see clearly, and those I don't. No matter which way we turn, I fear nothing good is going to come from this trial.* Angelique re-entered the room, but instead of heading back to where Attila lay sleeping, she curled up on the bed and closed her eyes.

Sleep still didn't come easy for Angelique. A vivid dream invaded her mind. In her dream, she saw a beautiful woman— young and vivacious—who seemed to be staring directly at her. The woman was crooking her finger and laughing unrestrainedly.

"I'm coming for you," she chortled over and over, "I'm coming for you all, and I'm going to take what is rightfully mine!"

Basarab lay with his arms around Virginia. He'd left Kardos in charge of watching Mia, feeling the worst of her transformation was over. The count needed his wife. He needed to make love to her, to hold her, to drink from her strength. He closed his eyes, envisioning their most recent moments together.

There had been no waiting for either of them; Virginia was as ripe as he was, but what came afterward was slow and deliberate. Basarab traced his fingers down one side of Virginia's body and up the other, hesitating teasingly at essential points on the journey. He relished in the way she moaned and arched her body, attempting to suck his fingers into her tempestuous depths. He would linger only a moment before moving on, knowing he was driving her crazy. Virginia bit her lip and felt the waves wash over her. She reached for his cock, attempting to direct it to its heaven, but Basarab moved it quickly away, despite his own massive desire, and continued on his journey.

Reaching her breasts, Basarab teased one with his fingertips, the other with his tongue. She began to curse him and thrash under his weight as more swells rocked her body. Virginia grasped hold of her husband's hair, yanking his head down to her mouth, twisting it to the side, then dug her teeth into his neck, drawing blood. He returned the favour.

Finally, when he could take no more, he raised himself up on his hands and spread her legs with his knee. Driving into her juices, the count and his beloved released their storms on each other.

For the first time, in a long while, Basarab closed his eyes and slept.

Ildiko turned furiously on her brother when they reached the doorway of her room. "What the hell are you doing, Gara? Why are you abandoning me like this?" She grabbed hold of his arm, thinking he was no match for her superior physical strength.

She'd thought wrong. Gara wrested his arm from her grip and glared at her indignantly. "You only told me half-truths, sister, and if it becomes known I know what you did, I will be as dead as you are going to be. I've decided I don't want to be. My suggestion is to go to Basarab, in private, and confess your part in the murder if that is truly what happened. Let him then concentrate on uncovering who drew first blood." Gara stepped back from Ildiko. "You are on your own, sister. Take this advice I have given you."

Ildiko watched her brother—her only genuine friend—walk away from her.

Samara and Lajos were returning to her room when they heard Ildiko and Gara talking. Quickly, they slid into an alcove and listened, each with a smile on their lips. Samara stood on her tiptoes and whispered in Lajos' ear: "She has no one now."

Lajos grinned but said nothing. He honestly didn't care. There was only one thing on his mind at the moment, and that was to fuck the temptress until she howled for mercy!

Santan paced around his room. Something was bothering him, but he couldn't quite put his finger on the problem. Mia's turning had unsettled his feelings for her. Not so much her turning, but her behaviour now that she'd joined his world. He was unsure if he even wanted her anymore. Santan knew his father had told everyone to not leave the house, but he needed a friend to talk to, and no one would even know he was gone. Closing his eyes, Santan transported to Carla's house in the country, hoping she would be there.

Carla was getting ready to leave the house when Santan appeared in her kitchen. She gasped in fright. "Satan! You scared the shit out of me! What are you doing here?"

"I need to talk to someone, Carla … someone I can trust … someone who is not a vampire." Santan's eyes pleaded with her to give him a moment.

With a resigned look, Carla threw her keys and purse on the kitchen table. "I need to call my office and tell them I will be late. Why don't you go into the living room and make yourself comfortable; I'll be right with you."

From the living room, Santan heard Carla talking to her secretary. A few moments later, she joined him and sat on the loveseat across from where he sat.

"What's on your mind, Santan?" Carla asked, curling her feet under her, and grabbing hold of a pillow to hug to her chest.

"You remember when I brought Mia here, the night her mother was killed?"

Carla nodded.

"I brought her here after her mother was killed, but she didn't know it was her mother we saw in the yard. She and I were out for a walk when we saw my father, Dracula, and Délia by the body. I discovered later, when my father told me, Katalin was the victim. My father told me Dracula had suggested that both Randy and Mia may well become a problem now, which might necessitate their elimination. It was for that reason I brought her here, to protect her.

"But something about her reaction, or should I say, lack of reaction, to her mother's death bothers me, Carla. Mia is showing no emotions. In fact, she's out of control. There are moments lately, when I watch her, I wonder if she is the one who killed her mother!"

Carla looked up in shock. "No way, Santan. Mia wouldn't kill her own mother. She might have been pissed off about everything that was going on, but she's barely more than a child … no … no … I don't believe it."

Santan shook his head in frustration. "I agree, but Carla, she's a vampire now. My sister took care of that. So Mia wouldn't be thinking like a human teenager, pissed off with her parents. Most human teens would say they wanted to kill their parents, but how many of them would actually do it!"

"Don't even go there, Santan. There's no way Mia killed her mother, any more than Randy could have killed Katalin. Neither of them was pleased with her threats to expose your family … I get that … but neither of them would kill her for that. Randy could explain to his daughter that Basarab would ensure Katalin didn't go to the police."

After a moment's silence, Santan looked at Carla, his eyes filled with worry. "Do you think my father killed her?" he asked, his voice barely audible. "You said Randy would explain to Mia that Basarab would look after things."

"Oh, Santan, I didn't mean the count would commit murder. You know, as well as anyone, your father has his way of dealing with matters. He wouldn't have to murder a mere human to get his point across to them!"

Santan shrugged his shoulders, thinking that Carla had no idea what his father was capable of. Even he didn't. "I guess you're right; but, I still can't shake the feeling Mia has something to do with this. I really hope I'm wrong."

Carla stood and walked over to Santan. She laid a hand on his shoulder. "Go home, Santan. Go to Mia and comfort her. Maybe she wants you to. She crossed over for you, and yet I'm getting the feeling you're ignoring her. Of course her behaviour is out of the ordinary, she's transforming, and she's learning how to deal with her new life. Give her time." Carla looked at her watch. "I'm sorry, Santan, but I really need to get to work."

Carla left the room, and the house, knowing Santan would return to his father's house when he was ready. She didn't mind her place being his haven—for now.

Santan, alone in the room, buried his face in his hands and wept. His biggest regret, still, was making the final crossing into his father's world. If he hadn't, he could have run away with Mia and she would never have thought it necessary to enter the darkness of the realm in which he lived.

Chapter Thirty-two

After rising from their sleep, the vampires, except the ones who would be interviewed by the police, were instructed to go down to the courtroom. Viktor had set out their evening refreshments. Basarab assured them the interview would not take long.

Before going their separate ways, Angelique motioned to Samara. "A word, please."

Samara looked puzzled but obliged. "What's up?"

Angelique guided Samara to a spot where they could have a private conversation, then pulled the diamond out of her pocket and showed it to her granddaughter. "Is this yours?"

"Where did you find it? I thought it was lost forever!" Samara exclaimed and reached out for the gem.

Angelique's fingers closed over the diamond. "Not so fast. I found it under the bed in Katalin's room. Any idea how it might have gotten there?"

Samara blushed and looked at the floor. "Must have been the night Lajos and I were looking for a secluded place to…"

Angelique shoved the diamond into Samara's hand before she could finish her statement. "Take better care of your things," she said, then walked away. *Thank goodness … it wasn't her!* Angelique walked to the room selected to meet with the police officers.

The select group sat quietly, none wanting to open a conversation. Each was thinking their own thoughts about the predicament Samara had put them in, but each would stick to the script Basarab had set out for them.

When the knock came on the door. Basarab thought the guests were early. *The sooner, the better to get things over with, I guess.* He stood and headed to the front foyer. However, when he opened the door, he was confounded by who was standing on his porch.

Radu and Elizabeth!

"Surprised to see us, nephew?" Radu smiled charmingly.

"Surprised is not how I would describe my feelings right now. Although, I have wondered over the years what happened to you, and thought maybe, sooner or later, you might show up! But her…" Basarab pointed at Elizabeth. "She should be dead!"

"Might we step in, nephew? I'll explain everything." Radu made a move closer to the door.

Basarab heard the crunch of car tires in his back parking lot and swallowed hard. Talk about timing! "Yes, do step in, uncle; however, your story will have to wait. I am expecting guests, and I hear they have arrived."

The count shuffled his unexpected guests through the door and headed to the study. Motioning to his father to come out, Basarab looked again at Radu and Elizabeth, still finding it difficult to believe what he was seeing.

"No time for explanations, father," Basarab said when Attila stepped into the hallway. "Take these two to one of the rooms in the basement, and ask a couple of our friends to stand guard until we are finished up here." Basarab cocked his head at the door. "Our other guests are here, as well."

Attila, hiding his shock as well as he could, nodded: "Follow me," he ordered.

Radu and Elizabeth both smiled sweetly and did as they were bid.

Basarab watched them walk away, not only thinking what lousy timing this was, but wondering why they were here, and how was it that Elizabeth Bathory still lived! Despite being anxious to discover the meaning of their appearance, he had other matters to attend to, and it was knocking on his door. Making sure his father and the uninvited guests were out of eyeshot, Basarab took a deep breath to calm his nerves, and answered the door.

"Welcome, gentlemen," Basarab greeted, motioning the three officers into the vestibule. He nodded recognition only to Captain Markus, despite having met both Nathaniel and Frankie, and directed the trio to follow him.

Entering the count's study, Nathaniel looked at the small group awaiting the police arrival. "Is this everyone?" he asked, turning to the count.

Basarab smiled coldly. "My father has been delayed a few minutes; he will be along shortly."

Viktor appeared in the doorway. "Might I bring your guests something to drink, Count?"

"Coffee for me," the captain said.

"Same here," Nathaniel and Frankie replied simultaneously.

Viktor nodded and headed to the kitchen, returning ten minutes later with a tray of coffees, cream and sugar on the side. Attila arrived at the same time and took his seat beside Angelique.

"Anything else, count?" Viktor asked, setting the tray on a side table.

"I believe that is everything," Basarab replied. "Thank you, Viktor."

"You not joining us?" Nathaniel asked, noticing only three cups on the tray.

"We just finished our evening meal," Basarab informed.

The count waited until the three officers fixed their coffee and returned to their seats before making further introductions. "Allow me to introduce my family," he started, "of course, you must realize this is my father, Attila, and the lovely lady sitting at his side is his wife, Angelique. My friend, Kardos, and my wife, Virginia, whom I believe you met the other night, and my son, Santan." Basarab sat beside Virginia. "So, what do you want to know?"

Frankie squirmed in his seat, wishing he hadn't bothered with a cup of coffee. He still had no idea why he hadn't just called and said he was sick.

Basarab was scrutinizing Markus, thinking the captain would be the one to ask the questions; however, it was the pesky cop who began.

"There was a crime committed behind the café beyond the railway tracks just over a week ago, and I know you are not staying here long and just dropped in to see to your property, but I think you, or one of your family members here, might have seen something that could help us find the perpetrator." Nathaniel leaned forward in his chair and stared at the count. *You might frighten my partner, buddy, but I'm an old-school cop and I've seen a lot of crap in my life and dealt with a lot worse than you!*

Basarab's smile was broad, having read Nathaniel's thoughts. Most humans were easy to read, unlike vampires who could put up a defensive wall. *You've never dealt with anyone worse than me!* Looking around the room at his family, Basarab asked: "Do any of you know anything about this crime?" He needed to end this interrogation quickly and deal with the more urgent matters at hand. Basarab tapped his fingers anxiously, something Nathaniel took note of.

Each vampire in the room, and Angelique, shook their heads.

Nathaniel was not about to give up so quickly. He looked from one individual to the next and swallowed hard, noticing all their eyes, except Angelique's, were similar in colour, all having a red ring around the pupils. "Our sources informed me that they noticed numerous people leaving your property and crossing over the tracks in the direction of the crime scene," Nathaniel stated. "Would that have been any one of you?"

"We did have a couple guests visit us one evening," Attila took the opportunity to answer. "I believe they went downtown, as young people will do." Attila leaned back in his chair and reached for Angelique's hand. "But they only stayed here one night; left the next day for home."

"Where's home?" Nathaniel queried.

"Brasov," Attila replied with a soft smile.

Nathaniel decided it was time to play one of his trump cards. "Is there anyone else staying here? One of the neighbours noticed a family of three arrive at the house a couple months ago … a tall man with curly red hair, and a young girl with long red hair. Our witness wasn't sure about the woman … said she sort of stayed in the shadow of the porch."

"Oh, that would be our friends," Virginia spoke up quickly. Basarab hadn't accounted for the fact that anyone would have noticed Randy's arrival. "But they left before we arrived," she added. "They only needed temporary lodging until they found a place of their own."

"There was a girl with you the other night," Nathaniel pointed out. "I don't see her here," he added.

"She has left already," Virginia replied quickly. "Homesick," she articulated, feigning a worried look.

"What's your friend's name?" Nathaniel's eyes narrowed in on Virginia, his pen hovering over his notepad.

Basarab stood and walked around to the back of the chairs where the officers were sitting. *Would this cop not give up!* "I don't think our friend's name is of any importance to you. They were long gone before we arrived, which also means they were not here when your crime was committed."

With the count standing behind him, a shudder shivered up Frankie's spine. He couldn't wait to get out of the house. *Why the fuck did I come?*

Nathaniel was thinking Basarab's son was being awfully quiet and decided to direct his next question to Santan. "Were you one of the young people who went downtown?"

"Not my thing," Santan stared hard at Nathaniel. "I prefer to stay in at night with my books and my computer," he explained further.

"It must have been nice, though, having kids your own age around," Nathaniel stated more than asked.

Frankie noticed a smile curl on Santan's lips and wondered what was so funny. If only he'd known that the 'kids' Attila had referred to were actually hundreds of years old!

"I prefer adult company," Santan stated.

"Santan has never been inclined to associate with those of his own age," Kardos confirmed protectively.

Angelique was eyeing Nathaniel closely, wondering what he was really up to by asking all these questions of them. She decided to go off-script for a moment, and confuse the police officer. "You know … Nathaniel, isn't it…? I was downtown a couple of days ago, having coffee, and I overheard some teenagers at the next table talking about an old man who was supposed to have been found dead behind the … um … yes, Station Coffee House, they called it." She smiled sweetly.

Nathaniel wondered where she was going with this.

"Well, what they were saying was that some old guy had been killed there, but that one of their friends had been up to the hospital for something … can't remember what it was … and he told them a story about some old tramp who'd been brought into the morgue and had miraculously come alive and actually walked out of the hospital on his own two feet." Angelique then turned to Captain Markus and directed her question to him. "Would that be the victim your officer is talking about, captain?"

Nathaniel was furious by this turn of events! And he was furious the woman had aimed her question to his captain, who, up to this point had said nothing.

Markus was startled out of his daydreaming mode. "I'm sorry," he said, "What did you ask me?"

Frankie noticed the scowl on Nathaniel's face and decided to fill the captain in on what he missed. "The lady is saying she heard some kids talking about an old man who was thought to be dead but who'd walked out of the hospital, and she wanted to know if he was the victim we're talking about."

Markus leaned forward in his chair, and instead of answering Angelique, he directed a question to Nathaniel. "Is it?" he simply asked, even though he knew the answer.

Nathaniel blushed, knowing he had nowhere to go but to the truth. He hadn't expected such an ambush; the news of Vincent's revival had not been made public, there'd only been a small, undetailed article about his death. He wasn't important enough.

"Well?" Markus pushed for the answer he knew had to be forthcoming, and also the answer that would get them out of the house and away from the count.

"Yes." Nathaniel glared at his captain, then at Angelique. She smiled at him.

Basarab feigned annoyance. "Well, gentlemen, it appears this crime you have come to ask us about is not a crime at all. I am baffled as to why you would waste my valuable time!" He strode to the door and opened it. "If you don't mind, I am a busy man."

"Satisfied?" Frankie asked Nathaniel as they drove back to the station. "Who would have thought such a secret would be busted by a bunch of teenagers, and someone from the house just happened to be in the right place at the right time to hear the story!"

"Yeah … who would have thought?" Nathaniel drummed his fingers on the steering wheel. "Somehow, I don't believe that is how she knows."

"I hope you aren't suggesting we return to the house?" Frankie said. "Haven't we embarrassed ourselves enough? There's nothing there for us to investigate."

"If we do return, it won't be when they expect us," Nathaniel's face was grim. He squinted at Frankie. "And I don't believe for one minute the count is leaving tonight, and I don't believe the little group he arranged for us are the only people—or whatever they are—in that house. The only way to prove it is to pay him another visit … maybe during the day, when they are sleeping late."

Frankie looked puzzled. "Sleeping late?"

"You'll see what I mean. Just follow my lead, rookie, and learn from an old cop!"

As much as Nathaniel didn't believe in actual vampires, he hadn't yet closed the door on the possibility he could be wrong, especially after meeting the Count Basarab and his family.

Basarab sent the family ahead of him to the courtroom. He walked to a window that gave him a view of the back parking lot and watched the police officers leave. He didn't like Nathaniel; he didn't trust that the man wouldn't be back. What the count didn't understand was why he insisted on this harassment.

As the cars left, Basarab turned and headed to the basement to deal with yet another issue besides the court proceedings.

"Why are you here, Radu? Why now? And, Elizabeth … how is it you are still alive?" the count asked himself on the way down the stairs.

Chapter Thirty-three

Adrianna watched with great interest as Basarab made his way to the lower level of his house. She watched as he strode with purpose to the room where he'd sent Radu and Elizabeth.

The two vampires standing outside the door where Radu and Elizabeth were waiting stepped aside when the count approached. When he entered the room, Radu stood and bowed his head, a sign of subservience.

Basarab drove directly to his point: "What brings you here, Radu, and why is that woman with you?" The count's words were severely delivered.

Elizabeth stood, ready to retort; however, Radu held his hand up to her, cautioning her to remain where she was. He would handle things.

"I miss my family … simple as that," Radu replied. "As for Elizabeth being with me, she is my wife now, and she will not cause harm to you or any member of your family." Radu glanced to where Elizabeth was sitting. "You learned your lesson, didn't you, my love … as did I."

Elizabeth nodded, but Basarab didn't consider her genuine.

"I would like to see my brother, and then I will explain everything to you both," Radu smiled broadly, an attempt at sincerity.

Basarab's brow furrowed into a deep frown as he tried to think of a way to handle the situation he found himself in. The arrival of an uncle, who had once tried to usurp his throne, and a woman who would have killed the mother of his children, did not sit well. "I am afraid you will have to wait to see your brother, Radu. In fact, I must keep you locked in this room until I figure out what to do with you. Forgive me if I don't quite trust your reason for being here." Basarab headed to the door; he paused and looked back: "I'll have Viktor bring you some refreshments. Make yourself comfortable until I return."

After Basarab left, Radu took a seat beside Elizabeth. He reached for her hand, but she snatched it out of the way. "Don't touch me! I don't enjoy being belittled," she hissed.

"You know why we are here, my dear, and you would be well to remember it," Radu warned. "We will bide our time, and we will be humble and civil, as Adrianna instructed us to be. She will be here soon enough, then we will be able to overthrow this regime and put the true heir to the throne in place."

Elizabeth looked away, shrugging her shoulders in disgust. Adrianna, who was still watching from afar, was not pleased with the woman's behaviour. Why wasn't her spell having total control over Elizabeth, as it should? She would deal with that issue later; for now, she would get a message to Rasputin to deal with the wayward vampire.

I hope you are not going to be a problem, Elizabeth, my dear ... if so, I will end the life I so graciously gave back to you!

There was a distinct restlessness in the courtroom when Basarab entered. He felt life spiralling away from his authority, something he was not used to. He'd always been able to deal swiftly with situations in the past. However, since the final crossing over of his son and daughter, everything seemed out of control ... Santan leaving ... the attempted murder of Ákos ... Samara dallying with Lajos while betrothed to Ákos ... Samara turning Mia ... Samara killing the old man ... someone murdering Randy's wife, Katalin, and still no clear picture of who committed the crime ... the cops harassing him for a crime Samara committed, but became a non-crime thanks to Angelique's magic, so why ... and now, old enemies showing up at his door, Radu and Elizabeth ... where was it going to end? What was going to happen next to upheave the vampire's tenuous hold on his world?

Basarab motioned to Dracula to meet with him outside the courtroom. Stepping into the hallway, Dracula closed the door, and noticing the worried look on his nephew's face, "What's wrong, Basarab? Do we still have a problem with these police officers? Would you like me to deal with them?" The grin flashed his lengthened incisors.

"The police have been handled; I don't anticipate their return," Basarab replied dryly. "However, we've received another visitor ... your brother, Radu!"

"Radu!" Dracula spit out the name of his brother with distaste. "Why is he here now?" *I thought, when I spared your life that day, I told you I never wanted to see your face again!*

"Claims he wants to reconnect with family, but there is more. Elizabeth Bathory is with him ... claims she is his wife."

Dracula had no love for anyone in particular, least of all his brother. Radu had always been jealous of Dracula, and angry with what he'd had to endure in the Turkish court at the hands of an overzealous Turkish prince, who used him as a sexual outlet and allowed his friends to do the same. Radu felt his older brother should have protected him. *Little did you know, brother, what I was enduring while you were being fucked in the lap of luxury! How many times I thought your exile was better than mine!*

Dracula didn't look fazed by the news, and Basarab thought this strange. However, his uncle was not a man to mince words or become emotional, and at the best of times, Dracula handled situations with swift delivery. "Shall I deal with my brother and his woman for you, nephew, and send them on their way?" Dracula's lips curled viciously.

Basarab shook his head. "Not now. I only wanted to let you know so you can prepare yourself for when we take a break from the trial. I have them securely locked in a room not far from here."

"Well then, I shall be thinking of what greeting I will give my brother, and wondering what it is he has to say to me after all this time," Dracula articulated. He motioned to the door: "Shall we proceed with the court?"

Uncle and nephew entered the courtroom, each moving to their places. Basarab nodded to Lardom to begin. The lawyer hesitated a moment, keeping everyone waiting for his next move. He was thinking of the brief meeting he'd had with Angelique before coming to the courtroom, and was still contemplating exactly how to approach the situation. Should he put Angelique on the stand and let her relay her dream, or should he call Ildiko back to the stand and let her fall into his trap?

He chose the latter. "I recall Ildiko."

After Ildiko settled into her chair, Lardom sauntered across the floor toward her. "Comfortable?" he asked.

Ildiko looked at him, puzzled at the question. "As anyone can be under the circumstances," she finally replied.

"Circumstances," Lardom repeated. "Are circumstances you find yourself in now making you uneasy?"

"Truthfully? This entire sordid affair of your witch-hunt toward me pisses me off!" Ildiko snarled.

A number of whispers sounded in the room as the vampires, especially those acting as jurors, reacted to Ildiko's statement.

Lardom gazed around the room, turning his back to Ildiko when he ventured further into his investigation. "What if I was to tell this court, and you, that someone actually saw you at the house on the night of the murder?" He waited patiently for an answer.

When it came, it was full denial. "I'd say whoever says such a thing is lying."

"Really?" Lardom remained with his back to Ildiko. "I'd say the witness on the stand is the one who has been lying to this court. For what reason, I have no idea … oh, wait … maybe I do have an idea." At this point, Lardom swirled around and drove a nail into Ildiko's arrogance. "I say it is because you were the one who drained the blood from Katalin and then threw her from the rooftop! I have a witness who saw the entire incident, so, I ask you again, Ildiko—were you the one who murdered Katalin?"

Ildiko searched the room for at least one individual who would stand by her side … she looked at her brother, he looked away … she looked at Dracula, he stared haughtily back … she looked at Lajos, his lips curled in disgust. Realizing she was cornered, Ildiko figured now was the time to come clean about her part in the murder, and maybe about what else she knew. However, she'd decide about that as she went along.

Heaving a deep sigh, "Okay, I'll admit to being there, but I didn't kill her. Let me rephrase that … I didn't strike the first blow! That privilege was someone else's."

Lardom was forced to wait until the courtroom settled down before continuing. "So, what blow was it that you struck?" he asked pointedly.

"I didn't actually strike anything; I just finished the job someone else started. The woman would have died anyway."

At this moment of the testimony, Lardom turned and directed his attention to the jury of peers. "So, there we have one piece of the puzzle, gentlemen. However, as you have just heard, there is still another piece we must solve. Once that fragment is in place, we will have solved the crime, and then it will be up to this court to pass the judgement and the punishment." Without looking at Ildiko, "You may step down, but be assured we are not finished with you yet!"

Ildiko was confused as she returned to her seat. *Why didn't you ask if I have seen or heard anything else? Am I to be sentenced on this? Maybe I should have just told him what I know and rock Basarab's world!*

Chapter Thirty-four

Lardom waited until Ildiko was sitting before calling his next witness. He had several options, with what Angelique had told him, but thought to call who might be the most obvious perpetrator. "I recall Randy to the stand."

Randy walked shakily to the stand, passing by Ildiko as he did. He paused a moment, his fists clenched, wanting to strike her, to pummel the life from her. Nevertheless, he knew that would not happen in this room filled with vampires; he'd be more likely to end up dead. He glanced to the front of the room, at his friend, and his eyes told Basarab everything the count needed to know. *I am trusting you, Basarab, to do what you promised.*

"When you were on the stand before, we established that the relationship between you and your wife was fairly shattered … would that be a correct statement?" Lardom opened with.

Randy's voice was barely audible: "Yeah."

"Let's move forward then. I think it would be safe to say the friction didn't end once you settled in here?"

"No, it didn't end." Randy heaved a sigh and cleared the tears from his throat. "I was faced with two irate females. Mia blamed her mother and me for taking her away from Santan. Mia figured she'd be able to keep in touch with him via emails; however, that wasn't the case."

"Oh, why is that?" Lardom already knew, but not everyone in the room was aware of all the details of the uprooting of Randy's family to keep Santan and Mia apart.

"Basarab and I had agreed to change all our emails and phone numbers so they couldn't contact each other. We were hoping at least one of them would move on. I also delayed the installation of our internet and phone connection, which didn't go over well."

"How did Mia feel when she found out she couldn't contact Santan?"

"Distraught, to say the least … angry … demanded I get the internet connected immediately … didn't believe me when I said all our contact information had to be changed. I tried to explain it was because our emails were attached to my company in Germany and that Canada had different servers … she still didn't believe me."

"How did Katalin feel about her daughter's continuous pushing to contact Santan?"

"In all truth, Katalin was hoping that being this far away from Santan, and having Mia attend a high school here, would take away her infatuation with Santan. But Mia threw a fit over that too, demanding to go home … actually, to Brasov, where she was hoping to have stayed at Basarab's castle while she attended the photography course she wanted in the city." Randy paused and ran his hand through his curls. Lardom knew he wasn't finished yet, so waited.

"This was the first Katalin had heard of Mia's desire to go to school in Brasov and stay at the count's castle. Mia and I had discussed the possibility. When Mia said she would be staying with family, that's when her mother lost it, saying they weren't family and she wouldn't have Mia near them ever again! Mia said it was her destiny to be with Santan; they were in love, and she added her mother wouldn't keep them apart. Of course, Katalin told Mia she was too young to know what love was.

"My daughter turned to me for support, and I tried to smooth things over by telling Mia her mother was terribly unsettled by what we'd witnessed during the ceremony, and I tried to convince my wife the vampires we knew weren't monsters—they weren't like the creatures portrayed in movies. But Katalin wasn't going to be convinced; said if she had to fight to the death, she'd not see our daughter married to one of you. Told me to choose my path wisely. Before she stormed out of the room, Katalin let slip what Basarab and I had arranged to try and keep the young people apart. Mia was furious … told me until I made things right she wouldn't do anything in this city. Said she would be in her room until I did."

Randy's shoulders drooped in despair as he rehashed what had gone on when first arriving to Brantford. He knew the upcoming questions wouldn't get any better. Lardom, feeling a touch of sympathy for the human, gave Randy a few moments to collect himself and relax.

"Shall we continue now, Randy? Would you like a glass of water, perhaps?" Lardom asked.

Randy nodded, realizing how thirsty he was. Lardom walked over to the side table where a pitcher of water had been set and poured a glass for Randy. Handing the refreshment to Randy, "Take your time."

Downing the water in a few gulps, Randy returned the glass to Lardom, not knowing what else to do with it. He shifted in the chair and straightened his shoulders, preparing for the next set of questions. Lardom set the glass on the table in front of Basarab.

"So, I understand you had a bit of time with just the three of you in the house, and then Basarab showed up with Virginia and Samara. Why was that?" Lardom raised his eyebrows inquiringly.

"Santan had left home; he wanted to know if I'd seen him."

"Had you?"

"No."

"What did the count say to that?"

"He felt if Santan had come to Brantford, the only one who might know would be Mia. He asked to speak to Mia after supper that night."

"How were you feeling about the count showing up, and the possibility Santan might be in the area, as well?"

Randy cleared his throat again. "How do you think I felt? My wife wasn't speaking to me … my wife and my daughter weren't speaking to each other … the count tells me Santan might have come to get Mia. My entire life was falling apart!"

Lardom was ready now to go in for the kill, which would reveal if Randy had been the one to strike the first blow, enabling his wife unable to fight off Ildiko. "We all know what was done to Mia, by Samara but what Mia wanted, so let's talk about the train of events that took place when you went to get Mia to tell her about meeting with Basarab."

"I went to see my daughter, but she told me to leave her alone. She'd only talk to me once she was able to talk to Santan again. I asked her if she'd seen him. She said no. I told her Basarab had arrived with Virginia and Samara and the count wanted to talk to her. She said she didn't want to talk to him. I asked her to be reasonable; if she had nothing to hide, just tell the count that and then he would leave. She turned away from me, so I left the room."

"What happened when you went to get your daughter for the meeting with Basarab?"

"She wasn't in her room. I went to find Katalin, hoping Mia had maybe relented and gone to talk to her mother, but she hadn't seen our daughter either, and suggested I check up on the widow's walk. Said Mia might want fresh air and not want to take a chance walking in the yard and bumping into us on her way there. But Mia wasn't on the widow's walk either."

"Did Katalin not question you as to why your daughter seemed to be missing?"

"She did, but I told her nothing was wrong and left the room quickly so she couldn't ask me anything more."

"How did Basarab react when you told him Mia had disappeared?" Lardom glanced from Randy to the count and back again.

"Upset, to say the least. He was even more upset when I told him I'd told Mia earlier that he'd wanted to speak with her. I told Basarab that Mia had said she'd not seen Santan, but I think we both felt maybe she had and that's why she was avoiding contact with the count. Basarab said if Mia were still in the house, she'd show up; if she'd gone with Santan, we'd have to find them. Before he left, Basarab told me it was time I informed my wife he was there."

"I see … how did Katalin take that news?"

"She lost it on me! Told me either they leave, or we leave. Said we didn't need Basarab's charity … asked if I was going to do what was right for my family—especially for our daughter. Asked if I was willing to allow one of those beasts to sink their fangs into our daughter and change her into one of them!"

"How did you feel about her attack on who you considered your family?"

Randy paused, wanting to choose his words carefully. He looked at Basarab, then at the jurors, who were watching him closely. The truth rolled off his tongue: "I was angry with her for insulting my family. I told her we wouldn't have had such a good life had it not been for the generosity of the count … that Mia had the best money could buy … that we'd never had to go hungry. I told her she wasn't the woman I'd married and," Randy paused again before finishing his answer, "I told her she disgusted me, and she was to treat our guests with the respect they deserved or she'd be the one to be sorry!"

Virginia was startled when Mia's hand reached out and grabbed hers. She looked at the newly turned vampire and noticed two things: a worried look in her eyes, and a peculiar smile on her lips. *You are a strange child, Mia, for that is what I consider you still to be, despite what has been done to you, what you asked for. You will never know the joy of finishing out your teen years, of having children of your own … you will just never know!*

Virginia wasn't the only one who noticed Mia's reaction to her father's statement. Basarab and Lardom were also concerned by what they saw.

Lardom faced the vampire congregation. "I would like to beg the court's indulgence and ask for a small break at this point. I am sure we are all ready for some refreshment." His request was met with several nods. "Randy, we are not finished yet, so upon everyone's return, you will be back on the stand.

Basarab, as anxious as he was to finish the court hearing, also wanted to speak with Radu and Elizabeth. "I think maybe we have had enough testimony for tonight," he said, standing. "I have another matter that has come up, which needs immediate attention." He nodded to Dracula, who was watching the count closely, just waiting for the moment when they would interrogate his beloved brother, Radu.

Dracula made his move to leave only after most of the others left. Basarab approached him. "I am asking my father and Kardos to join us when we speak to Radu and Elizabeth," the count informed. "If you don't mind," he added.

Knowing there would be no use in arguing with Basarab, Dracula nodded and headed to the door. "I'll meet you outside the room then."

As Basarab was leaving, he noticed Rasputin still sitting in a corner. He didn't like this Russian vampire and still couldn't figure out why he was here, why Volodya had brought him to Brantford. Rasputin was not present when Katalin was murdered, and he definitely was not part of the count's council!

Rasputin smiled and nodded to Basarab, then stood and made his way to the door, stepping aside for the count to exit first. Basarab shivered as he walked past. He couldn't help thinking Rasputin's smile was more of a smirk than a genuine gesture. Little did Count Basarab know just how right he was.

Chapter Thirty-five

Radu stood when the four vampires entered the room; Elizabeth remained seated, a look of disgust on her face. "I thought you might have forgotten us," Radu grinned nervously.

"Hello, brother," Dracula greeted, ignoring Radu's statement.

Basarab motioned to the empty chairs. "Shall we sit?" he directed as he took the chair closest to Radu. Giving Dracula a firm look, he added, "I shall take the lead if everyone does not mind."

Dracula drew in a sharp breath, not liking what the count said, but also knew better than to make a scene, especially in front of the unexpected guests. He took a seat, as did Attila and Kardos.

"What does bring you here Radu? How are you here, actually; I was under the impression you were dead!"

The smile didn't leave Radu's lips as he replied: "My brother didn't kill me, as you thought he did, and I see now he did not inform you of what happened. Despite what he did to me, which wasn't enough to end my miserable life but was enough to make me think long and hard about my next step, I lived. As for why I am here now, I miss my family and want to make amends for what I attempted to do. I was wrong."

"Took you long enough," Dracula hissed, not able to help himself.

Basarab threw his uncle a look. "Where have you been all this time?" he asked, redirecting back to Radu. "And, how did you come upon Elizabeth? I … we all thought she was dead."

"She almost was when I found her," Radu affirmed. "I discovered where Elizabeth and Peter took Virginia; Peter was supposed to bring her to me, but his plan changed. Honestly, she wasn't to be harmed; she was to be used as leverage to get you to give up the throne. However, Elizabeth told me later when she recovered, Peter was out of control, so she went along with what he wanted. Peter was not one to be denied."

"How do you lie so boldly to my face?" Basarab jeered, rising up from his chair and walking around behind Radu. He put his hands persuasively on Radu's shoulders and squeezed until his uncle moaned in pain. "My memory is sharp, uncle … you told us that day you had no use for Virginia … you told us it was all Elizabeth's doing … we told you what she did to Tanyasin and Jack the Ripper … remember? Remember, Radu? Yet, you, knowing Elizabeth was out of your control, allowed her to take Virginia out of your protection and then sent an even bigger monster after them!

"Didn't you tell me Peter was to bring Virginia back to you … he was to finish off Elizabeth … kill her … didn't you say you were going to let her go, begging us to believe you? Then, when we asked where Virginia was, you were ashamed to admit you had been betrayed by Peter.

"Do you remember me pointing out to you, uncle, that others might have their eyes on my throne, in particular, Elizabeth and Peter? Did you not admit how shrewd Elizabeth was? Jack, whom you thought was on your side, who was actually playing both sides of the coin, wasn't able to give you any concrete information as to his mistress' goings-on. You admitted that even he could be playing you. Well, we all know what happened to Jack, don't we? Virginia witnessed his demise!"

Radu looked at Elizabeth and saw the wrath in her eyes. She had no idea how much he had tried to place the blame on her. He cringed under her gaze.

"So, I ask you again, uncle … how did you come upon Elizabeth in the shed … and, how did you dare to bring her back from the throes of death?"

Adrianna was watching what was taking place in the small room in the basement of Yates Castle, and for the first time, she was nervous, second-guessing her decision to send Radu and Elizabeth ahead to stir things up, putting the Dracul family off-guard. Radu was still weak, as he'd always been. Her eyes focused on Elizabeth with the hope she could salvage what Radu was losing control of.

"When Peter didn't return with Virginia, and with Dracula's words still stinging my ears … he told me to make it right with you, Basarab, or he would hunt me down and finish what he should be doing. I remembered Peter having mentioned a shed close to a big park. I was hiding in the woods when you arrived, so I thought everything would be okay. You would find your woman and rescue her and I could just go on my way. I overheard the battle between you and Peter, and knew he was finished when I heard your victory howl!

"Then you left with Virginia in your arms, and your people went in and there was the sound of another horrific battle. I could hear Elizabeth's screams, but I stayed hidden, knowing I would not be able to save her. There were too many of you. After everyone left, I ventured to the shack and found her there, lying on the floor in a pool of blood, barely alive. I saw there was no hope for Peter, his head being severed."

Adrianna was impressed. Radu was pulling himself together and saying what she'd told him to. She looked at her mother's portrait, as was her custom when sitting in her office. "Soon, Mama … soon. Our revenge will be complete, and I will be sitting on the vampire throne!"

The four vampires in the room were listening intently to Radu, while at the same time watching Elizabeth's reactions to his words. She didn't look pleased; her lips were set firmly as though she were keeping herself from adding to his story.

Radu looked tired but he pushed on with his rendition: "As I knelt beside Elizabeth, she moaned. She looked so vulnerable, like on the day I turned her. I felt a pang of responsibility for the life I had returned to her that day, for what I created. It wasn't her fault … it wasn't her fault." Radu glanced at the woman beside him, moisture in his eyes. He patted her hand. She stiffened.

"I could not leave her, despite her betrayal," Radu continued. "I cut my wrist and began to feed her blood, a bit at a time. Once she gained enough strength to move, we left the shack and returned to my room, staying there a few more days while I made arrangements to return home to Transylvania. There we remained, until now." Radu finished with a sigh and leaned back in his chair.

Attila spoke for the first time. "What you say is all well and good; however, it does not really tell us why you are here now. What is it you want from us? How do you dare to bring this woman to Basarab's home? Do you think we forget so quickly or have forgiven your actions? Why should we believe you now after all this time, regardless of your outward show of regret?"

Radu squirmed in his chair. Adrianna had lectured him at length about what to say when questioned, but he was getting confused by Attila's multitude of questions.

"You appear confused, Radu," Dracula stated sarcastically. "Have you misunderstood some of what you are being asked?" he added.

"No. I simply want to reconnect with my family. I … we have been in a self-imposed exile, and I thought by now that maybe you would have forgiven me … us. Maybe, I am wrong."

Elizabeth finally spoke up in defence of Radu. "I understand you not wanting to forgive me," she began. "If my presence bothers you so much, I will leave." She waited, and when a reaction didn't come, "I was the one who convinced Radu to reconnect with his family. He didn't want to, but he was pining away, talking about you all the time, telling me how sorry he was for what he'd done."

Kardos leaned forward in his chair, ignoring Elizabeth's comments. Directing his question to Radu, he touched on something everyone else seemed to have forgotten: "What happened to all your rogues, Radu? We know you were building an army."

Radu looked surprised. This was a question neither he nor Adrianna had anticipated. Elizabeth bailed him out.

"When we arrived back to Radu's castle, the rogues were gone. We never discovered how they left, or to where. They just vanished."

Basarab, who had finally returned to his seat after pressuring Radu, stood. "I believe we have heard enough for now; it will soon be daylight and time for us all to get some rest. The night has been long already." He turned to Kardos. "Please ensure these two have some refreshment; I believe there are some bottles of blood in the courtroom. I will instruct Viktor to bring a couple mattresses; I believe that will be good enough for you two for the length of time you will be under my roof." With those words, Basarab left, Dracula, Attila, and Kardos on his heels.

Chapter Thirty-six

Before retiring, Volodya called his family together. Rasputin was not part of the meeting. The Russian vampire leader knew what a strain this trial was on everyone, but he also understood why they'd been called back—and it wasn't because Basarab actually thought any one of them was guilty of the crime.

"We had to be here for this trial," he began to explain, "Because we were in this house when the crime was committed."

"This court is a mockery," Petya commented. "We know who did the final blow to the woman…"

"But what we don't know is if Katalin would have lived if Ildiko hadn't gotten to her. And that is the reason Lardom must continue."

"I fear he may zero in on my mother again," Ákos said. "We must remember, Mother, you are the one who found the body and Lardom questioned you relentlessly about the possibility you killed her and to cover your crime, you fetched the count."

"He knows, and everyone else knows, I didn't do it," Délia said. "Even if Lardom said he would call me again, I doubt he will. He's looking for the one who struck the first blow," she added.

"Don't be too overconfident, Délia," Petya expressed. "Lardom is no ordinary lawyer; he's the best. He loves to play with people's minds. Look what he's doing with Randy right now, and he's the woman's husband! As far as I'm concerned, the man is innocent. I don't think Randy could kill a fly. You still might be called upon."

"I know that, and since I have done nothing wrong, I have nothing to fear."

Volodya stood. "No sense discussing something we are not able to control. Tomorrow is another night, and hopefully, this inquest will be over, and the count will have justice for Randy, and we can go home. Let's all get some rest."

Samara and Lajos spent the first hour in her room making love. When they finally finished, Lajos sat up in the bed. "Do you think she did the whole thing?" he asked Samara.

Stretching her naked body and sighing deeply, Samara replied huskily, her voice still saturated with sex. "Don't really care, but, for real … as much as I hate Ildiko, I don't think she did." Samara reached up and ran her fingers across Lajos' chest.

"Not satisfied yet, temptress?"

"Not really, lover. You know how famished I can be after a boring day of sitting around listening to … well…"

Lajos took up the challenge, and it was another hour before the two fell asleep.

Santan could not settle his mind. He hated what was happening in the courtroom, how Lardom was going after Randy. There was no way Randy could be guilty in Santan's mind. However, how far might Randy go to protect Mia if Katalin couldn't be stopped from going to the police?

His mind flickered over to Mia and her emotions—or lack of—over her mother's death. How much did she know of her mother's intentions? Was she capable of murdering her own mother? Not before, when she was still human. But she wasn't human anymore, so did that make a difference? Had she turned into a killer?

Virginia tucked Mia into bed, then left for her own room. As soon as the count's wife was gone, Mia climbed out of bed and paced around the room. *My poor dad ... whatever is he going to do? What am I going to do now? I thought this is what Santan wanted, but he's so distant now. Doesn't even want to touch me ... can't look at me without disgust. Samara didn't tell me how hard it was going to be ... why not? Poor Dad... poor Dad... what am I going to do, Dad?*

Finally, she returned to the bed and crawled under the comforter. She curled into a ball and cried herself to sleep.

Everyone in Yates Castle was finally in their rooms. The castle slept in the sunlight.

Across the world, an ocean and a partial continent away, Adrianna was making her final preparations for the trip to her self-professed destiny—to wreak revenge on the man who had given her life but destroyed her mother's!

Chapter Thirty-seven

Rasputin rose early and donned a heavy cloak. Pulling the hood over his head to block any possible rays of sunlight that might be lingering in the early evening hours, he headed out the front door. Moving quickly toward the downtown area, Rasputin went over in his mind the mission he'd been given. He didn't think it would be difficult to come upon a homeless person curled up in some back alley of the city centre.

The unlucky victim he came across was laying on a battered piece of cardboard box. Their eyes were open, yet they didn't see Rasputin when he approached. There was a faint moan as the vampire sunk his teeth into the man's neck. When he was finished, Rasputin picked up the lifeless body and transported it back to Yates Castle.

Looking around for a secluded spot to place the body, Rasputin finally decided on the perfect location—between two large trees, close to the sidewalk where a passerby would be able to see it.

For yet another night, the vampires gathered in the room in the basement of the house, settling into their chairs for what they all hoped would be the end of the inquest. Everyone wanted to go home.

"I recall Randy to the stand." Lardom stood, standing behind his table until Randy was seated on the witness chair. He approached slowly, looking puzzled. "The last statement you made to this court was that you told your wife—Katalin—if she didn't treat the guests with respect, she'd be the sorry one … am I correct?"

Randy nodded.

"Sorry, I didn't hear your answer."

"Yes, that's correct," Randy whispered, only loud enough for Lardom, and possibly Basarab, to hear.

Lardom turned to the jurors. "He said yes," the lawyer mocked. With a smirk, he turned back to Randy. "How did your wife take the disappearance of your daughter?"

Randy looked up at Basarab, licked his lips and ran a hand through his hair. *Shit! Can this get any worse for me … this guy is making my wife out to be a monster … no choice, though, but to tell the truth … he knows … the count always seems to know…* "She was distraught … wanted to call the police."

"Were you of the same mind?"

"Of course not. I told her we couldn't do that as long as Basarab was here."

"What did Katalin do then? I am sure she must have been furious with you for, once again, protecting … what was it she called the count and his family … oh yes … the beasts!"

Randy coughed. *Oh God!* "She asked Basarab to leave and let us handle the situation."

"Randy, Randy, Randy … are you trying to tell this inquiry your wife just asked nicely … really?" Lardom's lips curled in disgust.

Shifting nervously, Randy blushed. "Well, no, I guess she wasn't so nice about it."

"Fill us in … please."

Another shuddering sigh, "She accused the count of doing something to our daughter and she attacked him, calling him a monster."

"Your wife dared to attack Basarab! How did he react to such disrespect?"

"He held her off and told me to take control of her. I was to lock her up … we couldn't have her contact the police. Basarab promised we would find Mia."

Lardom walked back to his table and shuffled some papers. Randy was hoping his ordeal was over, but somehow knew it wasn't. *They're trying to pin this on me … they think I killed my wife to protect them … I'm doomed … Basarab promised to punish the killer … is this his way of getting out of it? Maybe it would be better for me … I wouldn't have this pain in my chest all the time … I wouldn't have to live with the pain of seeing Virginia and Basarab together … of seeing my daughter as a vampire, drinking blood to sustain her life …*

The courtroom was shocked as Randy broke down on the stand, sobbing like a baby.

Basarab decided to take charge of the situation. "I think Randy has had enough for now, Lardom … is there anyone else you can call to give him a break?"

Piling the papers he was shuffling, Lardom looked at the count, a slightly perplexed look on his face, but he recovered quickly. Approaching the count's table, "I call upon Count Basarab. However, I will question you where you are and Randy can remain on the stand. I am not finished with him yet!"

The count nodded.

"While all this was going on … what I mean is, while Katalin was telling you to leave and attacking you physically, did you know where Mia was?"

Basarab nodded. "Unfortunately, yes, I did." Without waiting for Lardom's next question, the count continued. "Mia was in the shack at the entrance of Brant Park; she'd been taken there by Samara. Mia wanted to become one of us, and unfortunately, my daughter took it upon herself to oblige the child."

"But you kept this knowledge from Randy and his wife?"

"I needed time to think of the best way to tell my friend … it was him I was concerned for."

"And you told him when?"

"After the confrontation with Katalin, I told Santan and Samara I would take charge of the situation. I told them Katalin would not be a problem once she knew her daughter had crossed over because she would not want any repercussions to come down on her child. I decided to speak to Randy first. I explained how Mia wanted to be with Santan forever and felt the only way for that to happen was to become a vampire. Unfortunately, for whatever her reasoning was, Samara obliged her. Randy was concerned about the possibility of Santan's involvement in the turning, but I assured him my son was in the dark about what his sister had done. In fact, I told Randy that Santan was furious. I stated we would break the news to Katalin that night, and bring Mia back to the house."

"Tell the court, please, how Randy reacted to this revelation?"

"All he said was he would like to go, and he would see me later. He was broken by what I had just told him—heartbroken."

"He was not angry?"

"No."

"Did he not threaten you, as he had his wife?"

"No."

"Basically, Randy accepted what Samara had done?"

Basarab leaned over his table, his eyes piercing, the flames around his pupils dancing angrily. "I will remind you, my daughter did not act alone; it was Mia who insisted on becoming one of us! As for Randy accepting the fact … I doubt he did, but he is also smart enough to know it was too late to change what happened!"

"Did you tell anyone else before informing Katalin?"

"My wife."

"How did Virginia take the news?"

Looking across the room and focusing on Virginia, the count replied: "Shock at first, but she also felt, as I did, Katalin would not go to the police and tell them about us because she would want to protect her child. Virginia said things would work out, they always did."

Lardom cleared his throat. "Let us move ahead. What was your next step to solve this problem?"

"Santan and I went to Randy, wanting to discuss how to handle Katalin. We knew we couldn't keep her locked in the basement forever. We devised a plan for Randy to tell his wife Mia had been found, and then to bring her up to the dining room, where we would reveal the circumstances. We also explained to Randy how dangerous it was for him to be around Mia until she learned to control her urges."

Lardom glanced at Randy. "How did Randy accept the fact he would not be allowed—able—to see his daughter alone?"

Basarab also looked at Randy, who was sitting dejectedly in the chair, a look of pure despair on his face. "He asked to be alone," the count finally replied.

"Thank you, Count." Lardom stepped back from Basarab and focused again on Randy. "I would like to continue with your testimony now," he declared. "Are you recovered enough to do so?"

Randy shrugged his shoulders. "As well as I will ever be," he mumbled.

Lardom sat on the edge of Basarab's table and began. "The count has informed us he was going to let you meet with Mia, and also Katalin, at which time your wife would be told about the situation with her daughter … who brought Katalin to the meeting?"

"I did."

"Why you?"

Randy glowered at Lardom, a hint of anger rising to the surface. "Isn't it obvious why it should have been me? There's no way she would willingly allow any one of the vampires to even touch her!"

"How was she when you went to get her?"

"She was curled up on her bed … she'd been crying … I tried to comfort her, but she pushed me away, angry because I'd allowed the 'beasts' to lock her up … told me I was supposed to protect her and Mia … that was my job as a husband! I finally managed to tell her Mia had been found, and she settled down a bit. Of course, she wanted me to tell her everything but, even had I wanted to, I couldn't … I just said we had to go."

"You were still protecting your friends—the vampires— by not telling your wife?" Lardom's one leg swung hypnotically from the table where he still sat.

"I wasn't protecting anyone," Randy retorted vehemently. "I simply didn't want to deal with Katalin by myself when she discovered what our daughter had become!"

"Carry on, Randy … let us enter the dining room where Basarab was waiting for you with your daughter. Describe briefly how things went when you and Katalin saw Mia."

"Katalin figured out right away something was wrong with Mia. Basarab took over and explained what had transpired … Mia's desire to be with Santan forever, and Samara's part in aiding her to do that. He also added that Santan had thought things over and was going to give her up so she could live a healthy human life, but it was too late.

"My wife was devastated … when I tried to reach out to her, she shoved me away … Santan tried to tell her no harm would ever come to Mia, he and his family would ensure that. At that point, Katalin went crazy. She attacked Basarab and drew blood … the scratches closed quickly and Mia tried to pull her mother off Basarab, but there were new scratches, and Mia became hysterical and turned on her mother … Santan rushed to assist the chaos, pulling Mia away and holding her … Basarab called Viktor to bring a bottle of blood, and Mia was given a drink … she calmed immediately.

"It was too much for Katalin," Randy carried on. "She told me it was my fault—and the vampires—then she turned her rage on Virginia, accusing her of having a hold on me … She accused the vampires of murdering our daughter … called me a fucking coward … said if I didn't have the guts to stand up to the vampires, she would!" Randy's breath caught in his throat, and he almost choked on what he was about to say next. "She said even if the only way she could stop her daughter from being a monster was to kill her, that's what she would do!"

Lardom, noticing the distress Randy was going through, "Take a moment, Randy … I understand how stressful this must be for you."

Randy stared blankly at Lardom. *Why did I ever open my door that day to Virginia … why did I allow myself to fall in love with her son and with her … why did I keep the relationship with Basarab, allowing him to control my life?* He turned his head to look at the count. *You've controlled me all these years by making it seem as if I couldn't exist without you … but it was me … my fault … I allowed it … I allowed it because I was afraid I would never see Virginia again!* Randy turned his eyes to the back of the room where Virginia sat.

"Okay," Lardom got down from the table and approached Randy. "Not much longer, and then you can take a break. What happened after Katalin threatened to kill Mia?"

Randy ran his hand through his hair. It pained him that he had to relive all that happened that day. "Basarab tried to remind Katalin of how the vampires had never harmed her, and that they had countless human friends; he reminded her it was Mia's choice, and, also tried to reassure her no one ever harmed her daughter. I believe Katalin felt threatened by Basarab…"

"Threatened in what way?" Lardom probed, interrupting Randy mid-sentence.

Randy shook his head. "Not sure. She just looked around the room and then stormed out. I remember Kardos tried to go after her, but Basarab stopped him, saying she wouldn't harm them. He did give permission for Angelique to follow her, though."

"I see." Lardom walked to his table and back again. "Did you go after your wife? When did you see her next?"

This is it … the final questions … then I assume they are going to pass judgement on me … better, probably … end this pain … better I leave this world as anonymously as I entered it. No one will know … no one will care … maybe Virginia … maybe Santan … but they'll forget me … Mia will forget me … well, here I go … moment of truth! "I went to try and talk to her later, but the first thing she did when I entered the room was start screaming at me for having allowed this to happen to Mia. Mia would still be human if I hadn't exposed the family to vampires! She told me she would go to the police as soon as she could get away … I said that would affect our daughter, too … she said she wouldn't turn her over to the police, but she would drive a stake through her heart so Mia wouldn't walk in darkness … I … I … I told her as long as there was breath left in my body, she would not kill our daughter! She was already dead, Katalin said … she told me to get out … told me to lock the door if I had to … told me I was a good patsy for the vampires … repeated that when she found a way out, the police would be coming for all of you, and for me!" Tears flowed from Randy's eyes as he broke down.

"Only one more question, Randy … I assume you left the room … did you go back and try to teach your wife a lesson, maybe strike her a bit too hard, hoping she would back off? Did you attempt to kill your wife?"

Randy, the tears still flowing, shook his head. "No … no, I did not try to kill my wife."

Chapter Thirty-eight

After a short break, the vampires filed back into the courtroom and took their seats. The inquisition resumed. Lardom called Santan to the stand.

"Do you believe Randy is capable of murdering his wife, or at the least, striking a near fatal blow to her?" Lardom's question was entirely unexpected. Nevertheless, Santan didn't miss a beat when he answered.

"No, Randy is not capable of such an act."

"Hmmm … protective of him, aren't you?"

Santan scowled. "I'm not being protective of him; I'm stating a fact!"

"Okay … let us talk about you now, and Mia. Can we do that?"

"Of course." Santan knew he had nothing to hide but still hoped Mia wasn't hiding anything.

"What did you do after Katalin left the room … after she found out about Mia?"

"I took Mia up to her room. After she fell asleep, I left and returned to my quarters."

"You did not think about trying to reason with Katalin again … pay her a visit? After all, she was threatening not only the existence of the vampires but of the girl you are in love with."

"Never crossed my mind," Santan answered easily. "I went straight to my room. I couldn't sleep though, so went to talk to my mother." He paused, unsure of how much he should declare of his confessions to Virginia. *Keep it brief and to the point ... best way.* "I apologized for running away from home, and told my mother I wished I had just left when Mia said she wouldn't come with me without consulting our parents ... I told my mother I intended to return for Mia, but after deeper thought, I had changed my mind, not wanting her to be part of the vampire world. It wouldn't be fair. I told my mother I had needed to talk to someone; I'd felt so alone at the time. Carla, the doctor who delivered Samara, was the only one I could think of who might be willing to listen to me, so I went to her.

"Carla felt sorry for me, but she told it was time to step up to the plate and follow the path my father had set out for me. Carla said if it were meant to work out between Mia and me, it would, but she also asked me to think about what Mia would be sacrificing if I drew her into the vampire world. Of course, this conversation was before Samara did what she did." Santan threw a disgusted look at his sister. Samara looked away, a smirk curling on her lips.

When Santan ceased talking, Lardom pushed for more. "What did Virginia advise you?"

"My mother told me my sister was impulsive. However, I should look on the bright side—now that Mia was a vampire, I would be able to marry her. We joked about my sister marrying Ákos, but my mother said she thought he had changed his mind." Santan pursed his lips. "It was good talking to my mother; she gave me perspective, told me how it had been too late for her to make her own choices the night she'd decided to see who lived in this house. She then told me to go and look after Mia, so that is what I did."

"Was Mia still in her room?"

"Of course, where else would she be. When I left her earlier, she was sleeping."

"How long were you with your mother?" Lardom asked, knowing it wouldn't have taken long for Mia to strike her mother and get back to her room if Santan had been gone long enough, even if she wasn't expecting him to return.

"Well over half an hour."

"Enough time to leave her room, do something, and return?"

"What are you insinuating?" Santan was angered by Lardom's insinuation, despite his own misgivings about Mia. "Mia would not have murdered her mother!" he added.

"Are you sure? She was angry at her mother … she knew her mother wanted to get her away from you. So I ask again, are you sure she wouldn't have, at the very least, gone to try and convince Katalin to back off, and then, maybe it wasn't her intention, but things got out of control…"

"Enough!" Santan stood and shook his fist at Lardom. "How dare you! Mia is just a teenager! She didn't want to come with me if her parents—both of them—didn't agree to us marrying! Does that sound like a girl who would kill her mother? Move on, councillor … Mia could never have done this!"

Lardom wasn't fazed by Santan's outburst. "Do I need to remind you, Santan, your sweet Mia is no longer human. She is a vampire—newly turned—and because of that, she just might have tried to sway her mother's feelings toward her kind." What he thought might be possible was revealed enough to give the audience food for thought. "Thank you, Santan. That will be all for now."

Police sirens resounded through the walls of Yates Castle. All the vampire eyes in the room turned inquisitorially to Basarab. What now? Only one set of eyes, at the back of the room in a shadowed corner, smiled. Rasputin.

Outside, at the edge of the property of the historic old house, several police cruisers and an ambulance surrounded a section of trees that had been taped off. Two old friends met, for the second time in the month, at the crime scene, which was familiar to the first one they'd been at. A victim drained of blood, with puncture wounds on their neck.

"Look familiar, Karen?" Nathaniel crept up silently behind the paramedic.

Karen stood and faced her former lover. "Very. Except for one thing: I don't think this victim was killed here."

Nathaniel gazed down at the body, then knelt in for a closer look. Standing he put his hands behind his back and walked around the victim. "Why do you say that?"

"Intuition … and, I know this guy. He never leaves the downtown area," Karen said. She paused, then pointed, "And look at the way the victim is laying, almost as though it was planted here."

Frankie approached at that moment, and his face blanched: "Oh, shit! This is Sam … he lives on the streets … usually sleeps in one of the alleys downtown … harmless old bugger." Frankie sounded on the verge of tears.

"Another similarity," Karen alleged. "A homeless person." She turned to Nathaniel. "Do you think someone is targeting the homeless?"

Nathaniel glanced toward the house and shook his head. "I honestly don't know, Karen. But, what I do know, is there is something creepy going on in that house there, and this time, with a body being found on the premise, I won't need a search warrant to question anyone. I have a feeling the count hasn't left for home as he said he was going to."

"Count?" Karen questioned curiously.

"Yeah … long story. I'll tell you about it sometime, maybe over a coffee, or lunch. Right now, we have a crime to solve, and I have some people who need to be questioned." Nathaniel turned to Frankie. "You coming, rookie?" he tested as he started across the lawn toward the house.

Frankie shuddered, not wanting to follow his partner's lead, but knowing he must. As he fell into step with Nathaniel, the sun sent slivers of light across the lawn as it rose for yet another day.

At the sound of the sirens, Angelique left the courtroom and headed to the widow's walk. As she stood, looking down on the scene, her heart beat faster than it had in a long time. "This is not good," she muttered.

Recognizing Nathaniel and Frankie milling amongst several other cops and paramedics, Angelique swore softly, something she seldom did. She squinted to get a better look at the victim. "Another homeless person … I need to get closer."

Whispering a spell, Angelique transformed into a bird and flew across the yard, landing in one of the trees close by the victim. The first thing she noticed was the body was drained of blood. *Damn!* She flew to a lower branch for a better look. *Puncture wounds … definitely vampire … but not Samara this time … she would not be that reckless with everything else going on … I cannot think of anyone in the house who would do this … Ildiko? No … then again, she's already convicted herself … is this maybe her way to remove the attention from her and stir up trouble for Basarab, taking his focus off the trial and off her punishment, giving her an opportunity to escape?*

Angelique turned her head and focused on Nathaniel and Frankie as they started across the lawn toward the house. *Damn!* Taking off immediately, Angelique flew back to the widow's walk, transformed, then made her way down to the front door. There was no time to notify Basarab about the coming visitors, or about what was going on outside on his property.

As Angelique entered the foyer, she bumped into Basarab's butler. "Viktor, I need you to take a message to the count. Tell him to keep everyone in the basement, including himself. There's been another murder, only this time the body is on the count's property, and that pesky police officer is headed this way right now. Tell Basarab I will handle this." Angelique continued on her way, not lingering to hear Viktor's response. She knew he would carry the message directly.

When the knock came on the door, Angelique took her time to answer. She mumbled a spell, and when she finally opened the door, she stood in front of the officers dressed in a sheer nightgown, which left nothing to anyone's imagination.

In a sleepy voice, "Officers … what is going on? I was awakened by the sound of sirens. Is there a problem?" Suddenly, as though realizing how she was dressed, Angelique folded her arms across her chest. "Oh dear … I wasn't thinking … just a moment, please, while I fetch a housecoat." She closed the door in the officers' faces and mumbled a few more words. When she reopened the door a few minutes later, she was wearing a housecoat.

Frankie was still blushing, but Nathaniel didn't look pleased with having his mission interrupted. "Can we step in?" he asked curtly.

"I do not see the necessity of that, officer," Angelique smiled sweetly. "It really would not be proper for me to entertain two such handsome men so early in the morning when I am all alone here; whatever would my husband think if someone were to see me, dressed like this, allowing men into my home…"

"Cut the bullshit … Angelique, isn't it?" Nathaniel mocked. "I want to speak with the count. Is he here?"

"Oh dear, you must not have just heard me," Angelique smiled sweetly again. "Did you not hear me say I was alone?"

"Yeah, I heard you, but, I don't believe you!" Nathaniel was thinking maybe he should just barge past the beauty blocking his way and shout out the count's name. However, he felt a hand on his arm. Frankie.

"Hey, boss … let it go … the lady says she's alone here … which means the count has already left like he said he was going to."

Nathaniel shook Frankie's hand off his arm. He was furious, and more assured in his mind than ever that something was going on inside the big house. "Okay, lady, you win this time. But know this: I don't believe you're alone here; I think the count is hiding behind your nightgown and you can tell him for me, I'll be back. Soon. With a warrant. Then, you and anyone else who might be lurking somewhere in this house won't have a choice but to let me in. Me and a whole team of police ready to tear this place apart!"

Angelique feigned distress, her hand fluttering to her throat. "Exactly what is the problem … Nathaniel, isn't it?" she asked, mimicking how he'd greeted her.

"You, and whoever else is in this house, will find out soon enough when we come back with a warrant!" Nathaniel turned and stormed down the steps, back to the crime scene.

Frankie lingered a moment, mesmerized by Angelique's fragile beauty. "There's been a murder, ma'am, and the body is on the count's property." He blushed, paused, then added: "Will you be okay?"

Despite the chuckle bubbling in her, Angelique manufactured a shocked look. "Oh, dear … that is terrible … no wonder your partner is so rude … but," Angelique laid a hand on Frankie's shoulder, allowing her housecoat to open slightly. "I assure you I had nothing to do with this crime, and there is no one else here, so please tell your boss it will not be necessary for him to return."

Frankie blushed and swallowed the lump that had formed in his throat. He nodded and turned to leave, but was stopped in his tracks when he heard a male voice. Spinning back, he saw Viktor approaching.

"Miss Angelique, should I bring your bags down for you?" Viktor was saying. "I have laid an outfit out for you, and there is room for you to put your nightwear in one of the bags. The limo will be here in half an hour to take you to the airport." Viktor stood solidly behind Angelique, his face expressionless.

"You're leaving?" Frankie mumbled. "But, you can't … not with a crime having been committed here, on the property … we'll have to come back and talk to you again." He paused, looking at Viktor. "I thought you said you were alone here," he directed to Angelique.

Smiling, Angelique replied: "Your partner was asking for the count, was he not? The count is not here, nor any of his family. He left, as did my husband. Viktor and I stayed behind to close everything up. So, as you heard, I will be leaving quite shortly and must get ready. As I already said, there is no need for you to return. The house will be empty. Good luck with your investigation," Angelique finalized the conversation, and shut the door.

Turning to Viktor, "Whose idea was that to have you appear when the cops are still here?"

"Basarab's instructions."

"I see. I assume he is trying to help."

"I assume so," Viktor droned. "But now, to carry through with the charade, I must call our limo service, and you should prepare to leave. The count wishes a word with you before you do."

Angelique nodded and whispered a few words, changing into a bird right there in the hallway. "The count will have to wait a few moments," she stated through an open beak. "I have a body to replenish first. Open the door for me, please."

Viktor opened the door wide enough for the bird to fly through. As Angelique headed to the crime scene, Frankie looked up and saw her.

"A bird, again," he muttered. "Always a bird at the crime scenes … looks like the same one that attacked our car, too!" Frankie shook the thought from his head. "You're going crazy, Frankie … get a grip on yourself!"

"What's that, Frankie … talking to yourself?" Nathaniel mocked.

"Nothing," Frankie garbled as he gazed up into the trees, searching for the bird. "Where's the body?" he asked, noticing it was gone.

"Taken to the morgue already," Nathaniel replied. "I asked Karen if someone took photos this time, and she said they did. I'm going back to the station … you coming?"

Frankie looked up at the trees again, hearing a rustle in the leaves. "Yeah, let's get out of here!"

Angelique watched from the tree. "Damn! Too late. I will just have to let this one go. Two bodies filling up with blood in a morgue would be more than questioned by the authorities." Angelique took flight back to the house.

As she did so, Frankie glanced back at the house, seeing the bird fly across the lawn. He was about to say something to his partner, but shut his mouth, not willing to be teased again.

Chapter Thirty-nine

Angelique went directly to the courtroom when she returned to the house. Basarab met her in the hallway and told her she must get in the limo and go to the airport. The police, in case they were watching, had to witness her leaving. Once in the plane, she could slip out and return to the house. Then, they would form a plan of action. Angelique agreed, and they went their separate ways.

Before leaving, Angelique put a spell on the door to the basement where the vampires were holed up. No human would ever be able to open it or break it down. Viktor followed her out to the parking lot where the limo was waiting, carrying two suitcases. Anyone who might be observing the leaving would have thought the cases were well-filled.

"She's leaving, you know," Frankie stated as Nathaniel was about to turn left onto Market Street.

"Really?" Nathaniel turned his blinker off and drove across the street into the cemetery. "How do you know that?" he asked as he circled around the entrance and stopped the cruiser, facing the road.

"After you took off, the old butler came and asked if he should bring her bags down for her … said the limo would be arriving in half an hour to take her to the airport."

"Well then, let's see if that actually happens! I don't believe a word coming out of that woman's mouth," Nathaniel snapped angrily. "I think we'll just sit here and wait for the limo to come down Buffalo Street; then, maybe we'll follow it to see which airport Miss Angelique is headed for!"

As the limo turned onto Market Street, Angelique noticed the cruiser parked at the entrance of the cemetery. She smiled. "Take me to the Hamilton Airport," she instructed the driver.

"But I thought we were headed to the…" the driver began.

"Change of plans. We have a tail. Therefore, I must make this look good. You will drop me off and then come back to Brantford; I'll make my own way back to the house." Angelique settled on the seat and grinned. *You cops have no idea who you are dealing with … pity … but if you get too nosey, Nathaniel, you are going to be very, very sorry!*

Nathaniel kept the car a discrete distance behind the limo, which wasn't difficult to keep in view due to its size. He slowed down at the entrance of the airport and watched from a distance as the limo stopped at the terminal entrance. The driver got out and assisted Angelique with her baggage, seeing her inside. A few minutes later, he exited and drove away.

"Satisfied?" Frankie asked sarcastically, fed up with his partner's illusions.

"Nope. I want to see her get on the plane. Then I'll be satisfied." Nathaniel put the car into drive and maneuvered the vehicle to the parking lot. "You can wait here if you want," he commented, getting out of the cruiser.

Frustrated, Frankie opened his door and followed the elder officer into the airport.

Angelique was annoyed at the delay. *You old dog! Can't let go of the bone! I guess I will just have to keep tossing you some more.* She walked over to security and lined up. Half an hour later, Nathaniel watched her get on a West Jet flight to Halifax.

"Satisfied now?" Frankie repeated his former question. "She's on the plane, man. Or do you want to get on it and go wherever it is she's going?" he added mockingly.

"I'm satisfied, for now. But, if you want the truth, I think there's still someone in that house, and I mean to find out who! A crime was committed—a body was found on the property— someone in there is guilty, or at the least, knows who is!"

"Yeah, probably the butler ... it's usually the butler that commits the crimes, isn't it?" Frankie laughed insultingly.

"Smartass," Nathaniel retorted as he made his way quickly out of the airport.

Angelique went to the washroom at the back of the plane. Once inside, she whispered the spell that would land her back in Yates Castle.

When Angelique entered the courtroom, most of the vampires were gathered in small groups. She looked around, and locating Attila and Basarab, maneuvered her way to them. "Sorry for the delay; the bloody cops followed me, so I was forced to complete the charade."

"They're satisfied?" Basarab raised his eyebrows.

"For now. However, I would not put it past that older cop coming back, despite everything we have done. We need to finish this inquiry and discover who struck the first blow, deal swiftly with both the perpetrators and get out of here!" Angelique could not have spoken truer words. "And," she continued, "I wasn't able to return any blood into the old man's body; to have followed it to the morgue and do what I did last time would have just been too weird and drawn even more attention to us. Especially, since the body was found on your property, Basarab."

Basarab strode to the front of the room and stood behind his table. "Fellow vampires, please return to your seats; we must finish this inquest as quickly as possible. I believe someone is attempting to frame us for another murder. A body was found on the property earlier, drained of blood. Before Angelique could replenish blood into the victim, he was removed to the morgue.

"The officer who has been harassing me even went to the extent of following Angelique to the airport. I believe, as does Angelique, he is not going to give up, despite the fact she told him there was no one here—everyone has left. I know you are all tired and want to go home, but I have given my word to my friend to see justice done for his wife. I now turn the floor back to Lardom to call his next witness." Basarab sat down.

Lardom stood and looked to the back of the room. He'd decided he had enough evidence gathered to finish the investigation with his next witness. "I call Mia to the stand."

Mia froze in her seat. She looked to Virginia for support. Virginia took the young vampire's hand, giving it a light squeeze. She leaned over and whispered in Mia's ear. "Just tell the truth of where you were when your mother was murdered. I am sure no one believes you would have done it." Virginia let go of her hand. "Go on now."

Standing and making her way to the front of the room, everyone could see she was shaking uncontrollably. Lardom approached Mia slowly, not wanting to frighten her. "Are you okay to answer some questions?" he asked softly.

Mia nodded, still shaking.

Lardom decided to lead her slowly in the direction he was headed. "You have had a lot of big changes in your life lately, haven't you?" came the first question.

"Yes."

"When did you fall in love with Santan?"

"I think it was on my tenth birthday. The count invited us to the castle to celebrate it … I remember being totally excited by it all, and Santan was so handsome." Mia wrung her hands in her lap.

"Is not Santan much older than you?"

Mia smiled for the first time since being called forward. "Yes, but he was so kind and paid so much attention to me—not like Samara. She ignored me all the time and treated me like I was a baby."

"In many ways, you were," Lardom articulated. "However, we are not here to discuss how Samara felt about your maturity level when you were ten, are we?" Lardom smiled, not really expecting an answer.

However, Mia gave him one, short and to the point. "Like I said, she treated me like a baby, and Santan didn't." Mia directed a nasty glare in Samara's direction. The temptress grinned mockingly at her.

"Let us return to the main subject, shall we," Lardom intervened before Mia could continue a tirade on Samara. "How long before you told Santan how you felt?"

"Goodness … not until I was fifteen."

"Did you tell your parents how you felt?"

"Oh no! Santan told me he felt the same way about me but we mustn't tell anyone yet. So we just corresponded by email and kept our secret." Mia relaxed and leaned back in the chair.

She glanced to Santan and smiled. Not wanting to upset her, he smiled back.

"I see." Lardom paused and looked to where Randy sat alone. "Your father loved his vampire family, as we have established here, but your mother did not. Right?"

Mia nodded.

Lardom aimed his next statement to the jurors. "Mia has also confirmed her mother did not love vampires—something we all know to be a determined fact by now. So," swivelling back to face Mia, "I ask you, Mia, did that bother you? After all, you were in love—at least what you thought was love—with a vampire! Did it ever occur to you your mother would not approve?"

"That's why we didn't tell." Mia looked at Santan again.

"Okay, let's move on. You were swept away to Brantford, as we learned, a plan devised by Basarab and your father to keep you and Santan apart, but Santan came to Brantford for you and tried to convince you to leave with him—correct?"

"Yes."

"Santan testified you wouldn't go with him because you wanted to make sure your parents and his, approved—right?"

"Yes."

"Let me understand this clearly … you wouldn't go with Santan, but then decided to become a vampire. I am slightly confused by your reasoning." Lardom leaned back on Basarab's table, but before Mia could reply, he continued. "Did someone convince you to cross over, or was it completely your idea?"

Mia sought out the spot where Samara was sitting. Their eyes locked. "No, it was all my idea. Samara asked me if I loved her brother and if I wanted to be with him forever. I told her of course, and then she said there was only one way I could do that. I have dreamed, ever since I fell in love with Santan, of becoming a vampire. Samara offered to help me, but only if it was what I really wanted," Mia emphasized dramatically.

"You did not stop and think how this would affect your parents?"

"No."

"Especially, the effect on your mother, whom you dearly loved?" There was a cutting edge in Lardom's tone when he asked that question.

Mia began shaking again. "No … I guess I didn't consider my mother's feelings at the time. I was just thinking how much I wanted to be with Santan … to be his queen. Samara asked if I was sure, and when I said yes, she said we had to move quickly before I spoke to her dad … I mean, the count. My dad almost spoiled everything when he came to my room but I got rid of him, just like he told you."

"At any point, did you want to change your mind?"

"Not really. Like I said, I want to be with Santan."

Lardom strolled over to his table and leaned on the edge of it. "Let's move on. You became one of us, and I understand your transition has not been an easy one. You do not have to answer that; I know how difficult transitions can be." He stopped for a moment and allowed the silence of the room to sweep over the young vampire on the stand. He watched her shift anxiously in her seat and look down to the floor.

Finally, he stood and returned to her, leaning over and resting his hands on the arms of the chair. "How did you feel about your mother when you realized she wanted to kill you because you were a vampire?"

It took a few seconds for Mia to reply to this question. "It scared me," she began, her voice fraught with nervousness. "But I didn't think she'd actually carry through on her threats. She loved me."

"Someone did. Someone was not pleased with her threats." Lardom grinned and waved a hand around the courtroom. "In fact, many individuals in this room could benefit from your mother's death, including your beloved father." A pause. "Do you think your father would do anything for you, Mia?"

Mia was smart enough to sense where this line of questions was going, and she didn't want to answer. She stared at her father.

"Simple question, my dear," Lardom pressed.

"What do you mean by *anything*?" Mia questioned, despite knowing what the vampire's answer was going to be.

"Come, come, Mia. I think you know what I mean. We have established in this court that your father was the last one, to our knowledge, to see your mother alive…"

"What about Ildiko?" Mia almost shouted. "Isn't she the one who drained my mother of blood and threw her from the roof? Wouldn't that mean she saw her alive and then killed her?"

"It only means, my dear, Ildiko found your mother at death's door, and being the vampire she is, she finished the job. She did not strike the first blow. So, I ask you again, do you think your father would do *anything* for you, Mia?"

Mia hung her head and stared at the floor. Nodding, she responded with a tremor in her voice: "He always said he would do anything for me."

"Even murder your mother because she made it clear to him that she would rather kill you than see you live as a vampire? Kill his beloved daughter—oh, how that must have pained him!"

"No! My father would never have done something like that! He loved my mother!" Mia's voice echoed hysteria now. "He would've found another way to stop her!"

"I think he loved you more," Lardom suggested.

"No … no … no!" Mia moaned. "He wouldn't have killed her! Not my father! Not my father!" Mia rocked back and forth in her chair, and her tears flowed.

Suddenly, Randy stood and shouted at Lardom. "Leave my daughter alone! You're a beast! Why are you trying to pin this on her? She's a child! My sweet child! If you want to blame someone, then it was me! I killed my wife! Is that what you all want to hear?

"I've wasted everyone's time—I did it. There was no way Katalin was going to stop until she got her revenge on my vampire family. She was determined that if I wouldn't do something about it, she would. She wouldn't stop … she was going to kill my daughter, and I couldn't allow that. So I killed her." Randy crumbled to the floor in a heap of emotional breakdown.

As everyone looked at the broken man, Lardom dropped his bomb at Mia's feet. "You see, Mia … your father will do anything for you. Even to the point of confessing to a crime he did not commit, just to protect the one who did!" Lardom gave Mia one of his famous smiles before turning to his fellow vampires and shrugging his shoulders, "There you have it, my friends … there you have it."

Every eye in the room turned to look at Randy. Murmurs of shock at this revelation echoed through the room, some of the comments spoken in anger at being so inconvenienced by this human. Basarab was shocked at the revelation as well, however, in his mind he knew Randy was lying to save his daughter's life. The question now was would she let him take the fall for something she obviously did!

Chapter Forty

Virginia went to Randy and assisted him back to his chair. She knew, in her heart, he hadn't committed the crime. She looked up to Basarab, her eyes pleading for mercy for their friend. "I do not believe you, Randy; why are you doing this?" she whispered in his ear.

Randy looked at her, but his eyes were blank. He tried to mouth the words that were in his head, but they couldn't penetrate through the thickness of his tongue.

Virginia looked at Mia, who was still sitting in the witness chair, looking traumatized. "You know your father did not do this, Mia. If you know who did, for God's sake, speak up!" Virginia's throat burned from speaking the word God.

Santan was also watching Mia. He was putting everything together now, especially her lack of surprise and emotion when he told her that her mother was dead. *What kind of monster did my sister create? Oh, my sweet Mia, what is to become of us now? Vampire law will condemn you to death—my father promised Randy the murderer would be dealt with under vampire law ... but, I cannot allow that ... I won't allow that ... and Ildiko ... she must also be put to death ... what are we to do?*

The room was bathed in silence as everyone waited for what they knew was the finale of their ordeal, allowing them all to return home to their dark lives. All eyes turned on Mia.

Lardom decided he'd waited long enough for the impact of Randy's confession to penetrate Mia's mind. "You said your father would never kill your mother, Mia. Yet he just confessed. Do you believe him?"

Mia shrugged her shoulders.

"Mia … Mia … Mia. Are you truly going to allow your father to take the blame for something you know in your heart he did not do?"

Randy attempted to stand again, but Virginia grasped his arm, holding him in place. "You did not do it, Randy; but your daughter knows who did," she hissed softly. "Let her speak."

Mia noticed her father's attempt to speak again, to come to her rescue, and how Virginia stopped him. *She knows … she knows my father didn't do it. Does she know who did? What am I to do now?*

Basarab decided it was time to end the suspense. He saw the picture clearly now. Leaning across his table, he looked directly into Lardom's eyes. "Finish it!" he ordered.

Lardom nodded. "You did it, Mia, didn't you? At least, you tried to kill your mother. You had no idea she was still alive when you left her room, but Ildiko did. She testified she was outside on the widow's walk, listening at the door. She may even have known it was you but didn't tell us, for a reason known only to her! Ildiko merely finished what you started." He took a deep breath. "Would you like to tell this court what happened?"

Mia looked around the room, her eyes brimming with tears. Randy struggled against Virginia's grip but she held him fast. Santan's heart was broken, knowing what was coming next, but he needed to hear how—why. Samara snuggled closer to Lajos and smiled, thinking only about how much closer she was to the throne. Ildiko waited for Mia's confession, knowing both their fates were sealed.

"I overheard my parents fighting," Mia began at last. "I was going to my mother to try and convince her to reconsider what she was thinking of doing. I was going to tell her I would always love her, and I was still her daughter, her little Mia. I stood outside her door and heard the hateful words she screamed at my dad, and I was just about to go in and stand with him when I heard him approaching the door.

"I slipped behind a pillar and hid in the shadows. I was fuming. I knew my mother was going to do what she said, so, after my dad left, I burst through her door. I didn't intend to kill her, but she looked at me with such disgust that I lashed out at her with the first thing I could lay my hands on, which happened to be a letter opener lying on the dresser. I didn't realize my new strength when I struck her, and when I saw her neck and the amount of blood pouring out, I panicked and didn't wait to see if I had killed her. I just turned and ran back to my room, and just in time, too. Santan arrived a few minutes after I crawled into bed. When he suggested a walk, I took him up on it, I needed to get out of the house … away from what I'd just done."

Mia couldn't stop now that her confession had begun. "When we were in the parking lot and saw the body in the yard, I knew it was my mother. I thought it would all be okay, that I wouldn't have to confess. I thought my mother had managed to crawl outside, to that widow's walk at the top of the house, and had accidentally fallen over the edge. I thought I was home free!"

"But, you slit your mother's throat, Mia, and you just left her there. You did not even try to help her." Lardom reminded her. "Therefore, you were not really home free, were you?"

Mia shook her head. "I can't let you take the blame for what I started, Dad … I just can't." Mia looked at the count. "So, do what you must, Count Basarab. I killed … I struck the first blow that eventually led to my mother's death." Mia finally collapsed, falling out of the chair, landing on the floor. Her shoulders shook, this time not from nerves, but with the tears that now released in a stormy torrent.

Randy struggled again against Virginia's hold. She finally released him. Standing, he rushed shakily to the front of the room and stood before Basarab. Slowly, he spoke, stuttering emotionally through his words.

"Let m-my d-daughter g-go, count, and Ildiko, t-too." Randy tried to get control of his speech. "I don't want revenge anymore. I … I couldn't handle losing my daughter, and as for Ildiko, well, I guess she was just doing what comes naturally to your kind. So, I'm begging you … I'm begging all of you … just let them go."

Basarab looked at his friend. He looked at Mia, still lying on the floor. He glanced at Ildiko, sitting alone. He looked at the vampires who had made their way to Brantford at his request to bring to justice the murderer of Randy's wife. Vampire justice dictated death when the taking of a life in the manner in which Katalin had been killed. But, looking at Randy, his human friend was asking for mercy, not just for his daughter, but Ildiko, as well.

Samara waited anxiously for her father's answer. How he decided would determine if she would be able to step up to the throne. She knew if the count didn't go along with Randy's request, her brother would not tolerate the death of his beloved, and he would leave for good, not wanting anything more to do with his father! Samara crossed her fingers and waited.

At long last, Basarab made his decision and presented it to the court. "I think there has been enough pain in this room. I am satisfied with what we have uncovered, although I am not pleased with either party in this taking of an innocent life. Despite Katalin's threats to our kind and to her daughter, I would have handled her. Therefore, I am going to grant my friend

Randy's request and allow both Mia and Ildiko to live—however, they will not go unpunished."

Turning first to Ildiko: "For the lies you have told this court and me, you are forever banished from the family. I never wish to see you again. For what you did in the past, and the exile you served, I would have thought you learned your lesson, but you did not."

Focusing now on Mia, the count walked over to her and helped her to her feet. "Stand, Mia, and receive your punishment."

Mia stood feebly to her feet, clinging to Basarab's hand. Her face was damp with tears as she looked into the count's eyes.

"I sentence you to five years of exile to be served in my castle in Brasov. You will live there in seclusion. I will provide you with your studies, so you may finish your schooling, and with the nutrition you need to sustain your new life. The only person you will be able to see, besides my servants, will be your father, but only once a year. You will not see my son, nor will you ever be his bride. At the end of the five years, you will be released from your exile and given leave to live wherever your path takes you, but, I remind you again, it will not be with Santan!"

Basarab turned to the congregation of vampires. "If anyone here has anything to say against my decision, let them speak now. If no one speaks, let this sentence be written down and carried out forthwith."

The room was silent. Samara hid her smile, as did Dracula. Their plans were finally coming to fruition, and not because of anything they had done, but because of a foolish girl who had fallen in love with the heir to the vampire throne!

"May we return to our homes now?" Volodya spoke up, expressing the sentiment of most of the vampires in the room.

"Of course," Basarab replied. "As soon as we are assured

the police will not return and the way is clear for us all to get to our planes."

As the vampires began to file out of the room, the sound of several police sirens sounded beyond the walls of the house. Basarab looked at Angelique, and she knew what it was she had to do. Putting a cautionary hand up to delay the departure of the vampires, Basarab moved aside for Angelique to pass through.

Making her way quickly to the top of the house, Angelique transformed into a bird as soon as she exited onto the widow's walk. What she saw made her heart skip several beats. A number of police cars surrounded the house, in the parking lot and all along the street. The yard was filled with officers in full combat gear, all advancing toward the front door. Angelique's eyes narrowed in on the one leading the charge—Nathaniel!

Chapter Forty-one

Angelique thought to put a protection spell around the entire house, as she had done to the castle where she'd hidden Ákos, but that was in another country, in the mountains. This was in a city where there were too many people who would wonder why suddenly they couldn't approach the house.

Flying from end to end, as though she were pacing, Angelique tried desperately to think of a way to stop the police from entering. Nothing came to mind. Finally, she returned to the inside and made her way back to where the vampires were all waiting for news.

"It is not good," Angelique said, her face grave. I have put a protection spell on the door leading to the basement; the police will not be able to open it. The only one left up there right now is Viktor, and I suggest we get him out of there and bring him down here with us. That cop, Nathaniel, is ruthless, and I would not want Viktor to be at his mercy."

"I will fetch him," Dracula stated, and not waiting for approval, he bound up the stairs. Angelique released the spell on the door at the top, just long enough for Dracula to make it through.

Stepping through the door into the living room, Dracula looked around for Viktor. Not seeing him anywhere near, he went toward the kitchen area and was rewarded with the sight of the butler preparing boxes filled with bottles of blood. He turned as Dracula stepped into the room.

"Good … I could use some help getting these to the basement," Viktor stated, picking up one of the boxes. "I see we have visitors again, and I want to make sure you were all well-fed in case the police stay longer than we hope." He paused. "These are the last of the count's blood supply, and I have made sure all the empty bottles were cleaned. If found, the police will think they are simply empty wine bottles."

"Good thinking, Viktor," Dracula replied as he grabbed the other box. "Basarab wants you to remain with us in the basement."

"As you wish."

Dracula and Viktor made their way back to the living room, and Dracula knocked three times on the basement door. Angelique released the spell for them to get through, then cast it again. As they were heading down the stairs, a loud knock came to the front door, and a voice shouted out: "Police!"

The crash that sounded a few minutes later resonated through the basement, and the vampires all looked at each other, realizing they must remain together and stay calm until the police left.

Attila suggested they change rooms; there was a larger one down one more floor—the one where Santan's naming ceremony had been performed. It was next to the room where the coffins were stored, if they should have to hole up for any significant length of time.

"What should we do about Radu and Elizabeth?" Dracula asked, approaching Basarab.

"Keep them where they are, but take them a couple bottles to sustain them," Basarab replied. He turned to Kardos. "Do you mind?"

Kardos bowed his head. "Of course not."

As the vampires made their way down another flight of stairs, they could hear heavy footsteps above them and furniture being turned over. Basarab was furious at the intrusion and went over in his mind what he was going to do when he had that police officer on his own. Nathaniel would be sorry he ever set foot in Yates Castle!

"Count!" Kardos pushed his way through the crowded hallway. "Radu and Elizabeth are no longer in the room!"

"Impossible!" Basarab almost shouted, taking heed at the last moment for fear of being heard on the upper levels.

"They are not there," Kardos affirmed. He glanced over the vampires that were in the hallway and noticed another one was missing. "Where is Rasputin?" he asked, turning to the Russian group.

Volodya shook his head. "I have no idea. I last saw him when we heard the sirens."

Petya stepped forward. "I noticed Rasputin sneak out of the room and head down that way." Petya pointed in the direction of the room where Basarab had locked Radu and Elizabeth. "But I lost sight of him when everyone started milling around and thought no more of him," he added.

Basarab was unsettled by Rasputin's disappearance and by Radu's and Elizabeth's escape. Something told him the two were connected, but why? *How do they know each other? They can't have gone far; it is daytime. But to where? If Rasputin is involved, he has probably scoped the place out and will have them well hidden.*

The count looked to where Dracula was standing at the end of the procession. *Do you have something to do with this, uncle? I know there is bad blood between you and your brother ... did you help them escape or did you do something to make them disappear, taking it upon yourself to serve out your own justice? Since you didn't finish the job you were given to do all those years ago!* Dracula caught his nephew's eye. He smiled.

Once everyone was in the room in the deepest reaches of the basement, Basarab looked around for his son. He didn't need to look far; Santan was approaching him. "Father," Santan's voice sounded strained. "I'm able to get some of us out of here if you want me to. I'm not sure how many I can transport at a time, but we can start with a few, and I can return for others."

"Where would you take them?"

"I thought, since you lived here a long time ago, you might know of a safe location," Santan replied.

"There is one place," Basarab looked thoughtful as he contemplated the possibility. "The Olde School Restaurant is located outside the city and has a private room in the downstairs. I know the owner, Gus, and I don't think he would mind if we used it."

Santan bowed his head in acknowledgement. "Tell me where it is, and who you want me to take out of here first."

Basarab gave Santan directions to the restaurant and told him to take Virginia, Samara, and Mia first. "I'll accompany you on the first trip so I can speak with Gus about our need for privacy; but, I will return with you. I must see this through to the end, and if these cops do not leave after finding nothing upstairs, I may be forced to make them!"

Samara, overhearing her father saying she was to leave, came forward with a pout on her lips. "I'm not going anywhere without Lajos!"

Basarab was about to refute her but thought there would be no use arguing any point. His daughter was headstrong and trying to make her change her mind would only waste precious time. To Samara's amazement, her father turned away and approached his Aunt Emelia.

Emelia was not thrilled about leaving Vacaresti behind. However, he urged her to go. "I will join you soon, my love," he crooned in her ear before giving her a gentle nudge toward where Santan was standing.

"Ready?" Basarab asked Santan as he approached him with a reluctant Virginia and Mia.

"Ready." Santan directed everyone to hold hands and close their eyes. He squeezed his shut and envisioned the Olde School Restaurant, as his father had described it. The energy surged through his body, and within seconds the group was standing in the restaurant foyer.

Basarab noticed Gus' car parked beside the building. "I hope Gus is still here. I will just be a moment," he said as he made his way up the steps. A few minutes later, he returned with a smile on his face. "All set. We have the private room in the basement for as long as we need. No one will bother us; the door will be kept locked. I told Gus we were not in need of any food at this time."

After seeing Virginia, Emelia, and Mia settled in the room, Santan transported his father and himself back to Yates Castle.

Nathaniel was frustrated. The raid was not giving up anything of any value, and they had searched the entire upper levels of the house. Frankie was just as frustrated, but more with his partner than anything else. He still couldn't understand why Nathaniel was so set on taking the owner of the big house down!

"We need to check the basement, boys," Nathaniel barked as he headed to what he hoped was the door leading down to the lower levels. Just a closet. He moved on to the next possibility. Another closet.

The third door he opened led into a tunnel. "I think I've got something here," Nathaniel hollered. "Frankie, take a couple officers and check this out," he ordered.

Frankie looked down the tunnel. "Doesn't look like it's been used for years … full of cobwebs."

"Check it out anyway." Nathaniel's face was beet-red, a sign his blood pressure was up. *Think I'll quit this job once I finish this investigation … before I end up having a heart attack … maybe Frankie is right … even I don't have any idea what's in my craw about this count guy!* Nathaniel left Frankie at the entrance of the tunnel and moved on to check out more doors, still searching for a way to the basement level.

Frankie stepped gingerly into the narrow passageway, his flashlight barely breaking through the darkness. Only one officer followed him through. "Bloody hell," Frankie cursed as a mouse ran across in front of him. To his further surprise, the passage ended at the entrance of what looked like an old-fashioned school room.

"Creepy," Frankie's fellow officer commented as he shone his flashlight around.

"Yeah, but we may as well take a look about while we're here." Noticing something shiny on the floor in the far corner, Frankie made his way over to it. "Looks like someone was drinking here … maybe an old school teacher after hours," he laughed nervously as he picked up a wine bottle.

Taking a whiff of the inside of the bottle, Frankie wrinkled his nose. "What the fuck … this sure as hell doesn't smell like wine!" he exclaimed. Detecting something liquid still in the bottle, Frankie tipped it upside-down. As remnants of the bottle dripped onto his finger, he began to shake. "Blood!" he hollered over to his companion. "A bottle with blood in it? Boy oh boy … maybe Nathaniel is right!"

"Right about what?"

"Never mind," Frankie replied, not wanting to get into a conversation with another officer about Nathaniel's theory of a possible vampire living in the house. "We need to get this to Nathaniel, stat!" Frankie said, and not giving a moment for any further questions, he headed back into the passageway, wasting no time reaching the central part of the house.

"Where's Nathaniel?" Frankie asked sharply as he re-entered the living area.

An officer pointed to the next room. "In there, trying to open a door that doesn't want to budge an inch ... let me rephrase that ... actually, can't even get near it!" He paused. "This place gives me the creeps ... can't wait to get out of here!" he added, turning on his heel and heading into another room, one closer to the front door.

Frankie approached Nathaniel guardedly, noting the fowl look on his partner's face. "Something to show you." Frankie held the bottle out to Nathaniel. "Found this in a little schoolroom at the end of the passageway." A pregnant pause. "Not wine in the bottle, but definitely the residue of something ... ah ... something you aren't going to believe ... ah ... blood, I think." Frankie waited to see his superior's reaction to the revelation.

At first, Nathaniel just stared at the bottle, then slowly, he took hold of it and sniffed at the opening. His nose screwed up in disgust. He tipped the bottle, and a drop of the liquid from within fell on his finger. "You're right, rookie; it is blood." And then, with a crooked smirk, "Believe me now?" Coming nose to nose, "This is our secret; I don't want anyone else knowing what you found. You didn't tell the other guy what was in the bottle, did you?"

Frankie looked away when he answered. "Sort of."

Nathaniel kicked the wall, leaving a large, black scuff mark on the paint. "Well, I'll just explain to him that you have an over-vivid imagination and all that was in the bottle was some stale wine. Get this bottle out to our cruiser and put it in the trunk. I'll decide what to do with it later."

The police captain received a call about the raid on Yates Castle just as he was about to go for a walk. It had been a long day with the investigation of the body found on the castle property. When he'd left work, he thought the issue was over. The body was in the morgue. There was no one home at the castle except the butler and the woman Angelique, and she had left for the airport. And now, he got a call on his cell that Nathaniel had taken it upon himself to get a warrant somehow—not from Judge Harris——and was raiding the count's house. Basarab was going to be furious when he found out!

Markus quickly dialled Judge Harris' number.

"Who the hell is calling me at the supper hour?" a gruff, pissed-off voice came over the receiver after the seventh ring.

"We have a problem, judge." Markus cleared the catch in his throat before continuing. "Nathaniel is raiding Yates Castle as we speak."

"He's what!" Judge Harris gripped his phone tightly, as though he were squeezing the life out of the wayward cop. "Get over there, Markus, and take control of the situation. Get Nathaniel and whoever he's dragged into this witch hunt of his, out of there! Pronto! Have I made myself clear?"

"Yes, extremely."

"I'll call Samuel and let him know what's going on," the judge added before hanging up.

On the way to Yates Castle, Markus went over a few scenarios of how to handle Nathaniel. He hated to demean a good officer in front of other cops, but Nathaniel had stepped over far too many lines of late. Maybe it was time to let him go from the precinct; he was close to retirement age, it wouldn't be difficult to arrange.

Stepping inside the house, Markus was appalled at the sight. The team had been anything but careful with their search. The captain called to an officer: "Get me Nathaniel!" he roared.

A couple minutes later, Nathaniel appeared, Frankie on his heels. Markus didn't wait for any sort of greeting; he dove right in with his mission to get the police out of the house: "Pack this up, officer! You've no right to be here!"

Nathaniel opened his mouth to reply, but Markus shut him down. "I don't know why you thought this was a good idea without consulting me first, and at the moment, I don't care! Pack it up and get out of here," he repeated, "And, I'll see you in my office first thing in the morning!" With that, leaving no room for negotiation, Markus turned and stormed out the door.

Most of the officers heard their captain and were hurriedly packing up to leave. Nathaniel was sullen and quiet. He hated it when his ideas were overridden by someone who didn't have a real clue about what was really going on.

"Close the door on your way out," he threw back to Frankie. "I'll meet you in the car."

Frankie looked around to make sure everyone was out of the house before he made his way to the foyer. As he was about to close the door, he noticed a bird sitting on a cage by the window. "You, again," he mumbled, then shut the door quickly and hurried across the lawn to his waiting partner.

Sure that all the police were gone, Angelique smiled as she transformed back to her human self and headed down to the basement to report to the count.

Chapter Forty-two

The majority of the vampires wanted to stay and refused to take shelter at the Olde School Restaurant until the police issue blew over. However, Basarab insisted his father and Randy leave.

"I need someone with a level head to watch over my wife and Mia," Basarab explained when his father showed some resistance. "And Randy. Despite Captain Markus' intervention, I do not trust that the police won't be back, plus, with Radu, Elizabeth, and Rasputin missing, I must remain here until we discover where they are. Those are three vampires I do not wish to have roaming around this city!"

Attila finally gave in, despite being hesitant to leave Angelique behind. "My wife…"

"I need her here," Basarab cut his father off quickly. "She is my eyes during the daylight hours should we have any more visitors."

Angelique stood by the count as Santan transported Attila and Randy to the restaurant. Basarab looked down at the woman who had captured his father's heart and saw the pained expression in her eyes. He laid a hand on her shoulder; she looked up at him.

"Basarab, there is something I must tell you, but in private?"

"Follow me," Basarab instructed, moving toward the door. Once in the hallway, he made his way to an alcove in the passageway and pointed to the bench there. "What is bothering you, Angelique?" he asked as he sat down.

"I know that dreams are dreams, Basarab, and, under most circumstances, they are not real … just figments of our daily lives trying to sort themselves out." Angelique hesitated, then drew in a deep breath. "However, I am having a recurring dream, and it is becoming more vivid. My sister, Tanyasin, is in it, and she is always warning me about the greatest sorceress that has ever lived, who is coming to claim what is hers. I have seen an immense stone fortress, set well within the heart of the Transylvanian mountains.

"The last dream I had, just two days ago, I saw the sorceress! And she, despite looking young and beautiful—almost an innocent air about her—she terrified me! Her eyes were penetrating as she stared directly at me; her smile was malevolent, and her voice, when she finally spoke, held no sweetness in the words—only malicious intent. She said she was coming soon and nothing was going to stop her from taking what was rightfully hers!" Angelique glanced at the floor, her shoulders slumped in defeat. Looking back up into Basarab's eyes, pain riddling her voice, "I do not know if I am strong enough to protect the family against one such as I saw in my dreams!"

Basarab sat beside Angelique, going over in his mind the similarities of her dreams to the visions Ilias had that were relayed to him. Basarab believed in dreams and the reality of them. When he and Virginia had been separated after Santan's birth, while he was in Transylvania and she in Brantford, their connection was kept open by dreams. He patted Angelique on her knee, stood, and headed back to the room where the vampires were awaiting further instructions. Angelique lingered a few moments, then followed.

Attila embraced his grandson before Santan returned to his father. "Watch your father's back, Santan. I fear there is more tragedy coming his way." Attila lowered his head and whispered so the others couldn't hear what he was saying. "Angelique told me about the dreams she is having," Attila said. He briefly told Santan what the dreams were about, then, "If they are true, Basarab will need you, and if things go badly, get him out of there; bring him here. Bring as many of the loyal vampires as you can; leave your father no choice in the matter—just do it.

"There is strength in numbers, Santan; make sure you utilize those powers, including Samara's. Convince her it is in everyone's best interest to defeat this tempest that may be coming. I fear it is a storm like we have never before experienced." Attila placed his arm around Santan's shoulders. "We await your return. May our ancestors of Wallachia protect you and keep you all safe."

Leaving Santan, Attila walked to where Virginia, Mia, Emelia, and Randy stood watching. After her son was gone, Virginia turned to Attila. "Is all well?"

"All will be well," he replied. "We must have faith in those we love and those who love us and will stand by our side, no matter the consequences. For now, we wait, my dear."

Rasputin, Radu, and Elizabeth hid in the corner of the courtyard of Yates Castle, which was shaded from the sun by overhanging branches of some large trees. Rasputin had managed to get out of the basement before Angelique put the spell on the door. Despite the police searching the house, he'd made his way to the outside door, and just in time. Luckily, the law enforcement officers hadn't bothered with the door leading to the outside enclosure and Rasputin hoped they would leave before he took Radu and Elizabeth back in the castle and up to the roof where they were to meet Adrianna.

"When is she going to be here?" Elizabeth asked Rasputin, her eyes glowing maliciously.

"Soon. I believe enough chaos has been created to confuse this regime, and they will have no idea what is coming at them when our mistress confronts them." Rasputin rubbed his hands in delight. He'd never had allegiance to anyone in particular, other than whom he saw to be the most powerful to raise him up to the glory he felt he deserved for his loyalty.

Radu leaned against the large wooden door—the same one Virginia had tried to get out of on her first escape attempt from the house. He smiled mockingly. "Personally, I cannot wait to see my beloved brother's face once he realizes Adrianna is coming specifically for him!" Radu's smile turned into laughter. "And when the pup's son realizes the throne, which has been his from the time of his birth, will not be passed to his son!"

"Why did the Gypsy curse Attila's son with the leadership?" Elizabeth pondered. "Her issues were with Dracula, as I understand it."

"Ah, Elizabeth, my love, do you not see what an affront that was for a man such as my brother? A man who was used to ruling, to being the leader of men? To have his young cousin's unborn child rule in his stead? Tanyasin knew what she was doing."

"What she didn't know, though," Rasputin added, "was about Dracula's love child, the one he made with the same witch who gave Tanyasin the means to curse him. The child who now seeks revenge for her mother's abandonment by Dracula, and for what she deems to be her birthright—the throne!"

Adrianna was ready to make her move. She gathered her super-rogues together, giving them last-minute instructions. "We leave tonight. Count Basarab's life is in turmoil; Rasputin has caused enough trouble to ensure the count's people are busy trying to put out a big fire. They will not be expecting us; they will not be expecting another conflict to be on their doorstep so soon."

The rogues grunted and started stamping their feet in anticipation of what was to come. Adrianna controlled their minds through telepathy, and not one of them ever questioned her authority—they were unable to speak.

"Prepare to be ready by the time the sun sets, and meet me back here," Adrianna instructed, then turned and left the room.

Entering her private quarters, she went straight to where her mother's portrait hung. She looked up into her mother's eyes as tears escaped her own. "It is time, Mama. Tonight I will have my retribution—your revenge. I will bring down the arrogant bastard that used you and then refused to even acknowledge your existence. Tonight, I will strike down Dracula, and he will be no more. I will burn his body and scatter his ashes on our mountain. And, when I am finished with him, I will deal with Basarab and his family, and they will either accept me as the true leader of the vampire world or they will join Dracula."

Adrianna wiped away her tears and blew a kiss to her mother's picture. Before leaving her room, she walked to the massive fireplace that took up an entire wall. It wasn't a real fireplace—Adrianna had no need to heat her fortress—however, behind the wall was a world unto itself, the place she kept all her spell books and potions. She murmured a slow chant, the secret code to open the wall.

Once inside the secret chamber, Adrianna went directly to her altar, which was laden with several decanters filled with various herbs and liquids. Her hand hovered over them until she saw the one she wanted. Selecting it, she poured some of the liquid into a marble bowl. Adrianna took a knife and slit her wrist, dripping blood into the bowl. As the two liquids combined, the fluid bubbled and steam rose, filling the room with a unique odour.

Adrianna chanted as she clasped the bowl in her hands. Her head swung around in a frenzy as her voice rose to a deafening crescendo. Finally, she quieted, raised the bowl to her lips and drank the contents. Her body quivered as the power of the concoction swept through her. With a keening shriek, Adrianna fell to the floor.

Moments passed as the sorceress lay there, comatose. Finally, her eyes opened. She stood and made her way to a mirror beside the altar. She smirked at her reflection, at the beauty she conjured, at her eyes that burned vehemently, the flames within them a rainbow of red, orange, and yellow.

Adrianna turned and left her secret cavity, waved her arms at the fireplace, and the wall closed. It was time to move. Her rogues would be waiting for her … Rasputin, Radu, and Elizabeth would be waiting for her … Dracula's time was almost up … Adrianna's was about to begin!

Chapter Forty-three

antan walked directly to his father when he returned from delivering Randy and Attila to the restaurant. "A word, Father," he pointed to the far corner, which was empty. Once out of earshot of the rest of the vampires, "Attila told me about Angelique's dreams; we need to prepare for this sorceress that is supposed to be coming. I suggest we tell everyone and stress the importance of standing together when she arrives."

Basarab nodded. He glanced over at the vampires, who had all broken off in small groups. "It might be a hard sell for some, but we can only do our best and hope our combined powers will be enough for whatever this creature is bringing. I would feel much better if we knew where Rasputin and Radu and Elizabeth are. Something tells me Rasputin is in league with the sorceress, and the appearance of Dracula's brother and Bathory … nothing about any of this is a coincidence."

"I totally agree." Santan returned. He kept to himself his grandfather's instructions about an escape plan should things get really ugly. "Shall we?" he moved aside so his father could take the lead.

Judge Harris was on the warpath when Captain Markus told him about the raid on Count Basarab's house. He picked up his phone and dialled Samuel's number and filled the retired administrator in on what Nathaniel had done.

Samuel shivered at the thought of what the count might do because of such an affront to his property. "What did the count do?" he asked.

"Apparently, the count was not present and the officer already knew he wouldn't be. Nathaniel went in anyway with an entire team."

"Did they find anything that might incriminate the count or any other member of his family in any of the crimes committed?" Samuel asked.

"Nothing, to my knowledge; however, we do have the body of another homeless person down in the morgue. We've had this one put into a locked drawer and have an officer guarding it. No one is going to tamper with this body!" the judge informed.

Samuel was puzzled, having forgotten about the circumstances of the first victim. "What do you mean by 'tamper with this body'?"

"Well, if you recall, the first body—Old Vincent—was drained of blood when the ambulance picked him up from behind the Station Coffee House; however, later in the morgue, while he was still on the table, miraculously his body filled with blood. And then, as you know, he sat up and asked for a drink. This new corpse was also drained of blood, and we aren't taking any chances of letting anyone near it," Judge Harris explained.

A low whistle reverberated over the phone line. "Are you suggesting some sort of sorcery might be involved here?" he asked, being reminded of the weirdness of the initial situation.

"How else would you explain such a phenomenon?" the judge inquired. "Besides, we know who, or should I say *what*, the count really is, don't we?"

The line was silent for a moment. Both men were unsure of whether to go there. Their knowledge of Count Basarab was a well-kept secret, and by the look of what was happening in their sleepy little city, that secret was about to be blown wide open unless they could do something to stop it quickly.

"What's Markus going to do about his out-of-control cop?" Samuel reignited the conversation.

Judge Harris coughed and cleared his throat. "Firing his bloody ass, I hope. Hang on, I have another line coming in … Markus … I'll call you back, Samuel." Pushing the link button, "Markus, hope you have some good news for me," the judge barked into the receiver.

"Only that I got Nathaniel's team out of the house. Place was dead as a cemetery on a dark night; I've got no idea what has gotten into Nathaniel, but I told him to be in my office first thing in the morning. Don't worry, your honour, I'll get to the bottom of this and if I have to let him go to stop him, I'll find a way!"

"What about the rookie?"

"He's not going to be a problem. I actually think, from the relieved look on his face when I got to the house and ordered everyone out, he was pretty happy."

"Okay, call me in the morning after you've dealt with Nathaniel." Judge Harris hung up and then sent a quick email to Samuel, letting him know what was going on. He didn't feel like talking about the subject anymore; his bed was calling him.

"I have something urgent to say to everyone," Basarab began when he and Santan rejoined the congregated vampires. "First of all, if what I am about to reveal to you troubles you enough that you do not wish to remain here, do not hesitate to speak up. Santan will transport you to safety with the ones who have already left. Does everyone agree to this?"

There were several nods of agreement and no one spoke up to say no.

"Good. Now, I ask Angelique to tell everyone about her dreams."

Ildiko couldn't help herself: "You're basing your assumption that something horrible is going to happen here on this witch's dreams?" she chided.

"I am." Basarab's eyes narrowed menacingly, "and I suggest you listen to what she has to say."

Angelique stepped forward and related to the crowd what was in her dreams. When she finished, she said: "I understand if some of you are wary about this situation—possible situation—but I assure you all, this dream was more than real. There have been rumours of a great sorceress in the mountains of Transylvania for centuries; my own sister told me of her with her dying breaths."

Angelique turned to Ilias. "I believe the woman you met in the mountains, on those two occasions, was the sorceress, and your experiences collaborate my dreams. I think she needed something from you to finish her plans." Looking now to the Russian vampires, "I believe Rasputin is in league with the sorceress, doing her bidding—Radu and Elizabeth, as well. I have a feeling it might have been Rasputin who planted the dead body on Basarab's property, which was meant to distract us and cause us more distress.

"I am sure Rasputin has been feeding the sorceress information about what is going on here with the trial, but I also believe she has a way to keep her own eyes on her ultimate goal. Exactly what that goal is, I do not know. What I do know is she said nothing was going to stop her from taking what was rightfully hers!" Angelique finished with.

"Thank you, Angelique, for this warning and for all you have been doing, and are still doing to protect this family. Is there anyone here who now wishes to leave?" Basarab asked.

Volodya stepped forward. "I wish for my son and daughter to be transported out of here," he stated. "My wife and I will stay and fight by your side."

"I wish my son to join Petya and Manya," Ilias said. Délia nodded her agreement.

Ákos opened his mouth to protest, but his mother threw him a look that said "shut it!" He looked at Samara and noticed the smirk on her face. Manya saw him focus on the temptress, and her face flushed with anger.

"Anyone else?" Basarab asked quickly, noticing what was going on amongst the younger vampires, and not wanting anything to escalate.

Everyone was quiet. "Very well, Santan, please take Petya, Manya, and Ákos to the restaurant. The rest of you, follow me," Basarab ordered, leaving and heading for the room filled with coffins. He cared not at this point if the cops showed up again. If they did, he was angry enough to deal with them—any way he had to.

Nathaniel walked into Captain Markus' office as he'd been instructed to do. Markus noticed immediately the large chip on his officer's shoulder.

"Sit down," Markus ordered. Tapping his fingers on the arms of his chair, "What do you think you were doing by raiding Count Basarab's home, Nathaniel?"

Nathaniel leaned forward in his chair, his eyes red from lack of sleep, his face flushed with anger. "Have you forgotten, captain, there was a dead body found on the count's property? That's what I was doing—investigating a murder, and I thought the best place to start would be with the people in that house, despite being told they'd left. I didn't believe a word that came out of that woman's mouth!

"Did you know there was one door in the house we couldn't get near? Like it was being blocked by an invisible barrier of some sort," Nathaniel scowled and reached into his coat pocket. "I wasn't going to use this, but under the circumstances, I believe you need to see what's inside it!" Nathaniel handed his captain the bottle.

"What's this?" Markus asked turning the bottle over in his hands. "Just an old wine bottle."

"Is it? It was found in one of the rooms in the house … no, let me clarify … it was found in a room we got to through a secret passage, and Frankie said it looked as if it used to be a schoolroom a long time ago. There's still some residue in it … check it out, captain, and tell me what you think it is. Then we'll talk some more about why I raided the count's house!"

Markus' eyebrows rose questioningly as he sniffed at the bottle's lip. He tipped the bottle over his hand, allowing some of the remaining liquid to drip out. "What the?!" Markus looked bewildered. "Is this blood?"

"As sure as I'm sitting here!" Nathaniel stood and walked behind his chair. He leaned on its back and glared at Markus. "I've been a cop a long time, and I've developed a great intuition about things over the years. One thing I know, when I feel there's something amiss, I'm usually right."

With Markus' knowledge about the count, he knew Nathaniel was telling the truth, but he couldn't acknowledge that. And what could he do about it? His understanding was that Basarab was not there anymore. His police force had no jurisdiction in the count's home country. In fact, they had no real proof the count had anything to do with the old man's murder, despite the body being drained of blood. Markus didn't think it was the count's style to go after homeless people and drain their blood.

"What's your orders now, captain?" Nathaniel interfered with Markus' musings. "Do I have your permission to return to the house?"

Markus got up from his chair and walked over to his window and stared out into the parking lot. Turning back to Nathaniel, "Give me some time to think about this … for now, stay in the precinct until I call you."

Nathaniel nodded and left the office. Frankie was standing outside the door. "What do we do?" he asked.

"We wait at our desks for further instructions."

Markus picked up his phone and dialled Judge Harris. His secretary said the judge was headed to court and wouldn't be available until late afternoon; he had a full docket today. He called Samuel next and got his answering machine.

"Shit!"

Not being able to get hold of either of them, Markus sent the judge and Samuel an email. Then, he sat back and waited for a reply, filling his morning with menial tasks, and telling his receptionist he was not to be bothered.

Chapter Forty-four

Adrianna landed on the widow's walk, her rogues surrounding her. Their tongues flicked in and out, anticipating the bloodbath their mistress had promised them. Adrianna walked to the door that led into the house and ripped it from its hinges. With a mighty force, she thrust it off the roof. Purposefully, she entered the house, followed by her entourage. On their way along the upper hallway, they met Rasputin, Radu, and Elizabeth, who had managed to leave the courtyard and make their way to the upper part of the house.

"Is all ready?" Adrianna asked Rasputin.

"Yes, mistress," Rasputin bowed.

"Are they still in the basement?"

"Yes, mistress."

"Good … showdown time!"

Basarab was taking no chances. He felt in his bones that evil was on its way—soon—and he didn't want to be caught inside the house. He told those who were willing to stand with him that now that darkness was upon them, they would take the battle, if there was going to be one, to a place of their choosing. His choice was the massive yard, under the light of the full moon.

Outside Yates Castle, Basarab circled the entrance of the building with his followers. They were all dressed in long black cloaks, which they'd retrieved from the coffin room. Santan stood by his father's side, as did Samara. The air around them reeked with anticipation.

Angelique appeared in front of Basarab. "She is here," the Gypsy informed.

"How many are with her?" Basarab asked.

"Besides the three already in the castle—Rasputin, Radu, and Elizabeth—she has twelve rogues with her. However, these rogues are like none I have ever seen before. They don't even look human—just sexless, transparent creatures wearing nothing but a layer of skin over bones. The only thing about them that appears alive is their eyes, which gleamed brightly in the hollows of their sockets."

"And the sorceress? How does she look?"

"Bewitchingly beautiful, like in my dreams."

Basarab sighed. "They are all inside the house now, and together?"

"Yes. Rasputin has taken them to the dining room. The rogues are in a frenzy, stamping their feet, groaning, slapping their chests, ready for battle."

"As are we," Basarab replied through clenched teeth. "As are we. It will only be a matter of time before she realizes we are not inside the house, that *we* have chosen the battlefield. When she comes, we will be ready."

The count smiled. Angelique's invisible cloak around the perimeters of the house had worked. The sorceress had no idea where the vampires had gone. However, it would only be a matter of time before she figured it out.

Markus didn't receive a reply from the judge until late afternoon, just as he was preparing to go home. His secretary informed him it was Judge Harris on the phone and asked if he wanted to take the call. Markus grabbed his receiver: "Finally! What took you so long?"

Judge Harris snorted derisively. "I was in court," came the curt reply. "So, your officer found a bottle with some blood in it," the judge proceeded right to the point of the situation. "So what! We already know what Basarab is, and I am sure we are smart enough to realize whoever is in that house with him—*was* in the house—is of the same persuasion. Leave it alone, Markus. I don't want to stir up a situation I don't think we'll be able to control, let alone win. Have I made myself clear here?"

"Yes, judge." Markus could feel his blood pressure rising. The judge had always been the one to call the shots, and at the moment it was pissing Markus off. Nathaniel had convinced him enough something was going on in the big house that needed further investigation, and he knew of no way to stop such a thing from happening, short of firing his detective.

"It was just a homeless man," the judge was saying, drawing Markus back to the conversation. "No one is going to miss him. Sweep this one under the carpet, Markus. Let the count go if he hasn't already left."

"Sir!" The police dispatcher burst into Markus' office. "There's a 911 call from one of the houses in the neighbourhood of Yates Castle. They are saying a crowd of weird people dressed in capes is surrounding the entrance of the place. They also said some weird noises were coming from inside the house and asked if we could send a couple cruisers to investigate. The woman sounded quite agitated on the phone. Mentioned she is alone with her four children and is afraid something is about to happen." The dispatcher stood waiting for an order to either proceed with the request or ignore it.

Markus lifted a finger, indicating to the dispatcher to wait. He returned to his conversation with Judge Harris. "We have a 911 call from someone living near Yates Castle. Something's going down there; we need to send some cruisers. Sorry, your honour … this is police business now." Markus shut the phone off and threw it on his desk. Turning to the dispatcher, "I'll take it from here."

Leaving his office, Markus headed straight to Nathaniel's desk. "We have a call; bring the rookie. I'll take my own car and meet you there."

Frankie looked at his captain, puzzled. It had been a long, dreary day having to sit doing desk duty. "Meet you where?"

"Where do you think, rookie?" Nathaniel answered for Markus. "This old nose of mine is never wrong. We're heading to Yates Castle to finish what we started—to arrest a killer! Am I assuming correctly, captain?"

Markus nodded. "All I know at this point is there's a ruckus of some kind going on in the yard, and a neighbour phoned in a complaint. We need to investigate."

Adrianna was frustrated at finding the house empty. She whirled around furiously, attacking Rasputin: "Where are they? Where is Dracula?"

Rasputin swallowed nervously. He knew from personal experience that one did not toy with the great sorceress. "I don't know, Mistress. They were all in the basement when I went to assist Radu and Elizabeth. I heard them say they were going down to another level; I assumed that is where they remained, hiding."

"Well, it appears you have assumed wrong!" Adrianna hissed. She raised her head and sniffed the air. "They passed this way not long ago, a great number of them. Follow me," she ordered and set off in the direction the scent was leading her.

The closer Adrianna got to the front door, the stronger the scent was. She opened it and stepped out onto the veranda. Looking down the stone stairway, the sorceress screamed out: "Dracula! You coward! Show yourself to me!"

Basarab looked at his uncle, surprise etched on his face. "It is *you* this sorceress comes for?"

Dracula, himself, was confused. "I have no idea why she comes for me. If it is the throne she is after, it should be you she calls for, nephew."

"Yet, it is your name she called out." Basarab turned to Angelique. "Remove the cloak, and let this woman see who she is up against."

Chapter Forty-five

drianna laughed when she saw the group of vampires in the yard at the bottom of the stairway. "So, you have chosen the field of battle?" she hollered out. "It will not matter where you fight me; I will win. It is my destiny."

Basarab stepped forward. "Who are you, and what is it you want from us?"

Adrianna ignored the count and zeroed in on Ilias. "Ah, there you are, Ilias. Do you remember me? I saved you twice when you were lost in the mountains. Is this how you repay me? By standing with this sorry lot?"

Ilias began to shake, recognizing the sorceress and remembering what he'd endured at her hands. Délia noticed her husband falter, and she laid a hand on his arm. "Be brave, husband. Stay with us."

The rogues, standing behind Adrianna, started stamping their feet and slapping their chests. The sound echoed eerily into the early evening. Adrianna raised her hand sharply, ceasing their movements. She motioned for them to place themselves along the stairs, six on each side. Radu and Elizabeth flanked her, and Rasputin skulked in the shadows, as was his custom.

"I am here for what is rightfully mine," Adrianna began.

"And what is it you think is yours?" Dracula stepped forward and cut her off before she could continue. His eyes blazed, and his hands clenched into fists, ready for battle.

Adrianna laughed again. "What is mine? What is mine? Dare *you* ask, Dracula? Do you not recognize your own blood?"

There wasn't much that could daunt Dracula, but Adrianna's statement took him by surprise. "What do you mean, woman? I don't know you!"

Running her tongue along her lips, savouring the moment, Adrianna chuckled. Then her face turned as hard as the granite on the mountain where she lived. "Do you remember the beautiful woman who found you dying on a mountain centuries ago?"

"I have met numerous beautiful women…" Dracula began.

"But this one," Adrianna cut Dracula off this time, "nursed you back to health. She sat by your side for days, for weeks, caring for you. And she fell in love with you—made love to you, and you to her, so she thought. Do you remember yet?"

Dracula dug deep into his past, and suddenly, as though someone turned a light on, he remembered. His lips curled into a sardonic grin. "Ah, yes, now I recall. She was a witch, I believe. She bewitched me into her bed and took advantage of me while I was yet unable to move well."

"Oh, you moved well enough to take my mother and release your seed into her belly!" Adrianna's eyes flamed, and her voice trembled with rage.

Dracula didn't miss a beat. "So you are my daughter?" Dracula shook his head. "I think not. I would know."

"How would you know, mighty Dracula? When my mother travelled to your castle to inform you of her condition, you spurned her. You didn't even deign to show your face. You sent your servant back with a horse that was supposed to pacify my mother, and she was told to go on her way and never set foot on your land again! Do you remember that, Dracula? Do you remember a woman coming to your gates, begging to see you?

"My mother was in love with you. You were the first man she truly loved; however, seeing you now as you are, I don't know what she saw in you. You are not handsome like your brother, Radu, here," Adrianna taunted.

Dracula's laughter filled the area. "Handsome! Like my traitor brother! Your mother would not have received much pleasure from him; he prefers boys!" he goaded.

Radu glared at Dracula and attempted to move down the stairs. Adrianna put a hand on his arm: "Not yet," she hissed.

Dracula took another step forward, looking up at the sorceress. "What is it you really want here, woman?"

"You call me a woman, yet not daughter … not my sweet child … not my heart. I came for you, father dearest! I came for you, and for the throne. My mother told me all about you, and she told me the part she played in the curse on your bloodline, the same curse that afflicted me! Did you know that? Did you know the Gypsy, Tanyasin, came and exchanged her great beauty for a curse on you, for revenge for what you did to her husband and son—impaling them on stakes? My mother didn't realize who it was Tanyasin was going to curse.

"So, Father, I was born before the curse, but being of your blood, I became part of it. My mother soon learned what was happening to the mighty Dracul family, and she did everything possible to protect me. But I had other plans, right from the beginning. I begged my mother to teach me all she knew, and I embraced her spells and magic as though it were a second set of clothing. Mother told me I was going to be more powerful than any witch she had ever known, and my power was escalated by the fact I had your blood flowing through me—vampire blood.

"I experimented with my mother's spells, creating many new ones of my own. I nursed my mother when she fell ill, into a deep depression with no end to it. She pined away her final days, longing for just one more sight of you. Longing to be held in your arms again, something she believed would save her. She took her last breaths longing for you, Father!"

Adrianna's voice rose to a shriek. "I swore on my mother's deathbed to avenge her. Oh, she begged me not to … she whispered to let it go, she was happy to sleep forever. I had the power to bring her back if I wanted to—if she wanted me to, but she shook her head and said no; I was to let her go, let her die! She died still loving you, Dracula! She died of a broken heart!"

Numerous vampires behind Dracula were getting restless, wondering where this was going. Basarab stepped forward beside his uncle, Santan and Samara close behind him. Angelique flanked Dracula on the other side.

Adrianna's lips curled into a snarl. "*These* are your soldiers now, great Dracula? The son of the pup who stood by your side? His half-human children? And you," Adrianna pointed at Angelique, "the sister of Tanyasin! How could you betray your sister by running with this lot she cursed? You think you have enough power to defeat me?"

Basarab moved another step forward. "Angelique may not be able to vanquish you, but as you can see, she is not alone!"

"And neither am I!" Adrianna's voice was filled with mirth. "Now, let us get down to business, shall we? All I want is the throne, which I believe is rightfully mine. After all, I am the daughter of the cursed one, the one who should have been on the throne all these centuries! What say you to that, Basarab? Are you willing to step aside to avoid bloodshed?"

Samara had heard enough. The fury inside her was building, despite trying to keep it under some semblance of control. "The throne will never be yours, bastard bitch!" she bellowed. "My great-uncle does not sit on the throne, my father does—the Count Basarab Musat. Only one of his children will follow in his footsteps, and only when he is ready to step down!"

Basarab looked at his daughter, gaining new respect for his wayward child.

Adrianna studied the young vampire challenging her. "Samara, isn't it? You and your brother are no match for me. Tell her, Lajos … tell her, and the mighty vampire warrior, Ildiko, and the one who crossed you over—my beloved father—tell them all where your true allegiance lies!"

Samara swung around, glaring at Lajos. "You are a traitor? You have dared to use me when you are in league with this demon?"

"You loved every minute spent with me, didn't you temptress?" But the grin on Lajos' face vanished as Samara attacked, shocking everyone.

Lajos was thrown across the lawn and Samara was on him before he could recover his feet, ripping his throat open with her teeth. Adrianna screeched to her rogues, and two of them flew to where Samara and Lajos were fighting. Mayhem broke loose as Kardos and Volodya flew up to intercept the rogues.

The sound of sirens echoed through the night, and two police cruisers screeched into the back parking lot. However, the bloodbath they witnessed from the top of the garden stairs was out of their reach. Try as they did, the barrier Angelique had constructed held them fast in place.

"My God!" Frankie exclaimed. "Is this for real? I thought they left."

"Apparently not," Nathaniel retorted. "Believe me now, rookie?" he added sarcastically. "We better call for more backup, captain."

Markus shook his head, horrified by what was before him. "Let it go, Nathaniel. There is nothing we can do here, no matter how many men we bring, we'll not defeat what is happening down there!" He returned to his car and placed a call to Judge Harris, filling him in on what was taking place at Yates Castle. The judge agreed with Markus and told the captain to call him when it was all over.

Despite Kardos and Volodya trying to assist Samara, they didn't reach her in time to prevent her from being attacked by the rogues. From the top of the stairs, Adrianna raised her arms and began to chant. As she did, the rest of the rogues attacked. Radu and Elizabeth zeroed in on Basarab and Dracula, and Rasputin flew toward Vasilisa, the Russian queen. He wanted a taste of her blood, remembering how many times she had scorned him.

Adrianna eyed Santan, then made her move to take out the current heir to the throne. To her surprise, when she landed where he was standing, he'd disappeared. She felt a tap on her shoulder, and when she whipped around, she came face to face with not a mild, meek young vampire, but one filled with rage and strength.

"Call off your rogues before you all die," Santan ordered.

"Never!" She attacked, but once again, Santan slipped through her fingers. She looked around to see how her army was faring, noticing a couple of them lying on the ground, not moving. But there were a couple of Basarab's vampires lying still, as well. The battle was not over. Still, she could not see where the vampire heir had gone.

Samara and Lajos were at it again, but Samara was winning over her lover, her fury besting him. Lajos had no idea just how powerful the temptress was, but he was finding out quickly. As she whirled around and around, Samara created a wind tunnel, which she whipped at Lajos, knocking him off his feet again. She dove in for the kill, this time ensuring her goal by ripping his head off and throwing it into the bushes at the side of the castle. Looking upward to the moon, Samara howled her victory—a howl which gave added courage to the vampires.

Basarab laughed as Elizabeth attacked him. He thrust out his arm, grasping hold of her neck, lifting her off the ground. As he squeezed his nails into her flesh, she snarled at him.

"Is this all you have, Count Basarab?" she mocked, bringing her hands up in an attempt to wrest the count from her throat.

Throwing her onto one of the statues, Basarab advanced on her, but she recovered quickly and stood to face him. Her tongue flicked in and out of her mouth as she delivered her message. "How is that pretty wife of yours, Basarab? Have you hidden her somewhere safe? She was so sweet, so juicy—Peter told me. And she loved every minute of what he did to her. I was so disappointed when you arrived just before it was my turn with her, but I shall not have to wait long now. Adrianna promised me I could have her all to myself as soon as she takes the throne."

Basarab tolerated Elizabeth's mocking long enough to allow him a good view of the main artery in her neck when she threw back her head and laughed at him. He moved in for the kill, catching her off-guard, tearing into her throat! Basarab grabbed hold of her head and twisted. "You will never touch Virginia again, and this time there will be no one to save you, Elizabeth Bathory!" With a final jerk, Elizabeth's head severed completely. Another victory howl echoed into the night, and with the smell of fresh blood in his nostrils, Basarab went to the aid of his friends.

Dracula and Radu faced off, centuries of hatred for each other gleaming in their eyes. Dracula, always the more powerful of the two brothers, flexed his muscles. "I do not wish to kill you brother, but I will this time if you force my hand."

"Why didn't you kill me when you had the chance all those years ago?" Radu asked as he circled around his prey.

"You need to ask why? You are my brother. I promised our father to look after you."

"You did a fine job of that in the Turkish court, didn't you?" Radu's lips twisted with scorn.

"You think you were the only one to suffer hardships there? You know nothing of what I endured. Where do you think I learned the techniques I used to win my battles, and how to punish those who betrayed me? It wasn't from *watching* our captors!" Dracula hissed. "Getting bum-fucked by a Turkish prince and his friends was nothing compared to the tortures I lived through!" he added.

Radu drew in his breath at the memories Dracula was recapping. He knew his brother spoke the truth; the prince had told him repeatedly how lucky he was to be living in the lap of luxury while Dracula lived in a hovel of torture. However, something triggered in his head, hardening his resolve to destroy his brother for Adrianna, his beautiful niece—his mistress. With his head down, he attacked, driving into Dracula's stomach.

Dracula, taken by surprise, fell to the ground, but recovered quickly, casting Radu across the yard. "So be it, brother," he muttered as he flew across the yard, going in for the kill. "No mercy this time!"

However, before Dracula could strike Radu, Adrianna met him in mid-air. "Not now, father dearest!" she shouted, slashing at him and drawing blood on his face.

The two dropped to the ground and began to circle. Radu got to his feet and staggered toward Dracula, with the intention of helping Adrianna. She waved him off. "He's mine! Help the others," she ordered.

While Adrianna was focused on Radu, Dracula attacked, knocking her to the ground. As he leapt to straddle her, aiming to rip her heart from her chest, Adrianna disappeared. Her lips cast a spell as she conjured a storm of her own from the widow's walk.

The trees around the property began to sway, stirring up the earth and stones around their roots, whipping them into the heart of the battle. Lightning flashed into the yard, followed by rumbles of thunder. Lightning struck the top of the house, sparking dangerously. Adrianna saw the carnage on both sides. She hadn't realized how powerful these vampires were, nor had she thought so many of them would step up to support Basarab.

Six of her rogues were dead, and Elizabeth and Lajos. They had served her well, but she was not about to cry over them. Adrianna watched Radu in battle. *How weak you are, Prince Radu ... you are not the asset I thought you would be ... it will not surprise me if you try to run from this battle, despite the hold I have on your mind ... I release you from me ... you are free!* As she let go of her mind control on Radu, he fell to the ground and began crawling out of the midst of the battle, heading for the tree line, fighting the earth and stones pelting his body.

Samara, seeing the storm Adrianna was creating decided it was time to create one of her own. She looked up to the widow's walk where Adrianna was sending lightning bolts to the yard below. Swirling around and around, Samara rose up to join the sorceress on top of the house.

Basarab, seeing what his daughter was about, found Santan in the heart of the battle, his face streaked with blood. Basarab bowled him over, out of reach of a strike from one of Adrianna's rogues, and whispered in his ear: "Get your sister out of here ... now!"

Santan looked to where his father was pointing and nodded.

"Take her to safety and stay with her. I will not have my children killed by this woman. Do you understand?"

"But..."

"No buts … I want you both out of here! Look after your mother and Mia. Tell my father, I will see him as soon as we are finished here … now, go!"

As Samara was about to land on the widow's walk, Santan grasped hold of her arm, closed his eyes, and envisioned the Olde School Restaurant. As Adrianna turned to attack, the two young vampires disappeared!

The three police officers were transfixed in their spot at the sight before them. No matter what they tried, they couldn't move, something was controlling them. There seemed to be no end to the carnage below.

Santan and Samara tumbled into the room in the restaurant basement, startling the few gathered there. Samara was manic as she turned on her brother. "What are you doing? Our father needs us!"

"He ordered me to get you out of there," Santan answered her.

"Oh, great!" Samara raged around the room impatiently.

Attila approached his grandson. "How goes the battle?

Santan shook his head. "Not good."

"I must go and help," Attila said. "What of Angelique? Does she still live?"

"Yes, last I saw, she was alive. But Basarab would not want you there. He meant for you to remain here to protect us. He said he would see us as soon as he finishes with the sorceress."

Attila accepted Santan's message from his son, but with deep sorrow. He hoped all would go well, but there was a sinking feeling in his heart that it would not be so.

Adrianna continued to watch the battle from the rooftop. Finally, deciding she'd lost enough rogues, she raised her arms to the sky and chanted another spell. The conflict froze. Adrianna could have done that from the beginning, but she had thirsted for blood. However, she wasn't willing to compromise any more of her rogues to these vampires, and her initial plan was going to have to be altered.

Adrianna jumped from the roof to the lawn, landing lightly on her feet. She walked through the carnage and examined the fighters who were still standing.

Coming across Ildiko's, Adrianna grinned. She'd heard stories of the mighty female vampire warrior who wanted nothing more than to be Basarab's queen. Lajos had said how pathetic she really was but that she was good in bed, so that made up for him having to listen to her whining about Basarab's choice in women.

"Well, you are nothing now, aren't you, Ildiko?" Adrianna commented, giving the body a kick. She looked around some more, searching the area for Dracula and Basarab. Both were still standing, fighting back to back, staving off two of her rogues.

Rasputin, too, was still standing. However, he was being held up by a sword that was piercing his heart, and at the other end of the weapon was Volodya, who had come to the aid of his wife. Vasilisa was on the ground, but she was still alive, trying to back away from Rasputin.

Radu was nowhere to be seen, and Adrianna assumed he was cowering somewhere close by, waiting for the battle to be over. *A pretty man, but selfish. I should have killed him a long time ago, but he did serve a purpose for me here—if only a distraction.*

Also missing from the scene was Angelique. *Where are you, Gypsy witch? Do you not have the courage to fight me either?*

Adrianna sighed. Things had not gone quite as she planned, but this was not the end. There were still six of her rogues left and a handful of vampires. Délia had survived, but Ilias was dead; the Russian king and queen lived; Kardos, Basarab's right-hand man; Gara, Ildiko's twin; and Lardom, the lawyer. Plus, Basarab and Dracula.

Once the vampires around the world were told their ruler was dead and his family scattered to the winds, they would accept her as their new leader. She would tell them the story of how she was Dracula's daughter, and it had been his and Basarab's dying wish for her to ascend to the throne.

Adrianna released the spell on her remaining rogues and instructed them to lay the dead bodies in a heap. Once this was done, she waved her hand over the pile, and it caught fire. Within seconds the magic flames left nothing to be seen by the naked eye.

The balance of the vampires was moved into a circle and Adrianna, and her rogues surrounded the still-sleeping bodies. The sorceress began her spell, the one that would take her home to her mountain fortress in Transylvania. Home where a room filled with empty coffins awaited her prisoners. She wouldn't kill them just yet; that wouldn't be any fun.

Epilogue

Released from their trance, the three police officers stared down at the immaculately kept lawn of Yates Castle.

"What just happened here?" Markus asked.

"No idea," Frankie said, scratching his head.

"I don't recollect anything either," Nathaniel started down the steps to the lawn. "But this old-dog brain of mine tells me something went on here—something big. I suggest we return in the daylight and check around."

Angelique sighed from where she was sitting on a branch in one of the trees. She'd cast a spell on the police to take away any memory they had of what they'd just seen, and any memories of anyone in the house that they had interacted with. She also ensured that their only memories of the property would be ones of a desolate, neglected house. It was the least she could do.

She'd realized early in the battle, she hadn't enough power to stop Adrianna; the sorceress was far too potent. At least she knew Basarab and some of the others were still alive. Angelique was thankful the count had sent Attila away, but she shed a tear for Emelia for she was going to have to tell her Vacaresti and Ilias were dead. She flew to the ground and transformed back into human form, then walked up the stairs and into the house. She needed a moment to recoup her thoughts before going to fetch the count's children, Virginia, Attila, Randy, Mia, Petya, Manya, Emelia, and Ákos. At least she would be able to tell the Russian royalty their parents lived and Ákos that his mother still lived, even if they were all taken prisoner. How long the sorceress would keep them alive, Angelique had no idea.

Angelique found Viktor cowering in a closet in the house, where he'd hidden away when he saw Rasputin, Radu, and Elizabeth coming through. She filled the count's faithful butler in on what happened. Despite his frigid demeanour, the man shed a tear. Once recovered, he asked what he could do to assist her.

"I am going to bring the others here," Angelique informed him. "Please prepare something for them."

"There is nothing left. All the bottles have been consumed," Viktor apprised Angelique of their situation.

"I see. Well, I guess we will have to make due until we can obtain more supplies. I will have Santan contact Carla; she will help us."

It was not a cheerful gathering of vampires in the basement room of the Olde School Restaurant when they heard Angelique's story of what had transpired in the battle.

Samara fumed. "Father should never have sent me here. I could have stopped her!"

Angelique laid a hand on the young temptress' shoulder. "No, my dear; she is too powerful. We must bide our time, grow our strength and skills before we go after your father and the others. I don't think she will kill them. If that were her plan, she would have finished them in the yard and burned them with the others."

"What do we do now?" Ákos asked.

"Now, we go back to Yates Castle. Santan, you need to contact Carla and ask her to bring us some blood; Viktor said there is none left. I will put a protection spell around the house so no one can step foot on the property."

"Including those cops?" Attila asked.

"Including them."

Angelique noticed Emelia sitting alone in a far corner. Her eyes were filled with tears, and her shoulders were shaking. Virginia saw her aunt, as well, and touched Angelique on the arm. "I'll go to her," she said.

Randy sat with Mia, hugging her to him, thankful that Basarab had saved his daughter and him from the massacre at the house. What he was going to do now, he had no idea. His wife was dead … his daughter was a vampire … the woman he loved was in mourning for the loss of her husband because there was no guarantee Virginia would ever see Basarab again.

Manya and Petya sat down at one of the little tables along the wall and reaching out to each other, they clasped hands. "It will be okay, Manya; we'll get our mother and father back if it is the last thing we do! Angelique is right; we must rebuild— together—and we must learn how to fight this vampire witch and destroy her!"

In the early hours of the morning, Nathaniel and Frankie drove by Yates Castle, disbelieving the disarray the property was in. The trees around the perimeter were thick with dense branches and bushes crowded their roots. The iron gate at the back-parking lot was closed and rusty with age, vines intertwined through the spikes. From the street, the two officers managed to get a glimpse of the yard, overgrown with weeds. Some of the statues were toppled over. The place was in darkness. They drove on, thinking it was time the city demanded of whoever owned the property to clean it up.

Iona had closed and locked her doors and windows after making the call to the police regarding the commotion at the big house. She'd hustled her children to the basement and there they'd huddled together, listening to the battle going on so close to them. She tried to distract her children, and herself, by reading stories and singing songs with them. But, they could still hear the strange, eerie noises.

At one point, Iona had to go upstairs to get a bottle for her baby, and looking out the kitchen window, had seen a large bonfire in the middle of the castle's yard. Her eyes had remained fixed on the spot, mainly because she couldn't believe the creatures she was catching glimpses of between the trees.

Just as Iona was about to close the blind, having heard the baby crying, she was shocked to see the fire extinguish and the people—or whatever they were—disappear into thin air.

Heading down the stairs to her children, Iona swore she was going to be moving out of the neighbourhood as soon as she could find another place to live.

Judge Harris sat behind his desk, frustrated. His last conversation with Markus had upset him greatly, the captain not having a clue what the judge was talking about when asked for details of what had taken place at Yates Castle. After calling Samuel, who told him he was leaving on an extended vacation and had no idea when he'd be returning, if ever, the judge realized he was on his own.

"Best to let a sleeping dog lie," he mumbled. "At least for now."

A month after the battle, Virginia entered Basarab's study. She walked around, remembering the moments they'd spent in this room. From the beginning, before Santan was born, it was the room where they'd bantered, where Basarab had told her stories, where they had fallen in love, although, in the beginning, neither one of them were aware of that.

She strolled to his desk and sat in his chair. Opening a drawer and pulling out a piece of paper, Virginia began to write…

It is with a heavy heart and a cold hand that I write this account of what happened here in Brantford, and I will add this page to the diary Attila has so meticulously kept over the centuries. He is unable to write the words now, his heart being heavy with the loss of his son, and he has turned the record-keeping over to me. Attila is also unable to lead us, as I felt would be the natural order of things until Basarab is returned to us, but the elderly count refused and turned the throne over to me for the time being. He said he and Angelique would support me, but it was not his place to rule—and, he added, Santan was not yet ready. I can tell Samara is not pleased with her grandfather's decision, but she keeps her tongue quiet—for now.

My heart bleeds for my husband, and I know not if the flow will ever be stopped. I know not if I will ever see him again, or any of the others. My children are still sullen, and the anger I see behind their eyes troubles me greatly. My children, and the children of Volodya and Vasilisa, and Ákos. They are all impatient, and I am thankful for the steadfastness of Attila and Angelique to keep the young vampires in check.

I have refuted Basarab's sentence on Mia. There has been enough pain, especially for her. I have also given my blessing to her and Santan, giving them permission to marry if they should still wish to do so.

Emelia dotes on Ákos, all she has left in her life. He is a dutiful grandson, allowing her the time to heal her losses. However, he, like the other young vampires, wants revenge.

Lastly, I write about Randy. He is lost in this world of vampires he finds himself in, and he has talked to me about the possibility of crossing over. He said there is nothing outside the walls of this house for him. His daughter is here, a vampire; his wife is buried in the basement. And I am here. I will keep his secret, for now, and encourage him to think long and hard about his decision to join my world. I have also told him that as long as there is hope my husband still lives, he must think of me only as a friend.

Carla keeps us well-supplied with blood, and Angelique has ensured our privacy from the outside world. I have seen the police car drive by once in a while; it slows but keeps moving on. Hopefully, the over-zealous cop never remembers what happened here—or anyone else who might have knowledge of who—what— —my husband is. I believe his secret was not as well-kept as he thought.

I will return to this page when there is more to say. For now, I must rejoin the family. I do not wish to remain as the leader any longer than necessary, and I will need to confer with Attila's and Angelique's wisdom to keep the young vampires in check, and to devise a plan to bring our loved ones home.

Signed on this 20th day of October 2010—Virginia Musat

About the Author

Mary M. Cushnie-Mansour resides in Brantford, ON, Canada. She has a freelance journalism certificate from Waterloo University, and in the past, she wrote a short story column and feature articles for the *Brantford Expositor*. Mary is the award-winning author of the popular "Night's Vampire" series and has also written and published several bilingual children's books, picture books, youth novels, mystery novels, collections of poetry and short stories, and a biography.

Mary has always believed in encouraging people's imaginations and spent several years running the "Just Imagine" program for the local school board. She has also been involved in the local writing community, inspiring adults to follow their dreams. Mary is available for select readings and workshops. To inquire about a possible appearance, contact Mary through her website—

http://www.writerontherun.ca

or via email

mary@writerontherun.ca